THE WEAVER

The Weaver

 A Novel

Allona Kagan

LUCE
Books

To my parents, who taught me much about love and joy.

The library of Congress has established a Cataloging-in Publication record for the title.

LCCN # 2023906621

ISBN: 979-98801-48-0-5 (paperback)
ISBN: 979-8-9880148-1-2 (Ebook)

LUCE
Books

T HIS STORY IS inspired by my connection to the unseen, other
realms of consciousness, and in particular a consciousness called
Lucien, *of the light*. The reader might feel the unconditional love of
Lucien shining through its words. It recounts the eternal magic of the
Weaver Woman, who resided in the forest, symbolic of the subconscious
realm. Tapping into this archetype we share in her wisdom. She evokes
goodness, healing and balance, and celebrates hope, love and joy through
awareness and a connection to nature.

The Weaver Woman is an archetypal form spanning many cultures
throughout the ages: The Goddess Athena and the three Fates from
Greek mythology; the Goddess Frig from Norse myths; the Goddess
Olorun from West Africa and Spider Woman, sacred to the Navajo people, are examples of weaving goddesses whose mythology recalls our
ancestral traditions–who we've been and who we can become. She is in
all of us, men and women. To tap into her wisdom and be transported
into her world, it is enough to uncover her in our hearts. She brings hope
to our lives, arranging its chaos of dark and light into an intricate design
of beauty. She mends the destruction of our world by assembling and
reassembling it in her constant weaving. She loves her work as she loves
life itself, aware of the eternal resonance of every gesture into which she
breathes her love.

This story is offered with the hope that the energies of the Weaver
Woman will flow into our reality. All that's needed is to open our hearts
and suspend our doubts. If you find that you resonate with her, then share
her with others, as together we can weave a miraculous world.

The dark threads are needful
In the Weaver's skillful hand
As the threads of gold and silver
In the pattern she has planned.

—Unknown

S HE WATCHED THE jagged cliffs nearing her face at a harrowing speed before she could even understand what had happened. Time stopped. She smelled the pungent mist of the ocean, heard the roar of its explosive waves. She knew she was about to be swallowed by them. *I wish I had more time with Will,* dread and regret in a single thought. *Time, more time!* repeated in a flash in the instant it was about to run out.

PART I

Striving

CHAPTER ONE

On The Run

J OYCE DASHED DOWN the three flights of stairs of her apartment building so quickly that for a suspended moment, she was flying. She was weightless and carefree, a puppy unleashed in a field. Nothing could stand in her way, not even the weight of her thoughts.

It was only at this speed that she could be free from the incessant preoccupations that flooded her days. At those moments, her mind focused on nothing but the course ahead of her and the brief flashes of whatever she encountered along the way. By racing forward, she could momentarily lift the anchor of responsibilities. Yet no matter how fast she ran, she couldn't erase the suspicion that she was running away from her thoughts. Away from herself.

She could hardly bring herself to admit that at this point in her life she had everything she ever wanted. *Everything, everything, everything.* The word bounced in her head with every stride. Through careful planning and conscious good decisions, she'd achieved the perfect life, although she wondered if she could sustain the high level of focus and intensity it took to stay there. She and Will had just celebrated twenty years of marriage, and they had plenty more years of achievement left. Yet he was always a stickler, telling even perfect strangers that they had been together since their junior year at Stanford. Still, they were already in their forties. *Forties, forties, forties.*

She hit the pavement in front of her building and picked up the pace to drown out the number, reminding herself how far they had come in all those years together. In a spark of pride, she thought of Will now managing a portfolio in the nine figures and of her promotion to run the biotech company specializing in neuro research that she had helped start and which was about to go public. She felt superstitious dwelling on their success, but she had to admit, at least to herself, that they were doing well. She smiled for the first time that morning, recognizing both the understatement and her pride. But she wasn't embarrassed by the pride. She and Will had worked hard to create a good life. She could honestly say she had it all.

She cleared the busy streets around their apartment building and began her usual run along the waterfront in the Marina District. Concentrating on as many details as she could at the speed she was traveling, she registered the blur of bicycle riders, dog walkers with a variety of dog breeds–although lately they seemed to be mostly some kind of doodled–delivery trucks, and yachts and sailboats on the Bay, each with an intriguing name. Her favorite, *Why Walk,* made her chuckle as she passed it.

She admired the grand houses with their manicured front gardens. They all became points of momentary focus as she sped by. She loved the exhilaration and sense of abandon her fast runs gave her, even while she retained a sense of control, through the detailed information she took in. She craved the adrenaline coursing through her body and her mind. When she was home, her morning run took her past the Safeway on the corner of Fort Mason and down the Bay along the Marina. Today she paused at Chrissy Field to admire the beauty of the Golden Gate Bridge, hovering right above her and the Bay, speckled by sailboats. She then circled back, retracing her steps, hustling to be home by seven in time to watch the morning news and feed Beau.

"Hello, Beau, did you miss me?"

Her goldendoodle was already at the door when she opened it, jumping excitedly in a determined effort to lick her face. He settled on licking her shoulder, which was the highest point he could reach, while she bent toward him to give him an edge.

"Settle down and give me a minute!" she said, still breathless from her run as she made her way to the kitchen to warm his frozen meat and vegetables package, the healthiest dog food she had found.

Beau rushed to the bowl she laid on the floor by the kitchen counter. She watched, amused, as he greedily chowed down with his face buried in the bowl. *Beau* had been written on the pretty white porcelain in black calligraphy, but she noticed that their darling had managed to scratch even more of the lettering off, leaving nothing but a few lines and curves.

"I love you anyway," she told him, rubbing his soft strawberry-blond curls. "And you love me."

As Beau licked the bowl across the floor, she downed a glass of water and filled a cup with coffee, already thinking ahead to her next tasks.

Will was long gone, as he had to be at the office at the opening of the New York markets, and she savored the quiet of the morning, just her and Beau sitting on the kitchen window seat overlooking the Bay. With each sip of coffee, she knew that her day was about to shift into a frenzy of activity. She was expecting a different kind of busy today because of the trip. A noon flight meant she had to hustle, so she hurried to the shower.

Under the cascade of warm water, she went over her plans, knowing that they could change depending on what happened at her first stop, Tel Aviv. The plan there was to hold a round of meetings to discuss a possible partnership, a merger with a startup whose app could track neurological states through non–invasive technology. After that she would travel to London to meet with bankers and discuss financing for the merger. At the brink of the company's public offering, a lot was riding on this deal, as it had the potential to significantly increase the value of the company.

Wrapped in a towel, she stepped into her walk-in closet and chose a comfortable outfit for the long plane ride, a loose beige blouse and wide-leg trousers, her usual business travel outfit. A few drops from her still moist hair dampened the blouse around her shoulders, so she quickly wrapped the towel around her hair, glad that the shoulder-length bob would dry quickly. No need to fuss with a hair dryer. She packed lightly since she'd be gone only three days, carefully folding her soft black wool pantsuit, a favorite travel staple that was warm and wrinkle-proof, a couple of colorful blouses and T-shirts into her carry-on bag. Since the trip was all business, she'd already decided not to bring any jewelry other than her mother's watch, her reminder of the reason she worked in her field in the first place.

She'd given herself a short window, only three days to achieve her agenda, cramming the meetings back-to-back in long focused days. She needed to be back by Friday at noon because she'd promised to spend the weekend with Will in their house up the coast. It'd been months since they'd been able to get away or even spend a quality evening alone together. She'd begun to feel the strain of their hectic lives on their relationship, part of that coming from Will. He was impatient with her lately and short-tempered, making mild but noticeable comments about how hard she worked or how little fun they were having lately. Will had always been her staunch supporter and was extremely proud of her achievements and mission. For him to be making those remarks was unusual, so she knew that she needed to shift gears soon and give their relationship more focus. She just had to wrap up this deal and everything would be fine.

She hurried downstairs to meet her ride.

Will could wait the three days.

Their love would survive.

CHAPTER TWO

Chasing Victories

WILL RAISED HIS arms in triumph after finally beating Don in their weekly squash game.

"You finally did it, man!" Don said, shaking Will's hand in his sweaty palm. "Congratulations, I owe you a drink, but it'll have to be a rain check. I gotta get home. Meg's birthday today, and I set up a surprise for her, but to play it right, I gotta get home before she does."

"No worries," Will said. "I won't call you a sore loser, even though that's the reason you never lose." He laughed when Don backhanded him with his racket.

"We'll go another time, and it'll be my treat. I know you'll need something to help you recover from the devastation of getting your ass kicked. Wish Meg happy birthday from me."

Despite their friendly competitive relationship, Will saw Don as an equal. They had both been athletes in college, him on the football team and Don on the tennis team, giving Don the competitive advantage on the squash court. Will had given up football in his junior year following a shoulder injury, an injury that still bothered him when he pushed himself hard in squash.

Their competitive natures didn't stop them from sharing tips about good investments to pass on to their clients, which they did over drinks after their weekly squash games at the prestigious Olympic Club.

They were the top performers at their branch, alternating almost yearly for the top position. Their friendly competition gave them the edge they needed to push themselves harder to achieve the success they both sought. Today Will finally beat Don at his game, and that made him happy.

Still wearing his dark blue sports clothes and sneakers, and his lucky 49ers baseball cap backward, Will ran up the stairs, eager to play with

Beau and shower before Joyce got home. She'd been returning from work late, so they'd have time for a walk before she got there. Marta, their cleaning lady, had had to leave early today, leaving Beau alone for a couple of hours. He probably needed to be let out before he had an accident. An accident Will did not want to clean up.

Will smiled and did an exaggerated Rocky dance when he topped the final step. Forty-two and he still had the stamina to run up the three flights of stairs to their apartment without losing his breath. Too many of his colleagues showed premature aging from the stress of their job—scalps balding, bellies protruding. Not him. He ran one hand through his hair, proud of his full head of hair despite the gray blended through the blond. He kept in shape working out in the gym five days a week. He was still in his prime, still full of energy. Though lately he'd been wanting their lives to calm down so that they could spend more time enjoying them rather than constantly running after more money and more success. He had success—shouldn't he and Joyce be able to enjoy it? Still, deep inside he was afraid to slow down. What if keeping up the pace was the only way to stay at the top? He unlocked the door, toeing his shoes off. He doubted that Joyce would be able to lighten her load any time soon, given the ambitious growth plans of the company she ran. He'd surprise her by taking her out to celebrate his win; he couldn't wait to tell her about it. Only when he entered the foyer and threw his keys into the change tray did he remember that Joyce had gone on one of her many trips abroad.

To drown his disappointment, he dropped onto the couch in the den and turned on the TV, flipping between news channels. Beau followed him and stared. "Yeah, yeah, you need to be fed." And he needed a glass of water.

From the kitchen he overheard the news anchor saying something about city of Shanghai being locked down. "How could that be?" he wondered. "Could they close down a city the size of Shanghai?" Surely he'd misheard the report. Regardless, he made a mental note to look into it, since something so major would affect the stock market. He hurried back to the den to hear better, but the news report had already moved on to another subject. He turned off the TV and stared at its black screen. The sound of street traffic mocked the silence in the room. He felt alone, a feeling he hadn't known until recently, when Joyce's work had taken her away from him more and more frequently.

He was thrilled by the spectacular rise of her career and the development of the company she had helped build into the billion-dollar success it now was. He also admired Joyce's mission to help humanity through scientific research of neurological disorders. But she'd become so obsessed with her work, it was all she talked about and focused on. Will didn't like what that obsession was doing to their marriage. She seemed to be swallowed by the rising tide of her success and drawing farther away from him. He missed the days she'd been entirely his, leaning on his strength, like when she grieved for her mother. The tragedy that had drawn them closer was now pulling them apart. His finger tapped on the glass of the coffee table, drumming away silence.

He'd been wanting to talk with her about how little time they shared lately, but there was never any time. Not for months now. He'd been feeling more and more like a small planet orbiting around the sun that was Joyce, waiting to receive a ray of its warmth and glow. He didn't know how to quiet his growing irrational fear that he might be losing her.

Recognizing that he was feeling sorry for himself, he reached for his cell phone on the coffee table and considered googling "events Shanghai." It seemed so far-fetched...

Instead, he dialed Gail's number. His sister answered instantly, sounding surprised.

"Willson?"

She was the only one who still called him by his given name, and hearing it propelled him back to the small town near Chicago where they grew up.

The memory of his father in front of the blackboard in his high school math class sent a nostalgic shiver through him. He'd inherited his father's knack for numbers, applying them to a more lucrative, if less rewarding, profession as a stockbroker. Still, that love for numbers got him to where he was now. He got his first job out of college as a trader, and was good at it, kept accumulating promotions and raises. He enjoyed the exhilaration of the intense focus his job demanded. Buried in numbers and graphs that constantly shifted on his computer screens from the start of the market to its close, he was transported into an enclosed circuit where only he and the numbers existed. Sometimes he would feel so aligned with those graphs, he could anticipate the direction they would be taking. He cherished the elation that the intuitive victories gave him.

His initial successes allowed him to save enough money so he and Joyce could buy their first modest house in the Avenues, where they lived their first five years as a married couple. It was important for him to provide a home for her, and for them, as soon as he could manage it. But that was a long time ago. They now occupied the sprawling penthouse floor of a four-story contemporary building on the Marina. Occupying it more than living in it, he thought.

"Is everything okay?" His sister's worried tone had him regret calling her. Gail taught English lit at the same school where their dad had taught and where they'd attended. Her close link to his small-town past was as reassuring as it was stifling, reminding him of how much he had changed in the years that separated them from the quaint childhood they'd shared. They'd drifted apart in the few years since their parents passed away, within a couple of months of each other after being married for fifty years. Aside from occasional phone calls on birthdays and holidays, he and Gail rarely spoke. But his older sister would rush to his rescue and drop everything she was doing if she smelled trouble. Unless he wanted her flying to San Francisco, the last thing he needed to indulge in was a pity fest.

"Everything's fine. Just saying hi."

"Are you sure?" Her persistence annoyed him.

"Yes, don't worry. I just wanted to check on you and the kids."

"Everything is fine out here." The conversation deflated before it had a chance to take off. There was so little he could share with her after their lives grew apart. Yet there was so much he *could* tell her about himself, about how alone he was feeling. But he didn't want to. Instead, the call dribbled into a vacuum of niceties, and he hung up feeling even emptier than before. As if sensing his loneliness, Beau lay his head on Will's thigh. Will caressed it absently.

"C'mon, Beau," he finally said, standing up. "We're going for a walk!"

Beau's ears perked up, and he twirled in circles a few times to demonstrate his excitement.

As they left the apartment, Will promised himself to speak with Joyce about what he was feeling as soon as they could find a moment alone together. Hopefully, she'd make it back without a delay to their weekend trip to the beach house. It had been too many months since they'd set aside career concerns to take on the slower rhythms of the beach. *Just a few more days*, he consoled himself, yet he was surprised at the wave of dread as subtle as it was unexpected, in place of the excitement he usually felt before their beach trips. "It's just been far too long!" he muttered, leaping down the stairs to chase the feeling away.

CHAPTER THREE

Returning

JOYCE WOKE UP Friday morning in her London hotel room with a splitting headache, and for a few seconds she panicked, not realizing where she was. She'd been traveling so much that sometimes it would take her sleepy mind a moment to recognize the unfamiliar surroundings of yet another hotel room. Each time it happened, she would be gripped by fear until she was fully awake and adjusted to the circumstances.

Nearing forty-three, she was the same age her mother had been when she was diagnosed with Alzheimer's. As that birthday approached, Joyce sensed in the back of her mind that she was entering the age of her mother's decline.

Covering her head with a pillow, she plunged into memories of her mother's long illness. Joyce had known that for her mother there was only a one-way road to hell with no hope of a cure. The only way to lift herself out of the dread she carried since her mother's death was to do all she could in her own lifetime to prevent that desperate route for other people suffering from neurological disease. For their families too. That mission gave her the stamina to work long hours and endure the incessant travel. But apparently it also came with headaches and sleepless nights.

It took Joyce only a few minutes to dismiss the worry over the horrible pain in her head and her momentary confusion, blaming both on exhaustion. She'd had a few instances of irrational panic lately, and each time she'd managed to brush off the panic by directing her attention to her next task. She gathered herself and looked around the room, recognizing the familiar elegance of Claridge's, where she usually stayed on her business trips to London. She breathed a sigh of relief as the sense of comfort and familiarity with her surroundings seeped into her.

Still in bed, waiting for the extra-strength pain medication to take effect, she reviewed her life.

Will and Beau were absolutely fine, and the company was progressing as planned. She smiled, the muscles in her face relaxing and jaw easing her headache even more, remembering the smooth negotiations with the Israeli company and the advantageous financing she was able to secure with the investment firm in London. It was all going according to plan.

She visualized her homes in San Francisco and Jenner. Pictured Will, herself and Beau driving along the beautiful California coast on their way to the beach house. She yearned to be there with them, and telling herself that was where she'd be soon, she was finally able to relax a bit. With the successful foundation set for the new venture, she could allow herself to take a break for a couple of days.

Her NetJets flight was scheduled for eight London time, so she'd be landing in San Francisco by noon the same day, which should give them plenty of time to arrive in Jenner before sundown. She checked her phone. It was already six thirty; half an hour had passed since her phone alarm had rung. After a brief shower she quickly packed her few belongings, threw on a long-sleeve silk white T-shirt and wide-legged black trousers, picked up her long gray cashmere coat and was on her way. She'd have her coffee and a bite to eat on the plane.

There was no time to waste. London traffic was dense at that hour, and the private aviation facilities at Heathrow were at least an hour from the hotel. She dozed off in the town car as they passed through the outskirts of London and opened her eyes when they slowed at the front office of the NetJets lounge. It was just after eight, but she was certain that they'd hold the plane, as she was the only passenger.

A neatly put together receptionist with slick black hair welcomed her into the lounge and asked her to wait there, much to Joyce's surprise. She'd expected that the crew would already be on board and wouldn't want a further delay.

A young man in a dark suit approached her.

"We deeply apologize, Ms. Woodland." His unemotional voice carried perfect British intonation. "Your plane arrived earlier this morning from Dubai, and upon inspection, the captain deemed that it was unsafe to fly. Unfortunately, it is the only plane available at the moment. We have sent to Frankfurt for another plane and expect it will be here shortly. In the meantime we can offer you a comfortable private room to relax in until your flight."

The situation was unusual, but Joyce was grateful for the precautions the captain was taking. She followed the young man toward the back of the lounge. There he opened a door to a room that looked like any business hotel room, complete with a king-size bed.

"I trust that you will be comfortable here." Joyce nodded her thanks. "Is there anything I could get for you? Breakfast, perhaps, and today's newspapers?"

"Just coffee, please." Her body wasn't awake enough for breakfast yet.

"Please call if you need anything else." He motioned to the phone on the desk before he stepped out and closed the door behind him.

Large windows overlooked the runway, and Joyce watched a plane take off, not 500 feet away. No noise, possibly thanks to the double-pane windows. The room was quiet and indeed comfortable, as the man promised. Coat and purse went on the couch and she sat at the desk. On it she found a card with the Wi-Fi name and password. She glanced at her watch, which was still set to California time. Twelve fifteen. Still okay to call Will without disturbing his sleep too much.

Except the call went straight to his voice mail. She wouldn't be bothering him at all.

The young woman from the reception area arrived with a tray and set up her coffee service. To Joyce's delight she found Stevia, her preferred sweetener, among the offerings. She didn't wait for the coffee to cool before taking her first sip. And since she was awake with extra time, she might as well catch up on her work. She had to get the points of the new agreement to the company's San Francisco law firm first thing in the morning.

She completed the email with all the contract information within an hour. With nothing urgent left to do and feeling too tired to read the paper, she decided to lie down on the inviting and elegantly made-up bed. Expecting to leave soon, she didn't bother to slip off her shoes.

She was awoken by a soft voice next to her.

"Excuse me, madam." It was another young woman dressed in the same NetJets uniform as the receptionist who'd welcomed her. This one had a blond bob and a very quiet voice. "Pardon the disturbance. We tried ring-ing several times, but there was no answer, so we figured you wished not to be disturbed."

"What time is it?" Joyce groggily reached for her phone. "What? It's five thirty already? That can't be right."

"We are so sorry, madam." The young woman sounded genuinely apologetic. "The plane that was supposed to arrive from Frankfurt had been booked by the time we reached the office in Germany, and there were no other planes available, so the NetJets mechanic repaired the part on your scheduled plane. Not to worry, madam. Everything is fixed now, and the plane is ready to depart." Her awkward struggle to smile was apparent.

"How could I have slept for so long," Joyce mumbled in her groggy state.

"Would you like to follow me? The crew is ready for you to board."

Still in a state of confused disbelief, Joyce packed her computer into her briefcase and grabbed her purse and coat. She has never been so late for anything in her life. She needed to call Will to let him know what had happened.

"You're back early!" Will's upbeat voice responded before the phone had a chance to ring. "Leave earlier than you planned? Beau and I are ready for the road. I even packed a picnic for our favorite rest spot." He paused long enough for a quick breath before adding, "I hope you were able to get some sleep on the plane."

"Honey." She searched for a delicate way to break the news to him but found no other way than to be direct. "My morning flight was canceled, and the soonest they could reschedule it was now. We're just taking off."

"You're just leaving London now? Why didn't you take a commercial flight when you couldn't leave earlier?"

She felt the accusatory tone that he tried to disguise. Felt the weight of his disappointment.

"I'm so sorry, darling, but it wasn't supposed to take so long. I'll explain when I see you. They're waiting for me to turn off the phone for takeoff." She was about to hang up when an idea struck. "Why don't you go ahead with Beau and head up to the house before I get there. It's been so long that airing it out might be a good idea. I'll drive up tomorrow morning, probably be there by noon." She hated the idea of Will moping around while waiting for her, so this seemed like a perfect solution.

"All right, I'll do that." He sounded resigned, and he hung up without his usual *I love you*. The phone went dead, and in the hollow moment of silence that followed, Joyce wished she had told him how excited she was to see him. How she couldn't wait to finally be alone with him. But in her rush to turn off her cell phone since the crew was waiting to take off, she didn't. With a sigh she let the thought drift off, determined to shower him with love when she saw him.

CHAPTER FOUR

Taking a Leap

T HE TWELVE-HOUR FLIGHT to San Francisco was uneventful. Joyce utilized the time to make detailed notes for the next steps of her plan. She visualized her moves ahead of each step and devised strategic variations for what might change along the way. Since her intentions for the trip worked out as the best-case scenario she had hoped and prepared for, she was now ready to meticulously lay out the next steps. She wrote memos to her staff and colleagues informing them of the schedules to come.

When she was done and her hands were cramping, she reclined into her leather armchair and tried to doze. But she couldn't sleep. Her long nap at the lounge refreshed her, so she found herself with several hours with nothing to do but relax. Yet relaxing had never come easily for her.

Listlessly she leafed through the pages of the few magazines displayed in front of her, but nothing drew her interest. She berated herself for not bringing the scientific journals she usually carried on her trips, but she hadn't expected the extra time for reading.

Her gaze drifted to the window and to the sky that stayed bright despite the hours that elapsed on their flight west, and for some reason she was reminded of the light streaming through her window when flying home from their first trip to Hawaii.

She'd been staring at the bright rays penetrating the small porthole when she reached innocently into the tiny chocolate box Will handed her. Expecting a piece of chocolate, she was surprised when her fingertips hit something hard. She pulled out a diamond ring. Will kissed her and told her how much he loved her, and she felt relieved when he finally asked the question she'd been expecting the whole trip. She admitted she'd been feeling a mild pinch of disappointment when it hadn't come.

He later joked that he proposed on the plane so she couldn't run away. Will liked surprises, so he chose to make his proposal at a moment she least expected. By that time there was never a question that she wouldn't accept. The memory made her smile, and she relaxed into the leather recliner. She missed his humor and their closeness. Knowing that they would soon be together in their beach house warmed her like the softest cashmere blanket. Her heart leaped with the excitement of anticipation.

When the wheels of the plane touched the ground, she texted Will. "Just landed, darling." *Heart emoji.*

"Welcome home, hon'!" Was the immediate reply. "Can't wait to see you!!!! Beau and I prepared the beach house, and a warm fire and a glass of Merlot await you." *Three heart emojis.*

Picturing their waterfront home and her by the fire on the comfortable love seat covered with cushions and a blanket, with Will by her side and Beau at their feet, made her body melt in relaxation. However, when she got into the chauffeured town car, she was dismayed by the return of her migraine. Reaching for her purse for a couple painkillers, she had an idea. She would ask Ravi to do an exam.

Nine-thirty was still early enough to call, so she pulled out her phone before she could change her mind and called Ravi Varadkar. The neurological research center at the company was closed, so she wouldn't reach Ravi, neuro-researcher extraordinaire, at his office. She prayed she didn't catch him out at dinner. Still, he was a friend, and her request was personal, not company related. She wanted to use one of the company's newest inventions, a project he spearheaded. A piece of technology that he knew inside and out. And she wanted not only the machine but Ravi's expertise.

"Joyce?" Ravi expressed surprise at her calling him on a Friday evening. "Is everything all right?"

Joyce perked up at hearing her old friend's voice. "Everything is great, Ravi. I just flew back from London and we nailed it! The merger is on. The trip went as well as it possibly could."

"Congratulations!"

She imagined his suspense in the silence that followed.

"Ravi, I need a favor."

"Anything for you, my pretty lady." His sweet humor had the desired effect of calming her nerves.

"I'd like for you to run the wave"–their nickname for the sophisticated device that measured blood flow to various parts of the brain–on me, but it must be completely confidential. No one must know, you understand?" She knew she could absolutely count on Ravi's discretion, but she wanted to hear him confirm it.

"Of course! I understand totally, but what's up? Are you ill?"

Joyce had to think quickly since she hadn't anticipated the question in her haste to call him.

"I'm absolutely fine. I just want to test the new equipment in case I'm asked about it in the meeting with the board next week." She blurted out the first thing that came to her mind, nodding when her words seemed like the perfect answer. "But so we don't raise any alarms, I don't want anyone to know. You know how fast and far gossip travels. This would be bad timing for rumors to go rushing out into the business world and through the scientific communities."

"Why don't you come by tomorrow morning? I can open up the lab at eight when no one is there and set up the equipment. It'll be ready for you by nine."

Not prepared to be examined so soon, she was taken aback. But that was exactly what she had asked for. And this way she'd be able to hit the road north by eleven and arrive in Jenner just past one.

"That'll work. Thank you so much, Ravi. Have a good night." She hung up feeling good that she'd made the call and was even excited to test the new equipment.

Her apartment welcomed her into its simple elegance of beige furniture and familiar lavender and jasmine aromas. It was past ten, and all she wanted was to dive into her comfortable, familiar bed as quickly as possible.

She awakened after ten hours of great sleep, feeling energized and refreshed. There was no trace of the migraine, and she felt silly over her alarm from the previous day. Nonetheless, she'd contacted Ravi, who was opening the research center on a Saturday morning especially for her, so she hurried through her coffee, put on her baggy jeans, a casual white shirt and a blue wool blazer, and was on her way. The Tesla was hooked to the charger and was completely charged. The full charge, good for three hundred and fifty miles, would be plenty to get her to the lab and back, and then to Jenner with eighty miles to spare.

At the lab Ravi welcomed Joyce with a warm hug. They hadn't seen each other for a long time, not like in their college days when they would meet up constantly for study sessions. His kind and familiar face send a nostalgic shiver through her for their intense student days' conversations about how they could improve neuroscience. Now they were actually doing it. She smiled to herself at the realization, and to him in gratitude for his friendship.

"Ready?" he asked, motioning to a white recliner that had electrical wires attached to it.

She sat in the chair and watched Ravi pull out the magnetic strip attached to the wires, which he then secured around her head. She felt excited to be one of the first people to test the "wave," Ravi's nickname for the sophisticated device he and his team created. Knowing how sensitive the machine was in detecting blood flow into the brain, she tried to relax as much as possible. Within a minute the computer beside her flashed several graphs of different colors juxtaposed on each other. Ravi leaned toward the screen. She studied his profile as he concentrated, and for a moment she thought she saw a shadow cross his dark face. Yet it was gone just as quickly as she blinked, and she decided that she must have imagined it when Ravi turned to her with a smile.

"You know, since you're here, why don't we do an MRI? It's not every day that I get to have a color print of that beautiful mind of yours. And we'll have additional info for comparison and to validate the readings."

As always, Ravi's charm and radiant smile worked their magic on Joyce. She acquiesed to his suggestion despite her limited time.

The machine shrieked stridently around her head. To make matters worse, time dragged to an eternity as she lay in the confinement of its tunnel. How antiquated it felt compared to the innovative device their company was creating. Trying to stay as still as possible, she fiddled impatiently with the space left empty on her finger when she removed her wedding and engagement rings before entering the machine, in a desperate attempt to disengage from the noise that surrounded her. She could hardly restrain herself from tearing out of it. Instead, she directed her thoughts to the drive up the coast to quiet her mind. She mustn't delay her trip much longer, she thought, with concern about Will creeping into her imaginings. He would be cross if she arrived later than expected. She wanted the weekend to be perfect, to cram all the love they had missed out on for months into those two days. She needed to catch her breath. She yearned for the peacefulness of the pine forest by their property. And Will needed her. She felt her throat tighten. *How much longer in this horrid machine? Was all this necessary?* Why had she bothered Ravi with these tests when she was perfectly fine? All she needed was a bit of rest. But right now, what she needed most was to get out of there and get going.

"All done!"

She finally heard Ravi's chipper voice above the noise. One more click, and at last, quiet. She was finally released, free to dash on her way. She let out a breath as the narrow tunnel opened above her.

"I'll get you the full report and charts on Monday," Ravi said, extending his hand to help her up from the MRI table. "My daughter is getting married this weekend, so I sneaked out on the preparations and need to get back quickly before anyone notices I'm gone."

"Ravi! I had no idea Kiara was getting married! Why didn't you tell me? There was absolutely no rush—"

"Not to worry, my dear. There's so much commotion in the house, it'll be a while before they realize I escaped, and by then I'll be back. Anyway, this gave me a chance to see you at this happy moment in my life. It's been too long."

She thanked him again and made a mental note to send flowers to his house the moment she got home.

"It's a traditional Indian wedding, three days and nights. We started the ceremonies yesterday. I didn't want you to feel obligated as I know how busy you are. I was going to share the highlights with you afterwards."

He had guessed her thoughts, although she'd assumed he'd had a logical reason for not inviting her and Will.

"We will have a separate party for our Western friends. I hope you and Will can make it."

"Well, I really shouldn't keep you, then!" she said. And she needed to go too. "Have a wonderful celebration and please congratulate Kiara for me. The last time I saw her she was a shy teenager. I can't believe she's already getting married!"

Ravi nodded. "Look at me, I'm already an old man, and you still look like you did when we were in college. No wonder you have not seen the time go by."

She shook her head and gathered up her belongings. "Ravi, you're hardly an old man. Maybe just a bit gray around the temples, that's all." She kissed his cheek.

Last task complete. Now she could head north with a free calendar and nothing to do but relax and cajole Will into a good mood if he was still holding on to the bad one. She'd remind him of one of the wonderful times they'd shared at the cabin. She had lots of memories to choose from.

CHAPTER FIVE

Reaching

THE FAMILIAR COAST road stretched in front of Joyce in all its glory. She marveled at its beauty every time she traveled it. It was ever changing, yet always powerful. Striking. The sky was particularly bright for a February morning, which made the landscape all the more vivid. Grassy hills had turned bright green and were seeded by white sheep, brown cows and, occasionally, horses. Small wooden farmhouses sprang from the sprawling expanse of sloping earth and grass. The vistas were open and welcoming—a very different feel from the closed-in city. Both were picturesque and arresting, but the sheer openness, the vastness, of the coast always made her contemplate the wider world. The world beyond the rolling waves. The world above the nearest stars.

Jaunts through the city neighborhood made her wonder about people, about where they were going and where they'd been. Time at the coast prompted thoughts of the earth, of nature and growth and eternity.

She began singing—loudly—glad to be exploring a vital part of her life that she'd been ignoring for too long. *Don't forget me I beg I remember you said.* Her voice rose, bellowed over Adele's song on the car's stereo. She guessed that Will had probably experienced the same freedom from the bounds of the city on his drive up the day before.

When she rolled down the window, aromas of sweet grass, pungent cow manure and soothing damp earth filled the car. She savored the reprieve from constant hyper-alertness. The car practically drove itself along the lightly traveled road.

Sometimes, like today, she felt a pinch of regret when she passed the quaint farmhouses that reminded her of an inner call to motherhood, a yearning that she had shoved into the recesses of her emotions. The cozy comfort of the farms tugged that craving back to the surface, reminding her of her ticking biological clock.

"There was never enough time," she said aloud. Sure, she and Will had discussed the possibility of kids every so often, as if idly playing with a candy bar that they ultimately set aside every time. Talking about having children—raising children—filled Joyce with intensely disparate feelings of joy and fear, and she could never settle on either of them. "It's not time yet," she reasoned again. After the company went public, they could think about it. Maybe they'd talk it over this weekend. But she knew that like all the other times, the talk would only be mind-candy and nothing more. She liked knowing that they could still consider the possibility of kids, but she seriously wondered if it made any sense at this stage. She changed the music theme on the car's dashboard. Glenn Gould's Goldberg Variations rolled harmoniously as the car glided along the meandering road. She was approaching the narrowing of the road with its twists and turns and craved softer classical music for this stretch of the journey.

There was also her charitable work to consider; How could she possibly have time for everything? She enjoyed serving on the board of ChildAid, a nonprofit that raised money for research for cures of genetic illness in infants. But for all the good she was doing, she sensed that her reluctance to give up, even momentarily, all that they had worked so hard to achieve in order to have her own child stemmed from a dreadful fear of loss hiding in the crevices of her subconscious, which she never felt brave enough to uncover. The constant motion kept that fear at bay. It also kept it in place.

"Damn!" She shook her head when she remembered that she hadn't told Will about the Sunday evening gala for ChildAid that they had to attend, the thought snapping her out of her reverie about motherhood. At her suggestion her company had bought a table for twelve, and she had to be there to welcome the guests. She *wanted* to be there. He would be irritated at having to head back to the city early on Sunday, especially since she hadn't even arrived yet. She'd need to tread lightly and find the right moment to tell him about it.

Okay, no more heavy thoughts.

The road narrowed, meandering along the rugged, dramatic coastline. Hovering high above the ocean, the expanse of deep blue water revealed itself in a panorama of eternal beauty. She loved knowing that from where she was, there was nothing but the vast Pacific all the way to Asia. She opened the window the rest of the way and thrust her arm out, flying it over the air. Perfect visibility made the endless blue particularly thrilling today, although she also loved those times when thick fog rose from the water to conceal the panorama with mysterious hues.

She was nearing the house at the bend where the piano concerto on her Spotify app would stop abruptly, so she turned it off at the end of a movement. There was no internet reception from that point until she reached the house.

She veered off the main road onto the unpaved path and let her car ease over its bumps. Every year they said they'd fix the bumps, and every year they never touched them, joking that they deterred trespassers. At the bottom of the path, she was grateful to notice that Will had left the wrought-iron gate to their property open for her.

The smell of pine and eucalyptus permeated the car from the surrounding forest. She inhaled deeply, clearing her sinuses and filling her senses before closing the windows.

From between the trees their dark brown wood house grew slowly larger. She parked in front, got her overnight bag from the trunk and walked in.

Entering through the shaded front porch, she was struck by the brightness from the huge living room window. It was a day for being outdoors. The window framed a view to the vast ocean horizon but was only the second-best view from the house. They were nestled on the edge of a cliff, and the view from their bedroom of the ocean surrounded by forest was even more glorious.

With the window slightly open, she could hear the roar of the fierce waves below. Yet inside, it was surprisingly quiet. Too quiet. She'd expected Beau to come running as soon as he heard her, jumping and yelping in excitement with Will at his heels, but no one was home.

She'd texted Will to let him know she was on her way, so it seemed odd that he wouldn't be there. She stepped into the kitchen, admiring the large bouquet of white lilies and yellow roses on the kitchen island. A note leaned against the vase.

Honey, I forgot to get bay leaf. Making your favorite dish tonight, so Beau and I ran out to the store. I opened the Burgundy to let it breathe. Please wait for me to have some. Tonight, we're celebrating!

"How adorable my husband is!" she called out, speaking to the flowers. She pulled a rose from the vase, inhaled the heady smell, and walked down the hall.

She upended her overnight bag on the bed of their cozy bedroom with its spectacular view to grab her leggings, a long-sleeved T-shirt and Nikes. The large bone she'd brought for Beau was tucked back into the corner of an inside pocket so he couldn't get at it before dinner time. She removed both her rings and mother's watch and set them on the bedside table on her side of the bed. Since the boys weren't home, she was going for a quick run to stretch her legs.

About a mile up the road, she parked at the vista point. Hers was the only car there, as tourists were rare during the winter months. All alone in nature, no human sounds, no one around for miles, just her in front of the endless ocean. She smiled, sensing the peace and freedom this special place offered her. She chose to run uphill on the trail adjacent to the road on the ocean side, primarily so she'd be running downhill on the return.

Right away cold air blew at her. She hadn't realized how windy it was, but that would be easier on the way back too. She gathered her strength for this final all-out exertion before she could finally let go completely once she was home.

The trail's familiar twists and turns beckoned, and that familiarity allowed her to give her mind over to a review of the trip and the tests Ravi had run. After ten minutes or so she didn't want to think of work anymore. She didn't want to think about headaches and the genetic component of Alzheimer's or what tomorrow might bring.

She increased her speed and turned her attention to the fierceness around her. She loved the intensity of nature, especially when she ran exposed to the elements. Exhilaration carried her higher up the cliff, but she had to turn back before she wanted to; Will and Beau would be waiting. She and Will could get in a longer run in the morning.

Dashing down the hill with the wind at her back, hissing and mixing with the rumble of the ocean, Joyce felt keenly the excitement of the moment. She sped up, wanting to match the power of the sea and sky, then cursed when at the same instant a dozen or so small rocks rolled down the road toward her. A sharp awareness of her surroundings was her special talent, yet even though she saw the rocks, she couldn't stop in time or hop over them. Resigned to a twisted ankle, she stuttered over a couple of the smaller rocks and then felt herself propelled backward at the bend in the road. Arms pinwheeling, she couldn't regain her balance and she plunged over the narrow barrier that separated the road and trail from the abyss. She had no chance to counteract the motion and the force propelling her into nothingness. She imagined herself suspended in midair, knowing that to be impossible. Falling backward, head down, she watched the wet rocks below her grow larger as she raced toward them and they toward her.

Her skull was about to be smashed on the rocks. "No, no, no, I refuse to die!" her mind screamed into the emptiness and her voice screamed into the air. The words echoed and echoed and echoed.

Arms and hands scrabbled for a branch growing out of the rocks, coming up empty. Then both hands locked onto a branch, a tree, a—

Pain. Pain and darkness.

And then only darkness.

CHAPTER SIX

Searching

A NNOYANCE WASHED OVER Will when he saw that the Tesla still wasn't there when he drove through the gate and toward the house. She must have gotten caught up on one of her endless business calls after she texted that she was on the way. No matter, he would start dinner anyway. The good thing about boeuf bourguignon, one of their favorite dishes, was that the longer the wine-based sauce macerated on the stove with the beef, carrots, pearl onions, mushrooms and spices, the better the meat tasted. He intended to spoil Joyce with a wonderful candlelit dinner. He opened one of their best bottles to let it breathe, a 1968 Domaine Rossignol premier cru that he'd been saving for a special occasion. This was their first weekend together at the beach house in months, and he wanted Joyce to know how special their time together was for him. He especially wanted to express his love, which he hadn't had a chance to do for so long. He could only imagine how exhausted she must be after the last round of meetings and flights—and that damned delay—so he intended to make her feel like the queen that she was.

Mick Jagger not getting *no* satisfaction accompanied him while he sautéed the beef. It was the song that had blasted from his roommate's boombox when he returned to their dorm room the day he met Joyce. As though a light came on in his mind, he'd suddenly realized what the words meant. Like Mick, he was so full of satisfaction that he couldn't possibly shake it off. *Hey, hey, hey.*

He'd noticed Joyce for the first time as he walked by the campus museum. She was sitting on the steps absorbed in a book, wearing black leggings, a tight white T-shirt and Puma running shoes. Her silky long black hair hung in front of her as she bent over the book in her lap. She was all he could see. Her slight figure was dwarfed by the massive building, yet her presence made it disappear. When she looked up and smiled at him, a wide-lipped, generous smile, his world changed forever.

Yes—hey, hey, hey—he couldn't deny that he was in love with his wife, even after all the years.

"Settle down, Beau." Beau was racing around him and then back and forth to scratch at the entrance door, but they'd just been out and Will was too busy savoring memories and cooking to let him out. But when Beau continued to annoy him, he finally let him go. Yet Beau came running right back, scratching to be let back in.

"What's gotten into you, bud?" Will asked as he let Beau in and went back to the kitchen to spice his sauce. A few minutes later Beau snuck by him with a large bone in his mouth and hurried to the couch in the living room, where he buried it among the many pillows and Joyce's soft orange throw. "Where'd you get that?" Will tried to pry the bone from Beau's mouth, but he refused to let go, clenching it with all the strength of his jaw.

Giving up on the bone but curious about where it came from, Will reversed Beau's path and headed straight to the bedroom. Hanging half off the bed with its zipper open was Joyce's black Vuitton bag that he gave her for Christmas two years ago. She was back! He smiled as he placed the bag on a shelf in the closet. Joyce must have gone out for a run when she got there and saw they weren't home. He checked her side of the bed. Yep, her rings and watch, which she never wore on her runs, were on the nightstand.

Humming, he went back to his cooking. He switched Spotify to classical piano in anticipation of her arrival.

As he stood over the stove, turning the dish over, its mouth-watering aromas permeating the room, he imagined their evening together. She'd be delighted to walk in and smell her favorite dish and the flowers he'd stashed all over the house. They'd cuddle by the fireplace after dinner, sipping on the exquisite wine. She'd tell him about her successful travels and meetings, and he'd tell her funny stories about what Beau had done while she was away, one of their favorite topics of conversation. Once she was relaxed, he would take her hand and lead her to the bedroom.

He was so lost in his imagination that it took a while for him to notice that one of the same concertos on the Spotify list was playing over again. The kitchen clock read half-past four, more than an hour since he'd gotten home. Unless she'd left just before he got there, she really should have been back by then.

Concern crept into his daydream. He got up from the sofa, where he'd joined Beau, and said, "C'mon. We're going for a drive."

He put on his baseball cap and leather jacket, and they were off, with Beau jumping into the open convertible. Will didn't bother to close the roof of the car and drove quickly despite Beau needing to adjust to the quick turns.

Thick fog was rolling in, obscuring the path ahead, but Will knew the turns and twists of the route by heart.

He intuitively drove north, assuming that Joyce would have headed to one of her favorite spots after the long absence. He spotted the red color from a distance and then the Tesla itself parked at the vista point, and he pulled up next to it. The car was locked, and there was no sign how long it had been there. He unlocked it with the app on his phone and looked into the glove compartment to see if she had left her phone, which would explain why she hadn't answered it. It wasn't there. Hands on hips, he peered over to the cliff below. The fog rising from the ocean was so thick that it obscured the rocks. What if the fog had come in quickly and she was stuck, unable to see the trail? But that wouldn't be a problem because she could always walk on the road.

He stared at the cars, but he pictured the trails. What if she'd had an accident and hurt herself in an area with no reception? A sudden pang of worry slapped at him. He was frozen by uncertainty for a long moment before continuing up the coast. If she was injured, she could be waiting for him on the side of the road. Or she could have sought help from one of the families who lived out that way.

When his search yielded no results, he walked back down the road with Beau by his side.

"C'mon, bud, help me find Mommy."

The fog was making it difficult to see anything now—had been for a while—so he returned to his car, reassuring Beau all the way. He closed the roof, turned on the heat, took his phone out of his pocket and dialed 9-1-1.

Sheriff Johnson from the local Jenner station answered the call.

"This is Willson Woodland." He gave his address and phone number. "I'm on the coast highway three miles up from the Jenner sign. I'm looking for my wife, Joyce. She went running and hasn't been back for at least a couple of hours." He managed to override his panic as he spoke. There was a brief silence before the sheriff's reply.

"Normally we wait twenty-four hours before we can take a missing person's report, and I'm understaffed this evening; it's only the new recruit and me here and he stepped out to get some warm food his wife just prepared and bring it back to the station. But I'll tell you what. As soon as he gets back, we'll drive over to meet you and see what's what. Where are you exactly?"

"I'll be waiting at the vista overlook in a silver Porsche next to a red Tesla."

Will hung up feeling vaguely reassured; at least he now had help. He put on the seat warmer and rubbed his hands together. The temperature was dropping quickly. Beau let out an impatient whine but settled when Will caressed his head.

"I know, bud, don't worry. We'll find Mommy soon."

About twenty minutes later, a police car parked next to him. It arrived without fanfare, no sirens or lights necessary on a quiet winter evening, as few ventured to that part of the coast.

"Hello, I'm Sheriff Johnson, and this is my assistant, Brad. Let's start with the basics—your license?"

Will passed it over, and Brad did whatever checking they did when a man reported his wife missing.

The sheriff said, "Mr. Woodland, do you have a recent photo of your wife with you?"

Will scrolled through his phone's photo library and stopped on a photo of them together at a recent charity gala for SFMOMA. Joyce looked radiant in her dark blue satin gown that angled off her slim shoulders. She wore her going-out makeup, and her shoulder-length hair was up in a twist.

"Here's one, but it doesn't really look like her. Not like how she looks every day. Let me find one where she looks more natural, more like herself." He was scrolling deeper and deeper into his photo library and growing flustered, unable to find any casual photos of Joyce.

"Let's see if we can find something on the internet," the sheriff suggested. "This vista is one of the rare pockets on the road when we can sometimes get reception."

"Of course, good idea." Will was surprised he hadn't thought of that. There were plenty of official company photos of her online.

"Her name?" Sheriff Johnson asked as he pulled out his Android phone.

"Joyce Woodland. J-O-Y—"

"I got it!" exclaimed the sheriff before Will had a chance to finish spelling her name. "She's quite a big shot, your wife, isn't she?"

"That she is." Will hung his head, annoyed at the comment and wanting the sheriff to get on with finding her.

All traces of humor left the sheriff's face. "I'll post an alert to the nearby stations to watch out for her, but right now that's all I can do." He gestured to the two cars. "She wasn't in a car accident, so we won't be searching for a car off the road."

"But she was jogging, so she could still be hurt somewhere on the side of the road." He ran one hand through his hair. "Beau and I walked the trail, but we didn't see her."

"I can go around looking," Brad volunteered.

"Your dog got tracking experience?" the sheriff asked.

"Not a bit. I thought he might be able to pick up on her scent, but if he did, I couldn't tell." Will had hoped Beau would find Joyce, but he'd shown no unusual reactions.

"I'll tell you what," the sheriff said. "It's getting too foggy and dangerous to search for her by foot on the slippery rocks by the ocean, but we can take a look at the forest on the other side."

Resigned to the limitation, Will nodded in resignation. He knew it'd be unlikely that she would have jogged in the forest right after she got there. However, there wasn't much he could do but follow their lead, and he preferred that over doing nothing. Besides, one never knows . . .

After a couple of hours of scouting through the thick forest, calling her name and shining an intense flashlight in all directions and Beau running around them in circles, they came up empty. And there was little they could see in the dark. They returned to their cars.

"I'll have a full crew here by six if she doesn't turn up at home before then," Sheriff Johnson told him. He shook Will's hand. "And you call us if she does show up, no matter what time it is, you hear? We might be able to get a helicopter by tomorrow morning."

The sheriff folded himself into the police car, and Brad joined him. "Let's hope the night will bring good news. Take care, Willson."

The house filled with her absence felt eerily quiet and very cold. He lit the fireplace, warmed a bowl of the beef stew. But he wasn't hungry. His stomach was tied in knots. He poured a glass of the Burgundy. The bold wine did little to calm his anxiety, but he sipped it absently until the bottle was empty. He stared at the fire trying to make sense of what had happened. Somehow, despite his confusion and anxiety, he dozed off.

He startled awake in the middle of the night, still on the couch. Still alone.

He sat up, body sore, head pounding.

Could it be true, or did he dream it? Was Joyce really missing? Or maybe she hadn't shown up at all? So many times she had canceled her plans to come home from a business trip at the last minute, he had stopped counting. He even half expected it now, a protective reflex to cushion his disappointments. Yet she had returned as she had promised; she was at the house before he got back from shopping. And then it took him a while to realize that she'd been there. She might have been lying somewhere, injured, the whole time he was cooking. That damned bay leaf! If only he hadn't gone out to get it.

The bowl on the coffee table was empty. What he'd prepared for their lavish evening had been gobbled up by Beau. He wondered how long it would have taken Joyce to realize *he* was missing if things were reversed. Would she miss him? Sensing he was spiraling into self-pity, he dismissed the thought immediately. It was all real, much too real, and he felt too miserable to go back to sleep. He drummed on the coffee table while trying to arrange his thoughts. Joyce was gone. She was supposed to be there, but she wasn't. He heard his breath growing louder and quicker. The sound of his pulse throbbing in his temples grew deafening.

He stared down at Beau sleeping deeply at his feet to slow the beat of his heart. How was it that he slept so peacefully with all that was going on? As if sensing his thoughts, Beau raised his head and looked up at him with a wide-mouthed yawn. He wasn't completely alone after all. Yet Beau had been no help at finding Joyce.

"Where could she be?" he said out loud, half to Beau and half to the empty room. Beau's perplexed brown eyes stared back at him. With a pang he remembered how miserable he and Joyce felt when Beau went missing the first time they brought him to the beach house as a puppy. They drove around for hours searching, Joyce weeping next to him. She couldn't stop crying until Beau showed up at their doorstep the following morning, tired and wet from his escapade in the forest but very much alive.

Joyce was resourceful, he tried to reassure himself. Maybe she found help along the way. But what if she trusted the wrong people? What if she was kidnapped? His breath grew heavy and fast again. His heart pounded violently. He put his hand on his chest and drew in a deep breath, willing himself to think only positive thoughts. She might turn up at the doorstep in the morning just like Beau did. The prospect reduced his panic, but he still couldn't go back to sleep.

~

Morning brought no relief. Sheriff Johnson telephoned at six, as promised, with an action plan, but there'd been no progress overnight. Still, they now had a crew of policemen and rescue workers from the surrounding area—meaning they knew the surrounding area—and a helicopter was on its way from the main station in San Francisco.

"We'll certainly be able to find her if she's around here," Johnson told Will.

The declaration was supposed to be reassuring, but Will wondered what he meant by *if she's around here*. Where else could she be?

After eight hours of searching, the crew found a smashed iPhone and an orange Nike sneaker by the waterfront. Will identified them as Joyce's. But there was no sign of her. No sign of what happened to her.

They brought more searchers to the waterline, to the inlets and outcroppings, and still nothing.

Had she been injured and carried off by the tide, which had been particularly high last night? Nobody could answer his questions. No one could relieve his fear. They'd continue the search the following day.

Will would be there with them. He wouldn't stop looking until he found her. That was his vow.

PART II

Awakening

CHAPTER SEVEN

The Awakening

N o time. No movement. No color or sound or scent.
There was no light and there was no darkness. Yet she was conscious of all of it.

Of the void. The endless void.

Then the light enveloped her. It was unlike any light she had ever known. She experienced it more than saw it at the essence of her being. It was overwhelming, yet warm and gentle. All she was, all she'd ever been, surrendered to the light.

In the stillness there was movement, and the movement gathered momentum, turning into a vortex so powerful that she got swept into it, spiraling deeper and deeper into its core. She was squeezed into a narrow space. Too narrow. Too constricting. She resisted. The momentum was stronger than her resistance. An eruption exploded from the pressure.

She awakened.

Her eyes blinked, adjusting to the dim light, and her body adjusted to the space it occupied. She lay naked on a hard surface covered in something damp. She or the hard surface smelled of rotting leaves. She attempted to pull herself up. Overpowering pain seized her. Then darkness.

~

When she was able to open her eyes again, she didn't stir. The space around her was bleak. A closed window above her cast streams of pale light into the air. Dust particles danced in the light. She watched the dance until heavy weights dragged her eyes shut.

~

A steady murmur came from her right side. She turned her eyes slightly. *Slowly.* A face emerged from the shadows and moved nearer. Dark, gentle eyes set in ancient face encrusted in deep wrinkles. She couldn't tell if it was a woman or a man.

"So, we have decided to awaken."

Soft feminine voice. The woman bent over her, adjusting something over her, tugging at something under her. She kept murmuring the whole time.

"Try not to move, dear," she whispered close to her ear. "There has been a lot of damage to this body, but it is mending, so it has a strong will to live stored in its cells."

Familiar words, *will to live.* They echoed within her, bringing relief. Bringing a recognition of strength. The echo called her to action: *remember.*

~

When she woke again—the next day?—she was able to move her head slightly and look around the room. It had an odd shape—too many corners, too many walls. Seven sides, so a . . . a heptagon? The old woman sat by her side, busily moving her hands. She worked at a red yarn, whispering in an unrecognizable language, her waves of murmurs drifting into a soft melody.

"All there is to do is rest," the old woman said when she saw that her eyes had opened. "Your body will do the rest. Your body and your will. Nothing is predetermined. The decision is yours. You have chosen this. The road ahead may be difficult, yet hopefully worthwhile."

She didn't understand what the woman meant—what had she chosen? And how was anything up to her when she was so utterly helpless? Who in their right mind would choose to be in such a situation?

"The mind has nothing to do with it dear," said the old woman, as if reading her thoughts. "The more you can rest your mind and body, the less your suffering will be."

That she understood. She drifted into deep sleep.

~

The aroma of bitter herbs filled the room.

"You need to regain your strength now." The gentle whisper was again by her side. "Try to swallow some of this."

A wooden spoon touched her partially open lips, and she allowed a liquid to glide down into her throat.

"Well done, dear!" exclaimed the old woman with a clearly satisfied expression. She offered the spoon and the liquid again.

The liquid, a broth, brought energy and a renewal of taste. She was able to keep her eyes open and study the room and the old woman. She was able to study herself.

She lay under a cover of leaves joined by strings of what looked like algae. The old woman replaced the leaves frequently and the algea less often, drawing both of them warm from a large pot in the center of the room. A fire burned under the pot constantly, casting a shifting glow that mixed with the shadows.

The old woman sang or murmured. She worked her red yarn. And she tended her.

The days flowed with little change. She had no sense of how long it took, but slowly she was able to move. To shift positions. She swallowed more of the clear liquid with its bittersweet taste.

She grew intimately familiar with her surroundings.

The room indeed had seven sides, made of what seemed like very old wood. There was only one source of light, the small window above her bed. The bed had revealed itself as some kind of large plank. There was one door, but she had never seen it open.

The old woman was always there, either busy at the large pot—a cauldron, in truth—in the middle of the room or sitting on a rocking chair and weaving. Her constant murmurs and quiet singing filled the silence.

The wet leaves were sometimes uncomfortable, but when she scratched or pushed at them, the old woman replaced them with new ones that she fished out of the cauldron. They were slightly warm when she applied them to her body, usually soothing and sometimes energizing.

The woman wrapped long algae around her head, which at first felt strange. But it too soothed.

She eventually noticed the pain subsiding and an improvement in her ability to move and stretch. She wanted to get up and be freed from her confinement.

"We're almost there," the old woman kept saying. "Not quite yet."

~

She awakened to bright light streaming onto her bed and birds chirping nearby. Fragrant pine and eucalyptus scents streamed through the open window. The *open* window.

The whole time she lay there—for what seemed like eternity—she never saw the door or window open, yet there was always a smell of freshness in the air despite the intense odors emanating from the earthenware cauldron.

"Time to try to sit up," said the old woman when she saw that she was awake.

She helped her into a half-reclining positing by wedging a diagonally slanted board behind her.

"How does that feel?"

"Good!" she replied. She lifted one hand to her lips, realizing that this was the first word she had uttered.

CHAPTER EIGHT

Tikvah

THE OLD WOMAN began removing the leaves from her body, although some just glided off when she sat up, revealing a thin and fragile form. The woman brought a small wooden bowl of water and a clean cloth to the bed and began wiping her face, chest and arms. The wet cloth was warm and smelled of fragrant eucalyptus. It felt refreshing.

"We cleanse this body of the traumas it endured," the woman murmured as she wiped her from head to toe. "We wash off the old energies so we can begin anew."

After she finished cleansing her entire body, the woman bent over a large wooden chest by the bed and pulled out a simple garment that looked like a large burlap bag.

"Let's slip this on," she said, helping to raise her arms.

The cloth dropped around her, surprisingly soft against her skin despite its rough appearance.

"Now we must fatten you up and strengthen your muscles," the woman said as she fastened a rope around her waist to hold the garment in place.

When the old woman removed leaves from the bed, she uncovered several crystals along the sides. They were of various shades and sizes, starting with a white one at the top followed by purple, blue, green, yellow, orange and red. She looked up; she'd already noticed the clear crystal that hung above her head. When light filtered through the window, the hanging crystal scattered small rainbows all around her. The colorful stones fascinated her, as light emanated from within them in all the colors of the rainbow. Their color and glimmer beamed each time the hanging crystal's rays brushed their surface.

"The crystals are for healing," the woman said when she noticed her looking at them. "All I've done here will become clear in time. How long that takes doesn't matter. It's the process that's important."

The enigmatic speech only added to her confusion.

"Where am I?" she asked.

"My cabin. It's a safe and blessed place for you to heal."

"How did I get here?" The words jumped out of her mouth before the other woman had a chance to continue. The old woman sat in her rocking chair and took a deep breath.

"Gabi found you." She pointed to a large fluffy dog beside her on the floor.

She sat up higher, amazed that she'd never noticed him before. She studied the beautiful creature who lay calm at the feet of his mistress. He woke with a huge open-mouthed yawn and opened his eyes, exposing a soft blue-gray glare. He had a majestic mane of gray and brown tones, and his head was larger than any dog she could imagine. Because of his size, she wondered if he might be a wolf.

"What do you mean he found me? Where? And how did you get me here?" She couldn't imagine that the old, hunched figure next to her had the strength to carry her to the bed from even the doorway, much less somewhere else.

The woman waved a hand over her shoulder. "In the ocean." She reached down to pat Gabi's head. "And we had help."

The ocean? She looked toward the window, picturing deep blue water pounding at the shore and disappearing out over the horizon.

"Gabi was the first to see you in the water. We were scouring the beach for long algae and kelp when he started howling at the ocean. The waves were high, so it was hard to see at first why he was running full speed toward the water. Then I noticed a group of seals swimming in unison, quite odd and unusual. They were holding something up, as though sheltering it from the waves. By then Gabi was in the water. I could barely see his head as he swam toward them. Then it disappeared into the swells. He kept to his course when I called him. When Gabi neared the seals, they dispersed, and he grabbed in his mouth what they'd been carrying on their backs. By the time I was able to get past the rugged rocks, he was back to the shore, dragging you out of the water. He laid you gently on the ground, and his brothers surrounded you. Uri had already run down to meet him, but Micha and Rafi stayed by my side until I climbed over the rocks and stepped on the sand."

She gestured toward the door. Another wolf-like dog lay at the entrance.

"That's Uri. He and Gabi usually stick together. The other two, Micha and Rafi, are outside guarding the cabin. There isn't any danger to us out here, but they like to do it, so I let them take turns outside."

"How did you bring me here?" The tale seemed surreal, and she was feeling impatient. No. She was anxious.

"Gabi and Uri lay beside you to keep you warm, and Rafi and Micha helped me scout the area. Much to our and your luck, we found a broken dingy that had washed up on the shore. I tied kelp to it with algae, and Micha and Rafi dragged it to where you lay. We literally scooped you up from the sand by placing the broken side of the boat next to you and rolling you into it." She laughed. "Maybe not a sophisticated idea, but definitely practical. I then tied you to the bottom with algae and kelp and used the kelp as rope; those four beauties dragged you up the hill, through the forest and into the cabin." She knocked on the bed. "You're *still* lying on the boat. All I did was saw off the sides and pad the bottom with leaves."

She knew she was gaping, mouth and eyes wide, but she marveled at the ingenuity of the old woman.

"Like I said, a lot of help, and not just from them." She patted Gabi again, and the second one—Uri?—padded over for a scratch behind the ears. "Thanks to all the wonderful elements of the forest and the sea, we were able to nurse you back to life. I'm so delighted to finally meet you. I'm Moriah. You're most welcome in my home."

"Thank you, Moriah. I— *Thank you*. And you too, Gabi and Uri."

"So, my dear, what is your name?"

She tried to summon a response from that realm where she'd drifted for eons in darkness and pain, where indeterminate thoughts and images tumbled without ceasing, but nothing came to her. The only thing attached to the word name was a black void.

"I don't know." She immediately felt like a failure for not knowing her name—a name was what identified a person. A name was—

"Not to worry, my dear," Moriah said, patting her leg just as she'd patted her dogs. "For now, I'll call you Tikvah. This will be your name until you remember." She stood. "But now you must rest." She moved to the bed and slid out the diagonal support. "But I'm certain your mind won't rest. And maybe that's for the best. Let your mind explore what you've just learned. You will be the one to provide the missing details."

She lay down, her thoughts spinning. Her rescue seemed unbelievable but also mysterious. Yet until she had more information, she'd accept it. She might not know her own name, but she did know that seals didn't perform sea rescues. The dogs? That part seemed plausible. But most disconcerting was the inability to remember anything from her life, anything about herself from before waking up in this place. She had no recollections and no way to trace herself back to who she was, not even a name.

"Time will show you the way and who you are," Moriah said, jolting her out of her confused reverie. "Do you know the meaning of *Tikvah*?"

When she shook her head, Moriah said, "Tikvah is the ancient Hebrew word for Hope. The word is derived from words meaning cord and to eagerly wait. To be patient. Unlike the current meaning, it held within it the sense of something which is going to eventually occur. It did not have the desperate connotation it does now of hope as the last resort. On the contrary, hope in its original meaning was a covenant that arose from an agreement, an expectation of a determined outcome." She eased back into her rocking chair. "The first time that Tikvah is mentioned in the Old Testament is in the book of Joshua and the story of Rahab, the woman promised by Joshua's spies that she and her family would be spared from the Israelite invasion if she tied a crimson cord on her window. So *Tikvah* also means a cord. In its origins it had a tangible form. Hope ties us to a destiny which is expected. The expectation creates anticipation. We take actions and make plans to fulfill the expectation, all out of hope." She began rocking. Forward and back, forward and back. "This name will guide you to who you are and to the life you expect, to the future you imagine."

Moriah rocked, the dogs slept and *Tikvah* pondered what she had learned.

Much later, Moriah asked, "What is your hope, Tikvah?"

Tikvah responded without hesitation. "I hope to be healthy and joyful and to know who I am and where I belong."

CHAPTER NINE

Moriah

A S HER BODY strengthened, Tikvah began to go outside. She often sat on the shaded bench in front of the cabin, observing the steadfast changes in the front yard with its neatly arranged rows of plants that Moriah grew for food. Yellow and orange butterflies hovered around the plants and the air buzzed with insects and bees. The high-pitched chirping of birds emanated from the nearby forest during the early hours of every day. Sweet scents of grass and flowers permeated the air from the wild field beyond the vegetable garden.

The dogs soon became her companions. She quickly learned to distinguish their markings and personalities. Moriah had named them after the four archangels: Gabriel, Michael, Uriel and Rafael. Their joyful protection and canine—or was it angelic?—intuition filled Tikvah's days with fun and comfort. They played with and around her, often panting at her feet in the shade, and they clearly accepted her as one of their pack. Gabi spent the most time with her, and she treated him like the big brother of the group. She felt welcomed by their constant close frolicking.

Moriah started work in her garden when the sun rose, and by midday a delicious aroma would fill the cabin. Tikvah had a good appetite and became stronger each day. Moriah began teaching her the attributes of the vegetables and herbs she cooked.

"This will not only strengthen your body but also your mind and memory," she said of more than one herb or vegetable.

Tikvah still had absolutely no recollection of the accident or anything from her previous life. She knew that her body had physically died and that a part of her hadn't come back from that death. She feared the missing part and was reluctant to reclaim it. She felt safety in not seeking the unknown and in the acceptance of things as they were. And yet she recog-

nized that the absence of anxiety wasn't usual for her. Knew that she was
hiding from something she should be facing. But Moriah didn't push her
to face that fear and therefore she chose not to push herself.

She did wonder how she'd come to be in the ocean, but since Moriah
said nothing more about the incident, Tikvah didn't demand answers.
She didn't want to lose the peace that Moriah's home provided. Her fear
of what she'd learn was stronger than her curiosity, although she doubted
that would always be the case.

She settled into the slow rhythm of waking, playing with the dogs, eating, learning in the afternoons and sleeping at sundown. It was a sweet
gentle existence in which she felt loved, nourished, content and safe. She
had no past and no future, and she was happy experiencing the life around
her moment by moment.

Moriah's incessant activity filled their days.

She carried their water from an underground spring and filtered it
through a cloth to remove dirt and other particles. Moriah would then
bless it, as she did everything she touched, by murmuring indecipherable
words and holding her hands over it. Her gnarled fingers, molded by constant digging in the earth and her daily chores, would dance in the air as
if they were magic wands igniting a spell.

Tikvah's first impression of Moriah as being ancient changed with
time. Her face was covered with deep wrinkles, her white hair was set in
a high bun, whisks sticking out in all directions, casting a halo of light
around her face as the sun caught them. Yet in the brightness of the day,
she appeared youthful and even beautiful. Maybe it was her brilliant dark
eyes that lent her the youthful appearance, as they always seemed curious,
joyful and kind. Her energy was incessant and gleeful, as though every
action ignited in her a playful delight. She tended her vegetable garden
with the same devotion with which she'd nurtured Tikvah. When she
made her daily gatherings of carrots, onions, eggplants, a large variety of
squashes and herbs, she laid each on the outdoor stone slab that they used
as a table, as though they were ornaments to be admired, before scooping
them up to be chopped and cooked in her large stoneware cauldron.

Her cooking was infused with ritualistic gestures that made her
slightly crouched figure seem as graceful as a dancer. Tikvah watched her
with constant fascination.

The meals her cauldron produced were gourmet elixirs and body-fattening stews. In the mornings they ate a porridge made of wild oats speckled with berries gathered from the forest. The afternoon meal was a feast of vegetables spiced by Moriah's herbs and wild plants foraged from the forest.

Some mornings Moriah disappeared into the forest for what seemed an eternity as Tikvah anxiously awaited her return. She always reappeared before the sun rose high in the sky, her arms filled with herb, shrubs, tree barks and at times, even mushrooms. She would hang her finds inside the cabin to dry before grinding them into fine spices.

After their afternoon feast, they sat together on the outside bench until the sun disappeared behind the cabin, casting long shadows over the yard. Moriah always brought out bundles of red yarn and a large wooden loom and began weaving an intricate cloth.

She spoke while she worked, teaching Tikvah care of the garden, the forest and the animals.

Everything in nature was organized around an energy cycle and the balance of the elements. The plants that nourished them were nourished by air, sunlight, water and the earth. The nourishment they consumed was returned to the earth to start the cycle again, Moriah told her on several occasions, as though she never tired of marveling at the natural cycle of death and rebirth. And Tikvah never ceased to be fascinated by Moriah's explanations about the intricacies of nature's creations.

Even the dogs' angelic names were linked to the elements. Gabriel was a master of water, Uriel of earth, Michael of fire and Rafael of air.

When Tikvah asked about them, Moriah taught her about the crystals that she'd placed in her bed while she was recovering: a white selenite above her head, a purple amethyst next to her temple, a blue turquoise next to her throat, green tourmaline by her heart, a yellow citrine by her abdomen, an orange moonstone by her sacrum, and a red fire agate by her pubic bone. Each stone corresponded to a different energy vibration and meridian in her body; Tikvah remembered—no, not remembered but knew—that meridians were used in acupuncture.

"The crystals transmitted their energy to those vital areas to help heal the cells of your bones and organs as well as your spirit," Moriah explained, as she lifted them one by one and pointed to the areas in Tikvah's body that received their healing.

Tikvah stared at the magical stones, enthralled by their healing power.

Beyond their visible beauty, they appeared to hold secrets she could not comprehend. Despite having to stretch her imagination to understand Moriah's teachings, Tikvah drank in her words, eager to learn, wanting to understand her own healing process.

"These majestic crystals have been around for millions of years," Moriah told her. "They hold the memories of the ancients. Someday even they will return to dust. Yet their consciousness will remain intact, and they will be reborn again from the cosmic dust as stars."

Tikvah tried to imagine the vastness of time it would take the stones to crumble to dust and reassemble into stars. She felt her mind expanding beyond her own threshold of vision, beyond vision itself to a realm where ideas are born. She wondered if Moriah meant it literally or it was a metaphor to describe the endless undying cycle of all things, even of stones. Regardless, she felt reassurance in the sense of their eternity as it connected her to the indestructible eternal part of herself.

Dusk would send them back into their cabin. Moriah had changed the makeup of Tikvah's bed, placing a thick layer of hay at the bottom and covering it with a cloth. The bed was a bit noisy when she turned, but the padding was much more comfortable than wet leaves.

While she drifted to sleep, Moriah sat in the rocking chair, weaving and humming and singing softly.

Tikvah's sleep was deep and often filled with intense dreams, and she woke with glimpses of images from another life that she could not decipher.

The dreams unsettled her. As much as she wanted to chase away the questions they brought up, they returned to her each morning. Who was she and where was she from? Did she leave loved ones behind? She knew Moriah couldn't help her with these questions, so she didn't ask. But how could she find out? Where to begin? Could her night visions provide her hints of answers? For the moment, her dreams were shrouded in a jumble of images, and she couldn't even find the words to ask Moriah about what those images might mean.

To her wonderment, each morning she woke up to find the crimson cloth that Moriah spent an entire afternoon and evening weaving the day before completely undone. Why did she go to all that trouble?

Just like her night's dreams, Moriah's world was shrouded in mysteries, which she hoped to uncover in time.

CHAPTER TEN

The Acorn

ONE AFTERNOON, AS Tikvah sat in her usual spot on the bench in front of the cabin, she was astonished by a swarm of delicate orange petals that suddenly swirled around her head.

Butterflies? Her mouth formed the word syllable by syllable, as though of its own accord. Immediately they lifted up and flipped their orange wings toward the meadow. She drew up from the bench and followed them, spellbound. There in the meadow an explosion of colors—purples, blues, yellow, and red greeted her. She twirled, arms extended, as if hugging the ocean of colors to her, inhaling the sweet scent of the meadow with each deep breath. Only then did she realize that she was moving without pain for the first time, and not just moving, but floating through air as the butterflies had sifted the air around her face. She spun and spun, arms wide open, head tilted back, her laughter spilling until dizzy, she fell and rolled into the sea of color. The dogs surrounded her in a flurry of fluffy fur, wet tongues and squeals of joy. She truly was one of the pack, now that she could run and spin and roll as they did. She pulled herself up and smiled and noticed that the flowers around her returned her smile. She gathered a bunch of yellow, blue and red smiles to take to Moriah with her gratitude.

Moriah was overjoyed, tears filling her eyes as she hugged the bouquet and Tikvah.

"Thank you; they're beautiful. And your trip to the meadow ... Do you realize that this is the first time you spontaneously ventured so far on your own?" She pointed down and laughed. "And on bare feet! This is the sign that your physical recovery is complete." She took the flowers into the cabin, where she placed them in a clay jug.

When she came out, she carried something wrapped in craft paper.

"This is a moment of celebration, dear one, and we must mark it appropriately." She winked. "And that means presents."

Tikvah unwrapped a pair of leather moccasins, soft to the touch and sporting a thick leather sole.

"I made them in anticipation of this moment," Moriah said. "May they carry you to many marvelous discoveries."

She helped Tikvah lace the long leather straps, binding the leather up her ankles and calves. They fit perfectly, and Tikvah danced around the yard in joy, elated by the freedom to move about as and where she pleased.

After an afternoon celebration, feasting on an exquisite vegetarian meal, Moriah skipped the usual lessons and let Tikvah enjoy playing with the dogs in her newfound freedom.

The following morning, after breakfast, Moriah said, "Today you can help me tend the garden."

Tikvah was thrilled at being able to put her many lessons into practice. The sun beamed as they worked, while a cool breeze chilled the air. Moriah showed her how to prepare new plots for planting by plowing and by mixing compost with the soil, then watering the ground and letting it sit for a day for all the nutrients to be absorbed into the earth.

She enjoyed the moist earth under her fingers and the stretching of her body.

Next they brought out the grains that Moriah had dried from the previous harvest. They planted some of the seeds directly into the plots, but some were planted in small containers to be allowed to germinate before being put into the ground.

There was a separate plot where they planted mostly lettuces and greens. Moriah dedicated that plot to the insects and rodents and asked that they feast there and leave the other plots undisturbed.

"A proven method to protect a crop from invading creatures of all sizes," she assured Tikvah.

Weary after the intense morning activity, Tikvah dozed after lunch on the bench shaded by the cabin. She awoke refreshed and peaceful, the afternoon sun caressing her bare arms and legs. On the ground beside her was a woven basket.

"I'd like you to do something for me."

Moriah was by her side, drying her hands on an apron.

"Please go into the forest and find the grand oak tree at the end of the path. You'll see it on the ridge to your left. I'd like you to get the biggest acorns you can find on the ground underneath it and bring them back here."

She motioned to the basket, indicating to Tikvah that she should take it with her to collect the acorns.

The request was quite unusual, but Tikvah was happy to help. Even happier, if a bit embarrassed, when she realized she'd never once offered to help Moriah.

She'd also never been inside the forest and now wondered how she'd be able to find one specific tree. She stared at the trees at the edge of the forest and shook her head.

Moriah grinned when Tikvah hesitated. "Don't worry. You'll recognize it the moment you see it."

Tikvah picked up the basket and made her way toward the back of the cabin, where the thick forest extended itself to a mysterious world beyond the familiar.

"Make sure you stay on the path. It's the only way you'll find your route back."

She waved, and Moriah's voice faded as she penetrated the shadowed darkness. She was immediately struck by a sharp scent that penetrated her nostrils, filling her head with freshness. *Pine?* It took a moment to adjust to the darkness. Where was the trail Moriah promised? She bent down and studied the terrain, realizing that she was standing on an actual path overgrown by moss and ferns. As she pushed deeper, she was able to distinguish it better among the trees, but she needed to concentrate to stay on course.

The forest grew in thickness, the trees closer together, the farther she got from the entrance. And she guessed that the path might once have been a brook or stream, so differentiated it was from the rest of the terrain. Her intense focus chased away the fears that periodically crept into her mind with the increasing obscurity. She intended to return before sundown, because it would be impossible to recognize the path in the dark.

She fleetingly wondered why Moriah had entrusted the task to her. It was likely to be a lesson, but maybe she just had a hankering for acorns.

Tikvah laughed and pushed on.

The time could be measured only by the darkening sky between the thick canopy of trees and by the cooling of the air.

She stopped when she reached a point where she couldn't advance unless she climbed over fallen trunks. Just as she raised her head to study the terrain, she saw a huge tree to her left hovering majestically on the slight incline of a hill. Its branches, extending in all directions, obscured the horizon beyond it. Moriah had been right; there was no mistaking the chosen oak whose large acorns covered its extensive branches.

After a few steps, Tikvah stood under its vast canopy, where she gasped in awe at its magnificent grandeur. For a brief instant it reminded her of her first glimpse of Moriah's face when she opened her eyes in the cabin.

Majesty and eternity radiated from its monumental twisting trunk and its enormous crown of leaves. She felt silly that she had the strangest urge to hug it, so she reached out and touched its weathered trunk instead.

She stepped closer, a loud crackle under her feet, and only then noticed that the ground was buried under giant acorns the size of her thumb. She was jolted out of her wonderment and into the task of finding the biggest acorns she could to bring back.

While engrossed in concentration, she suddenly sensed a dark and ominous presence. Standing upright, she was confronted by a ferocious sight: a dozen coyotes creeping toward her, grinning teeth on display. She dropped her basket; the sudden thump made the coyotes growl as they smoothly crept closer. She was afraid to move, but there was nowhere to go anyway; her back was nearly flush against the huge oak trunk. She closed her eyes and imagined the coyotes scattering into the forest. She had no idea what she could do to cause them to do that, since they were completely fixated on her as their prey. Yet she *expected* them to leave. She refused to believe that after all she'd been through and her miraculous recovery that Moriah would send her to such a violent death.

An earsplitting howl rang out from the hill above her. Was it the alpha calling for the rest of his pack and telling them they'd located their prey? She shivered.

Could she climb the tree? And if she could, would that even help?

The raucous howling continued—got worse—and she finally dared to open her eyes. She gasped. Three coyote tails, the last of them, were disappearing into the thickness of the forest. Within moments Gabi was at her side, jumping on her and licking her face. Tikvah laughed in relief and thanked him, squeezing him hard. That was the second time he'd saved her life.

"You're such a good boy, Gabi." Still praising him, she quickly gathered the acorns that had fallen out of the basket and retraced her steps, this time accompanied by her guardian angel.

The flickering cabin light appeared when she neared the edge of the forest. The return felt a whole lot shorter than had her journey to the tree. By the time she entered the yard, dusk had fallen, bringing its long shadows to the day's farewell.

They were welcomed joyfully by the three other dogs, and Tikvah called out, "Moriah, I'm home."

Moriah smiled when Tikvah rushed inside, holding the basket over her head like a prize. The aroma of soup sent Tikvah's stomach rumbling, and she handed the basket to Moriah while gratefully accepting the bowl that Moriah poured for her.

"What an adventure I had," Tikvah said around a spoonful of soup. "Have you seen coyotes in the forest? There were at least a dozen." She swallowed more soup and pointed at Gabi. "But Gabi ran them off. He was a hero again."

"An adventure indeed," Moriah said.

"I didn't know what to do, and I was afraid, but I knew they were going to leave. I just knew it."

"Eat first. We have the whole night for stories."

While Tikvah ate, Moriah carefully inspected the acorns and laid them one by one on the wooden table. She waited for Tikvah to finish eating before picking up the biggest acorn.

"You did well, my dear." She held the acorn high. "This one is most robust; it'll be perfect."

She leaned across the table and trapped one of Tikvah's hands under her own. "I am so very proud of you," she said. "You persevered despite the impending dangers you faced, and you conquered them with your hope."

She handed the large acorn to Tikvah.

"This acorn in its very essence contains the hope of the entire oak to become a grand tree. Let it be a symbol of your triumph. Now you have truly mastered hope. Its power courses through your spirit, and you'll be able to draw on it whenever you chose. It's a most creative tool for the living of your life." She took the acorn back from Tikvah, placed it on the table and surrounded it by the seven colorful crystals. "We'll keep these here. This is a shrine to your hope and courage. The crystals will enhance the power of both."

Tikvah marveled at her small shrine and gathered its meaning, hope and courage, inside her heart. She wanted with all her will to believe Moriah and hold on to this moment, knowing that she could summon hope when her path was obscured or threatened. Still, she couldn't shake the troubling memory of the vicious beasts surrounding her with sharp, bared teeth. She focused on the acorn to chase away the image, gathering its hope to become a powerful and majestic tree as a reminder of strength. She recalled her own hope that she shared with Moriah when she first woke up: to be healthy and joyful and know who she was and where she belonged. She had been shoving these hopes to the recesses of her mind during her convalescence, unwilling to face the inevitable questions that they evoked, afraid of the answers they might rouse. As she stared at the prized acorn surrounded by the glorious crystals, she sensed a shift within herself. A rise of courage. Her hope to find out the truth about herself might actually be granted, but where to start to piece together the mystery that shrouded her past?

"Moriah, I've been wondering about the day you found me. Were there any clues about who I might have been? Where I came from? Why didn't you take me to the hospital to get help?"

She gazed at Moriah with determination, yet her voice faltered.

Moriah smiled lovingly. "I have been anticipating these questions and knew they would come in good time. I am so glad that you are finding the way to self-discovery and that you are finally having the courage to face your hopes." Her eyes drifted towards the door and beyond the cabin, as she continued.

"When Gabi brought you out of the water, all the breath had gone out of you. I didn't know how long it had been that way, but I wanted to try to help you, nonetheless. Your rescue by the seals was an indication that the universe wanted you to live. They kept you afloat, and Gabi delivered you to the safety of the sand and laid you at my feet like an offering from the heavens. I knew then, or rather hoped, that you would live again and that I had a role to play in your life. In the state we found you, doctors wouldn't have been much help. But I understood at that moment that destiny had united us in this miraculous way. So I did all I could to bring you to safety and heal your body. Just as your body's hope to live led you to your miraculous recovery, your hope to know who you are and where you belong will lead to your destiny. And I am here to help you with that in every way I can."

This wasn't the answer Tikvah expected. But she understood that it was the best response she could possibly receive. Moriah couldn't offer her concrete answers about her past, but she could help her find her own way. Moriah's calm reassurance filled her heart with determination and fired her resolve, and those feelings woke up a faint wave of remembrance of who she had been, as if she began waking up to herself. Her sigh transformed into a yawn; this had been a long evening, and an even longer day, and there was much digesting she needed to do of everything that she had discovered about herself. She kissed the acorn and then Moriah's cheek in gratitude before turning to her bed. But she had a hard time falling asleep as the same stubborn questions kept churning in her mind. *Who am I, and where do I belong?* The questions bellowed from the depth of her being.

CHAPTER ELEVEN

The Pinecone

N IGHTMARES HAUNTED TIKVAH the entire night, their theme consistent; she had to get somewhere, deliver an important message, but couldn't reach her enigmatic destination, couldn't be heard, or didn't know the direly important message that it was her duty to deliver, and which would prevent some catastrophe. She tried every means to reach her destination—by boat, by car, by foot—but each time her intense efforts were thwarted, and she found herself in the place where she began, a dark cell.

In one of her more pleasant dreams, she was in a room with a man and a dog. She cared deeply for both of them, yet for some reason they weren't able to see her. She spoke to them and even yelled that she was there, but they went about their business as if she didn't exist. As though they occupied parallel planes of existence.

Another dream revealed a woman falling into a deep abyss. Tikvah reached out, trying to catch her, but was pulled by the woman's weight and swept into a vortex of darkness.

She finally awoke in a fit of sweat after dreaming that she was surrounded by giants wearing white robes. They told her that she hadn't completed her mission and would need to start over and that she must return to her post; the safety of the planet depended on her success. Even awake, she felt the responsibility of the dream, and she huddled in terrified dismay, paralyzed by fear and shame because she couldn't remember what her mission was.

Moriah was stroking her arm when she opened her eyes. Both Moriah and the sight of the familiar cabin brought instant comfort, and Tikvah sighed.

"Just relax, dear one," Moriah said, wiping her forehead with a warm moist cloth that smelled of lavender. "It was just a dream. You're safe." She moved the cloth slowly. "Nothing to worry about."

Tikvah focused on the room. From the long rays upon the dark walls, she deduced that it was late morning; she'd slept longer than usual. She got up and gratefully accepted the warm herbal tea that Moriah extended to her. She recognized the fragrance of valerian root.

"This will help calm your heart," Moriah told her.

Outside, Tikvah was welcomed by the dogs, all four eager to play. But still under the spell of her nightmares, she wasn't in a playful mood. The lingering dream shadows were a stark contrast to the reality of the bright sunny day, the beauty of nature that surrounded her and the peaceful life that she'd been enjoying in Moriah's company.

"What's happening to me?" she asked.

"Nothing to alarm yourself over," Moriah said as she sat by her on the bench. "Dreams, right?"

Tikvah nodded.

"It's to be expected. Your subconscious is trying to tell you something and is doing a pretty good job of shaking you up. It's its way of jolting your memory. Before you came here, you had programmed your subconscious along a certain story, a personal myth, if you like. Since you haven't yet recovered it or replaced it with another one, with a new image of yourself, your subconscious is trying to bring you back into its paradigm. It's the only way it knows to feel safe." Moriah spoke gently while caressing her arm. "Even though you're not in your old life anymore, you've carried anxieties from the past into your current reality. They must be faced in order to be released."

Tikvah angled toward Moriah, feeling helpless and searching for answers.

"How am I supposed to face fears and anxieties if I don't know what they are? Was I supposed to accomplish something important? Was that part of my destiny? Was that the reason I was saved?" An image of a man and a dog flashed across her mind. "Did I abandon loved ones?"

Questions were gushing at her faster than she could think or ask them. Moriah took a long breath and gazed at Tikvah with the kind of deep gaze she used to penetrate into her and yet also span far beyond her. The stare was uncomfortable but not unkind, and although Tikvah blinked several times, she didn't turn away.

"There once was a beautiful little girl with long black hair," Moriah said. "The girl had only her mother, whom she loved very much. They lived in a comfortable house by the bay. Her mother would brush the girl's long hair every night while she told her how beautiful and smart she was and how much she loved her. One day her mother revealed that she was sick and that she might not be there very much longer. She asked her daughter to be brave when she was gone and do all she could to be happy.

"The mother's disease progressed, and even before the woman died, she was absent. She didn't respond to her daughter or even recognize her. The little girl took care of her mother and the house because no one was around to help. She fed and washed her mother, and while she combed her mother's hair in the evening, she told her that she was being brave as promised and that she'd be happy if only her mother came back. She never did and died a short while later. As the girl watched her mother on her deathbed, she vowed that she'd find a cure for the disease that caused her to go away. When she grew up, she dedicated her whole life to her promise. Remembering her promise to her mother, she did all she could to create a happy life, while continuing her quest to find the ultimate cure. A part of her believed that finding the cure would restore her mother's love and fill the gaping hole in her heart. That, of course, could never happen. She had sacrificed her whole self to her mission, to a point of obsession, and in the process she lost herself."

At the conclusion of her story Moriah stood up.

"Wait, what's the lesson here?" Tikvah wanted to scream. "Isn't there supposed to be a happy ending, like in a fairy tale? And why are you telling me this story? Was I that girl? Did *my* mother die?"

"To be continued," Moriah said after a long moment of silence that felt like an eternity, much to Tikvah's frustration.

"Why can't you tell me now?" The cry escaped from her throat. Tears stung her eyes and she willed them to dry. She didn't want to be that girl. She wasn't ready to know. She yearned to climb back into the cocoon of blissful ignorance. Moriah only smiled faintly, her eyes narrowed, and she turned to go outside.

Tikvah was in no mood to play with the dogs who kept jumping on her to get her attention. She wasn't inspired to tend the garden either, so Moriah weeded and watered the plots by herself. Tikvah ate her lunch listlessly, barely tasting the food and staring into the distance. She felt numb to the world.

"I'd like you to do another errand for me," Moriah told her after lunch, handing her the woven basket. "I'd like you to find the smallest pinecones you see and bring them back. Take Gabi with you; he'll show you the way."

Tikvah took the basket reluctantly. She'd had enough adventure the previous day and wanted to be left in peace. But peace wasn't to be found, as she still felt disturbed by her dreams and the story Moriah told her. Searching for tiny pinecones couldn't make her feel any worse.

She entered the path into the forest behind the house, with Gabi leading the way. He didn't stay on the path this time but meandered between the trees in the direction of the sun. He swiftly skipped between fallen tree trunks and high bushes as Tikvah climbed breathlessly, trying to keep up. He sniffed and advanced, unconcerned by the difficulty she had in following him. Her dark thoughts only augmented her confusion and worry. The carefree days of her convalescence were apparently gone, and she didn't understand why Moriah had told her the sad tale and what was in it for her to understand. Was *she* the girl from the story? A surge of pain rose in her as she pondered this possibility without being able to come up with any certain answer. And she continued to be haunted by the fear that she had left someone behind. Someone she loved and who had loved her. Someone who might be searching in desperation for her at that very moment. Her inability to ease that person's sorrow and the inability to remember those she loved made her heart break.

Even with her apprehensions, her survival instincts told her to keep a close watch on Gabi, who advanced easily through the treacherous terrain, not bothering to look back for her. She gave herself over to tracking the dog and playing catch-up. She would have sworn that he was playing with her, getting just far enough ahead to make her have to hurry before she lost sight of him.

"I know what you're doing, Gabi," she called out once. "And I don't think it's very funny." But she giggled with relief when he disappeared only to pop up from behind a tree a moment later, tongue lolling and tail wagging, before he raced in a circle and disappeared again.

About a hundred trees later, as she dragged herself up one more pile of rocks after him, she noticed that the heavy thoughts that had clung tight and darkened her mood had been gone for some time. Not only her thoughts, but even her body felt lighter, and she sighed contentedly when she got to the other side of the rocky mound and saw that Gabi had finally stopped and was sitting tall and staring back at her.

Beyond Gabi, the thick forest gave way to a sparsely planted young pine grove. The view was so clear and open that she could see the ocean hovering on the far horizon. Even from this distance, it glistened in the setting sun, the thin silver line on the horizon mesmerizing in its beauty. She stood arrested for a few moments before realizing that she needed to hurry to her task before the sun set completely and she'd be unable to see Gabi leading the way back to the cabin. She decided to waste no more time taking in the vista and rushed toward the small pine trees. She collected some of the pinecones from the ground but found smaller ones that she picked directly from the trees. Those on the trees were closed and green, while those on the ground were brown and open. She had no idea why Moriah sent her on a seemingly innocuous mission but hoped it might have something to do with the story she had begun that morning. Perhaps her hunt was supposed to help her make better sense of the tale. If so, her trip into the woods hadn't yet been successful.

When her basket was full, she straightened up, catching another glimpse of the blue sea peeking among the trees in the distance. For an instant she was drawn to it, wanting to explore what lay beyond the woods and beyond Moriah's protective cocoon. Yet when a large cloud passed overhead, darkening the bright day, it took but a moment for fear to overtake her, rising like a cold column inside her, a shield blocking her desire, and causing that desire to retreat just as quickly as it had sprung up.

She excused her fear by telling herself she needed to get the pinecones to Moriah and ask her about them, and there was still that mysterious tale about the little girl and her mother that was unresolved. She had questions for Moriah that needed answers, and she was resolute to continue the conversation they had begun earlier.

So maybe her explorations *had* accomplished something.

Gabi lay panting and drooling under the shade of one of the taller trees, but as soon as she called him, he leaped to his feet and headed in the direction of the mound where they'd entered the field. This time he stayed close by her side, bumping into her companionably every few strides.

It was even more difficult to climb the rock mound with the heavy basket on her arm, yet Tikvah managed it awkwardly while Gabi waited for her at the top. The thick forest stretched in front of them when they got to the other side. Its density stole Tikvah's breath; she felt she could never manage to find her way back on her own. Luckily Gabi never left her side, and together they negotiated the complex route, climbing over fallen tree trunks and bulging roots, circumventing thorny bushes until they found their path forward again. Tikvah could do nothing but trust that Gabi and his keen senses were capable of getting them back. As they progressed, the journey made more burdensome by the full and heavy basket, the sky—which was mostly obscured by the heads of trees—seemed to grow unusually dark. Clouds were gathering and the wind picked up dramatically. The whispers of the rustling leaves became a roar. Tikvah, reassured by Gabi's presence, nevertheless braced herself for the approaching storm. It seemed that the brooding sky and the torrid air were a reflection of the storm that had been churning inside her all day.

The sky exploded its torrent of rain just as they arrived at the meadow, a short sprint to the cabin, and they rushed inside. Moriah took her into her arms in a warm embrace.

"I'm so glad you're back safe before the storm hit. What perfect timing."

Tikvah laughed and shook her head, scattering raindrops. Gabi did the same, shaking and flinging water across the room. Moriah ran a hand over Tikvah's hair and said, "Well, almost before it hit."

Tikvah couldn't help but feel bewildered by Moriah's ever-present good spirits and optimism. She allowed herself to slump on the bed while Moriah fixed warm soup for her. A fire was lit under the cauldron, warming up the room and releasing its endless delicious aromas.

All four dogs were inside, since the rain had become torrential. As she ate, Tikvah listened to its loud thumping on the roof as well as the howling wind that encircled the cabin. Inside, however, all was still and calm. Full and exhausted by the stress of the day, she allowed her eyes to close.

"You did well again today, dear one," Moriah said. "A full basket. Now rest. Tomorrow will bring its wisdom."

Tikvah gladly took Moriah's suggestion, leaving her worries outside the cabin.

~

The rain was still tapping on the roof when Tikvah woke. The room was in almost complete darkness, with faint light seeping from the small window on such a cloudy day. The flickering ambers under the cauldron sent strokes of amber light into the darkness of the room. The dogs lay huddled together to conserve their heat. Moriah was already busy at the table, hunched over it and biting her lip, seemingly lost in concentration.

Tikvah stood and stretched. Able to see better, she saw that Moriah was carefully placing the many pinecones one by one into a deliberate pattern on the table.

"The deep breathing of pine you enjoyed yesterday invigorated and awoke your senses. There is nothing like the scent of pine to overcome ailment of the heart and body. And it is a great boost to the immune system."

Tikvah drew closer, curious to see what Moriah was doing with the pinecones.

"Look, dear," Moriah said, not lifting her head from her task when Tikvah approached. "Here is your collection. Some of these found their own way to the ground; others you picked from the trees. Now, please pick one, the one pinecone that really speaks to you."

One that spoke to her? All the pinecones looked slightly different, but she didn't feel particularly drawn to any one of them. She chewed on a thumbnail—was this some kind of test? An initiation perhaps? She didn't want to disappoint Moriah by showing too much hesitation, so she pointed to one of the open pinecones, the smallest one she spotted, remembering yesterday's instructions.

"An excellent choice, small but perfectly formed. It contains the essence of a pinecone in the most concentrated manner, and it's a beautiful choice indeed." Moriah lifted the pinecone high and admired it in the dim light of the embers below. She placed the pinecone in Tikvah's palm. "Don't look at it but feel it and describe it to me."

Tikvah closed her eyes in concentration, unsure of what was expected of her.

"It feels very small in my hand," she began hesitatingly. "It's hard and fragile at the same time, as though it could scrape me, but I could also easily break it."

"So it's powerful *and* vulnerable?" Moriah fisted one hand and then loosened her fingers and waved her hand softly in the air.

"Yes!" Tikvah agreed. "That's it exactly."

"Now tell me how it smells," Moriah continued without pause.

Tikvah brought the pinecone to her nose and without missing a beat, said, "It smells of the forest."

"The smallest piece of the forest smells like an entire forest—isn't that amazing!"

Moriah smiled as she took the pinecone from Tikvah and began tying a red cord around its top end. She twisted a long piece of her yarn, tied it off, and then hung cord and pinecone around Tikvah's neck as a pendant.

"Let this pinecone serve as a reminder that when you feel vulnerable, you are powerful, for it is in our vulnerability that we know our true strength. And just as this small pinecone smells of the entire forest, so is the entire wisdom of the universe contained in each one of us. All that's needed is to recognize this truth and connect to it."

Tikvah lifted the pinecone and studied it. She understood what Moriah was getting at, yet she didn't know what to do with the information. A pinecone might smell like a forest, but she wasn't as sure that all the wisdom of the world was inside her. Actually, she rather doubted it. There was so much she didn't remember; wouldn't that mean that she was missing a whole lot of that wisdom?

She had a lot of questions for Moriah, but she settled for asking, "How can this be?"

"There's a small gland in your brain called the pineal. It looks just like the pinecone you picked but is even smaller. It's located between the two hemispheres of the brain, and it's stimulated by light—daylight primarily. Today's modern science defined it as a gland that secretes the hormone melatonin. But Western philosophers and theologians have known for centuries about its importance to our connection with divinity; there's a sculpture of it in the Vatican. The French philosopher Descartes called it the seat of the soul, and in Eastern spirituality it is regarded as the third eye. Their intuition was on track, as it's one of the most important energy centers in your body, and it connects you to divine knowledge and wisdom and thereby orients you toward love and joy. You've been distraught and disoriented because of your memory loss, which is quite understandable. By connecting to this part of yourself, you can find your way, not through your personal memories but through the divine guidance of your intuition, an inner knowing that helps you discern your truth. This source of direction is a much more powerful guidance than knowledge from your past. Through it you will find your way to your true life, a life born of your divine essence that creates an abundance of love and joy for yourself and others. Whenever you feel at a loss, all you need to do is touch this small pinecone hanging from your neck, connect to your own love and joy, and you will know your path forward. Whatever originates from the flow of these emotions will bring even more of them to you. Your life will be guided and grounded in love, joy and peace."

Tikvah's hand lifted, gliding down her neck, and settled on the tiny pinecone hanging down her chest by the string which Moriah had tied to it. Her fingers fiddled with it as she concentrated to take in what Moriah had just told her.

How could such a small gesture create a shift in her that could be so defining? She hoped that Moriah's words were true, as her counsel seemed a way out of the fear and uncertainty she'd started feeling about her past, her future and her very existence. She didn't know how to do it, but she assumed that just as her hope came naturally to her when she was threatened in the forest, so would her intuition spring up when she needed it. All she had to do was believe it would be possible. But would she heed its message? She already knew how fleeting peace and joy could be. *Believe!* She willed herself to think and feel, suspending her doubts at least for a moment, and felt immediately more spacious, more accepting.

"So when I'm looking for guidance, all I need to do is touch the pinecone and the answers will come to me?" Her voice was hesitant, although she didn't want to sound incredulous.

But Moriah didn't seem to mind. "As you touch the pinecone, connect to the feeling of love and joy in your heart. The pinecone will remind you to connect to your emotions every time you touch it. Then once you feel the emotions, imagine what will bring more of these emotions to you. Those visions will be clear indications of which directions to choose, which acts to follow. That's the way of intuition, an inner knowing beyond knowledge." she concluded with a smile while looking intently at Tikvah.

"I'll do that, I promise." Tikvah responded enthusiastically to Moriah's inquisitive stare. "But I do have some questions." Some questions? She had dozens.

"Wonderful!" Moriah exclaimed. "Let's discuss them over warm porridge and tea."

As the delicious oats and herbal tea sweetened with wild honey warmed her belly, Tikvah was eager to continue the conversation, with the questions that she'd mulled over the previous day exploding within her. She needed to know the answers as quickly as possible.

"Why did you tell me the story about the girl who lost her mother and then lost herself in trying to bring her back? Was that my story before I came here? If you knew who I was, why didn't you tell me sooner? And if that is about me, why don't you take me back to my home and the people I love?"

Tikvah's hand was fisted in her lap. Moriah pulled it out, laid it on the table, and stroked the tight fist. The drumming of the rain on the roof erased the silence.

"My darling girl, that story came to me through my own intuition. It's one story among so many other possible ones. That girl may have been one aspect of you, yet there are so many other stories that could have been created or are already created and not yet told. It will be up to *you* to invent your own story. You've already been realizing it by healing yourself and by opening up to the wisdom that nature shares with you. During this time here you have unknowingly been creating your beautiful story, and there is so much more to come."

"But don't I need to know where I came from in order to continue? What foundation do I have to build on? And what about my mission that I must achieve, the reason I was saved back to life?" Her voice rose as she was overwhelmed once again with questions and with the vastness of the unknown.

"Dear one, I hear your frustration; it's a brave act to ask questions that arise from your deepest fears. Only by facing your fears through inquiry can you transform them rather than repress them and be ruled by them. Essentially you are alive because you saved yourself. You wished for it in every fiber of your being and summoned the alliance of the universe, so the help came. You do not need to be worthy to receive universal love and help, and you knew that when you were determined to live. You weren't granted life because you deserve it, but because you chose it with your love for yourself. Your mission is a life choice that guides you toward your self-fulfillment, and your greatest joy; it is not a condition you must achieve in order to justify your worthiness and your life."

Moriah's response was so direct, so bold, that it shook Tikvah to her core. She felt dumbfounded by the realization that she could have such power over the creation of her life. That it was up to her to find her destiny by following her love and joy. At once she felt the burden of responsibility that it was up to her and her alone to find the path to who she was and where she belonged. Moriah taught her how to connect to hope and intuition for help, but she still didn't know how to go about it. All she had was Moriah's explanations of those powers, and at this point she couldn't find either of them. Moriah's enigmatic responses to her questions only flooded her with more confusion and angst.

"Then why did you tell me that story?" Her voice choked with grief and surprisingly with anger as she confronted Moriah for the first time, heart racing, amazed at her own intensity. Yet all Moriah did was stare without saying anything, peering through Tikvah as though she were transparent.

She felt a part of her melt under the blaze of Moriah's gaze. Rage, fear, loss and abandonment rose in her, swallowing all other emotions in a violent eruption. She didn't know where the feelings came from, didn't know what to name them, but felt as though she was about to be crushed by the wave that rose inside of her. She suffocated under its weight as it swelled. She wanted to run as fast and as far as she could, and when the impulse overcame her, she ran.

Moriah didn't stop her as she dashed through the cabin door, and she didn't call out her usual warnings. Silent and resolute, she let Tikvah go. Tikvah ran. Where, she didn't know. Rain hit her face, dripping down her cheeks, into her collar and along her body, but the pain lodged in her chest didn't yield its grip. Branches and tree trunks confronted her at blinding speed, yet they surrendered the path to the fury-filled beast racing through them. She stumbled on a root and fell. Blood mixed with wet dirt smeared across her knee. The forest swallowed her when she fell to earth, receiving her stream of heavy tears that mingled with the raindrops.

After what seemed like an eternity, the rain subsided and there were no more tears left in her. Her chest felt empty and hollow, her limbs and back throbbed in exhaustion. She lay on the ground, letting the moist warm earth cradle her. Her mind wandered to the trunks of the pines that surrounded her in a neat circle. They welcomed her as one of theirs. A soft breeze dried her face, soothing it with its gentle caress and cool whispers.

Soon there was no trace left of the flood that had erupted from her eyes. There was only the breeze that carried on its gentle wings the smell of pine, the sweetness mixing in her nostrils and calming her breath, whose flow and that of the wind were becoming one. She eventually got back on her feet, brushing off the leaves and earth that clung to her. She looked around to check where she was, and all she saw were pines. In a moment of panic, she couldn't catch her breath, but almost immediately she remembered Moriah's words and reached for the pinecone that hung around her neck. Her hand rested against her heart, a heart that felt whole and filled with a nectar of its own goodness. The pounding speed slowed, and she lifted her head. She took another look around, and this time she spotted the majestic oak protruding above the forest.

She rushed to it and climbed as high as she could toward its canopy, clawing her way through the bulging bark, pulling herself up its thick branches as though its strong arms were lifting her toward itself—closer, higher, closer still.

At the top and nestled in its majestic crown of leaves rising above all that she'd known and all that she'd seen, she felt invincible, the tree's courage to stand tall through the ages coursing through her. She focused on the horizon seeded by trees, trees and more trees as far as her eyes could see. Her spirit attached itself to the hawk circling above her and soared to dizzying heights.

"If only I could stay here forever." Perhaps from this vantage point she could finally calm the whispers that churned in her heart, calling her to find the loved one whose absence left the gaping and bleeding hole she held there. Maybe at the top of the ancient tree could she find respite from the cries of loss that bellowed from her core. She feared that she would have to climb higher still to escape them, yet she knew that she could never get high enough to silence their call completely.

Gabi found her once again, alone in the tree and lost in reverie. His howls pleaded with her to come down and follow him back to Moriah and their pack. She yielded, knowing that he wouldn't give up on her.

Moriah sat weaving by the fire when she entered the cabin, eyes glimmering in the dimness of the room to radiate that wise knowing that was an integral part of her. Moriah didn't say anything but pulled moist leaves from her cauldron to clean and patch Tikvah's knee. The aromatic soup she handed Tikvah glided into her like a warm caress. Tikvah felt love.

She felt peace. She was home. Her concerns were still brewing, yet she chose to savor the gentle joy that swelled in her heart.

CHAPTER TWELVE

The Night Sky

"WAKE UP, MY dear!"

The whisper at Tikvah's ear felt like a caress of the wind as she emerged from her deep slumber.

"Come!"

Moriah motioned for Tikvah to follow her, and she stumbled out of the bed, her eyes blurry with sleep. She followed Moriah to the door of the cabin and outside to the front yard.

"Look at all these stars!" Moriah exclaimed, lifting both hands high.

After rubbing her eyes, Tikvah opened them to the most extraordinary vision she had ever seen. The night sky was so completely seeded with stars that the air seemed illuminated. She could almost feel their light upon her skin, just as she felt the sun during the day. She gasped and spun in a circle, arms wheeling, head tilted back. The storm had driven away the layer of clouds that usually hovered over the cabin, clouds produced by the proximity to the ocean. At that moment the air was completely clear and warmer than usual. An eyelash moon hung gently in the midst of the ocean of twinkling stars.

"Do you feel the earth below your feet?" Moriah asked.

Tikvah nodded, silenced by awe. The earth, moist and cool from the day's rain, invigorated her bare feet.

"Do you feel the sky encircling you?" Moriah asked quietly after a brief silence.

That was exactly how Tikvah felt. As though cocooned by the vastness above her.

"This is when you know that you belong, my sweet girl. Your feet on the ground, your head under a canopy of stars tells you so. You belong to this earth, to this planet and to this time and space. Your place among the elements matters. It completes them, just as they complete you. They belong to you, and you belong to them. And most importantly, you belong to yourself. Keep this feeling with you always, and you can find belonging anywhere you choose."

In the depth of her being, Tikvah felt what Moriah was describing. She felt rooted to the ground and at the same time she soared into the sky, and the two sensations held her in the exact place where she stood. She also felt rooted in herself in a way she had never felt before. A deep peace settled over her.

Only then did she notice that the four dogs had surrounded her. They were standing very still, like she was, so she hadn't felt their presence until one of them brushed against her foot. They stood quietly, heads slightly raised, as though they shared her reverence in the sanctity of the moment.

"Let's sit and enjoy the spectacle with a nice cup of Chamomile tea."

Tikvah lifted her feet to the bench and wrapped her arms around her legs, still amazed by the light show as she waited for Moriah. A few minutes later Moriah handed her a warm cup of sweet tea.

They huddled on the bench, bookended by two dogs on each side. Rafi broke the silence, letting out a long melodious howl aimed toward the sky, and the others followed suit. Tikvah and Moriah joined them, lifting their voices high before breaking up in uncontrollable laughter. Tension drained from Tikvah, taking with it the stresses of the last couple of days.

"See the cluster of stars over there?" Moriah raised her gnarled index finger and pointed to a line of three stars. "That group is called Orion's belt. Follow it down, and to the left there's a star that shines brighter than the others."

Tikvah followed Moriah's directions until she spotted the brightly twinkling star. She nodded.

"That's Sirius, the star of our origin. If you're ever lost at night, it will lead you on your way."

"The star of our origin?" Tikvah turned toward Moriah and for a split-second thought she saw the star's light reflected in her dark eyes.

"Our soul's knowledge comes not only from what we experience in this lifetime but through the vastness of time and space, even other dimensions. Some ancient cultures, such as the Egyptians and the Dogon tribe of Africa, believed that we were handed knowledge from distant civilizations from Sirius. Some even believed that their souls had inhabited Sirius in another incarnation. It is possible that this outer planetary knowledge was passed to us even if we are not cognizant of it. If we bring it to our awareness, we could connect to this wisdom even though thousands of light years separate us from the star we see."

Tikvah gazed at Sirius and wondered if someone on that star could be gazing back at her thousands of years earlier and holding memories of her that she no longer possessed.

"How did the ancient civilizations know about Sirius?" she questioned.

Moriah seemed lost in the heavens in contemplation, and she took so long to respond that Tikvah wondered if she had heard her.

"There is cosmic memory," she finally said. "That memory contains all that you are and all that you have ever been, and since there is no time in its realm, all that you could ever be."

The concept was hard to grasp, so Tikvah listened closely.

"Memories from a particular life mostly hold what the subconscious deems important for survival. The subconscious cannot possibly hold every action and thought; it must be selective. True memory is held in other realms called cosmic memory. And then of course there is divine memory, which is even vaster."

Tikvah was wide-eyed. "Can we really access cosmic and divine memory?"

Moriah nodded with a slight smile and continued. "Many people throughout the ages have done so. In ancient times they were considered to be prophets. More recently, in the turn of the twentieth century, Rudolph Steiner and Edgar Cayce, who were spiritual teachers, called this kind of memory the Akashic records. They claimed to be able to access the Akashic records and draw information about past civilizations lost to history."

The history lesson was intriguing, but Tikvah was getting flustered with the explanations, as she didn't understand how it was possible to draw information out of the cosmos and why that would be of value. As Moriah spoke, her mind drifted back to the stars, where it got lost.

She snapped out of her reverie with a question. "So what does all this have to do with me, anyway?"

"Since you have been granted the gift of being lifted from this life's memories, you are much more open to connect to the cosmic and divine memory that can guide you to your true and higher self, as it is not obscured by the self that your subconscious selected for the purpose of its preservation. You are already receiving its wisdom without being aware of it. Your true life is so much bigger than the life you had thought you lived since your last birth. It is the life of your eternal soul."

Tikvah's head was spinning with everything Moriah was telling her. She tried to relax by opening herself up to the cosmos to fill her with its memories, but nothing came.

"Cosmic memories aren't cognitive memories," Moriah said as Tikvah closed her eyes. "These are more intuitive, like whenever you have a feeling that you already know something that you supposedly are learning or discovering for the first time. The knowledge was already within you, but it took your being confronted with it for you to realize that it already existed inside of you. The more you allow this inner knowledge to seep into your life, the more fluidly it will come to your awareness. The life we live is only a reflection of what is inside of us."

Moriah's words were bewildering, but they resonated as true in Tikvah's heart. She was connecting to a part of herself that was eternal, that had always been there beyond the life she couldn't remember. The fear she'd been feeling because she was so unsure of herself and of her past began to subside. She could and would trust that inner guidance. She didn't need to possess logical knowledge in order to trust; her inner consciousness was as infinite as the entire cosmos, and the answers would come as the events of her life unfolded rather than the other way around. As she acknowledged this newfound vision, she breathed a deep sigh of relief.

Rafi and Gabi began licking her face—maybe they were feeling her joy—which made her even giddier. It seemed that the whole cosmos was laughing along with them as the glimmering stars danced their eternal dance. Perhaps her beloved was staring at these same stars at this very moment, and their gazes connected in the flickering heavenly lights. She smiled and hugged the possibility close.

She felt hope expanding within herself and connecting her to all that she loved in the universe. To all that loved her in return.

CHAPTER THIRTEEN

The Geese

A RAUCOUS DIN woke Tikvah at dawn. When she stood, she felt the exhaustion of too few hours of sleep. But she'd so enjoyed the warm night and the spectacle of stars, staying outside even longer than Moriah had. She stretched, hoping to stir up some energy, before stumbling out of the cabin barefoot. The sun's halo caressed the horizon, sending its timid rays into the yard. Moriah was already tending the garden and singing one of her endless exotic chants. Tikvah waved even though Moriah's back was turned, then followed the noise to the back of the cabin and quickly found its source. Seven huge white and gray geese were honking at the four dogs that surrounded them. Suspicious of the new inhabitants while not daring to approach them, the dogs circled the birds at a short distance, their nostrils flaring. The geese were determined to protect their new territory with their mighty cries. Beaks open wide and necks protruding, they hissed and honked at the four dogs. Tikvah called the dogs over and they reluctantly left the geese. The birds' cries immediately dissipated. Tikvah wasn't very sure of the new arrivals either and settled down at a safe distance to observe them.

The geese turned quietly to the business of moving leaves and digging the ground with their large orange beaks. Tikvah frowned, angling to see what they were doing. When two of the geese uncovered snails and quickly swallowed them before diving back into the dirt, Tikvah understood that they were searching for what must be marvelous delicacies.

Once they settled into their feeding routine, the geese looked beautiful in the white and silver feathers that sparkled in the dawn's pale light, and not at all threatening as they'd first seemed. Even the dogs relaxed, gathering around Tikvah to watch the activity. The more Tikvah watched, the more amused she was by their dichotomy of characteristics. On the one hand they were graceful when they were still or when they stretched their necks down to the ground to uncover layers of wet leaves. On the other hand, when they walked, wobbling from side to side, they were comically awkward. Their raspy honks were strident and not at all as soft as one would expect from their angelic attire. Tikvah marveled at their complexity and welcomed the new and fascinating presence into her world.

Suddenly Moriah appeared behind the cabin, waving her arms. "Ah, here you are, my girl! We have a problem!"

Tikvah had never seen Moriah distraught, and she jumped up, wondering what could have put her out of sorts. Quickly she followed Moriah to the garden, searching for danger or the unexpected, but she didn't see anything that would raise an alarm.

"Look!" Moriah stood over a leafy plot, inviting her to inspect the ground. Tikvah had to kneel to get close enough. To Tikvah's amazement, there appeared a cluster of another type of intruder. "Snails!"

They clung to the underside of every leaf of every plant, hanging on like grapes on a vine while chewing a slow procession through the leaf.

"What are we going to do?" Moriah turned to her in quiet desperation. "Our entire crop will be ruined."

Tikvah mulled over the situation. They needed to remove the snails from the leaves, but there were so many of them, it would take more than a day to get rid of all of them with only four hands to the task. By then, much of the crop would be destroyed. At the sound of a subdued honking, she remembered the geese and an idea came to her.

"Moriah, why don't we direct those very hungry geese to the snails in the front garden?"

Moriah hugged her with relief. "A wonderful idea. But how can we get them to come around the cabin and out here? They seem very territorial."

"We'll get the dogs to help!" Tikvah said with confidence.

They called to Micha, Rafi, Gabi and Uri to join them at the back of the cabin, and the procession—dogs leading the way—circled the building. At first the geese resumed their aggressive honking, but when the dogs approached from the forest side and didn't retreat, the geese's bravado abated and they began withdrawing toward the front of the cabin. The dogs continued their approach, abiding by the encouragement of their mistresses, until the geese reached the front yard. Tikvah called the dogs to the bench on the porch, knowing they needed to be out of the way if the geese were to explore. From her vantage point, she watched the geese work their way energetically along the garden plots, removing clusters of snails in big gulps. The plots were quickly cleared of snails and the garden saved, thanks to Tikvah's idea and the cooperation of the animals.

"You did good today!" Moriah said when Tikvah brought the dogs into the house to keep them away from the geese. Moriah had been able to salvage many of the plants that the snails had begun eating and made a delicious potato, carrot, Swiss chard, kale and mushroom stew with them. It was spiced by wild garlic and onion and selections from her large collection of dried spices. "You're integrating all the things you've learned so well!"

Tikvah swallowed before smiling back at her, grateful for the acknowledgment.

"You didn't lose hope when you realized that we were quickly losing our crop. On the contrary, your hope combined with intuition allowed you to create an ingenious solution immediately. You came up with your idea without knowing what was even possible, with no prior knowledge. That's pure creativity."

"Well, it was just lucky that the geese were here this morning!" Tikvah modestly dismissed the praise.

"And you think that the geese just happened to be there when we needed them?" Moriah asked with a mysterious smile as she passed a bowl of mashed potatoes to Tikvah.

The question hung in the air as Tikvah replayed the morning's events. She'd assumed that the help of the geese was just pure luck. She had come up with the plan that seemed obvious after observing the geese that morning. But it never occurred to her that it was *all* part of a plan.

"Not exactly a plan." Moriah interrupted her musing. "More like reality creation."

"Reality creation?" Tikvah let the words play on her tongue and in her thoughts.

"My dear girl, a part of us is always creating our reality. We may not be aware of it. We may think that everything that happens is a coincidence, that things just happen and we react to them. But what if it were the other way around? What if we are constantly creating even without a conscious awareness, and reality is responding to our subconscious thoughts and beliefs?"

Tikvah tried to wrap her mind around the concept Moriah was sketching out but found it difficult to accept.

"If that were true, then why would I have created my drowning?" She couldn't imagine that she'd been responsible for her accident.

Moriah swallowed a bite of stew before saying, "Maybe it was for you to learn certain truths that your reality at that time wouldn't allow you to access. Or perhaps it was a process you needed to go through for your highest good." She pointed a finger at Tikvah. "Or it could be that the accident saved you from a different path that would have been even more damaging."

"More damaging than breaking my entire body, losing my memory and an entire life?" Tikvah suddenly felt quite miserable thinking about her loss, something that she hadn't felt in days.

"There is a much greater mystery involved with the living of life than what meets our cognitive understanding," Moriah said. "But realizing that we create our lives for our highest good gives us the power to do it consciously rather than at the mercy and whims of whatever comes. There is growth at every experience. Unfortunately for many people, growth happens through pain, but we also grow through joy. The path we take is ultimately our choice, and that choice gives us the power to create a reality that matches it." Moriah broke her explanation to take a deep breath, and Tikvah leaned forward in her chair, eager to hear more. "When the snails invaded our garden, there were many possible outcomes, but you created one that was beneficial for you and us. The one that led you on a path of joy and growth through learning. I call it the path of self-love. This is what I congratulate you for today."

Tikvah sat silently thinking. If everything that happened to her was her own creation, then that gave her the ability to create the outcome rather than be at the mercy of it.

Moriah poured them both some tea and waved Tikvah back to her seat when she got up to clear their dishes. "Knowing that we create our reality gives us not only a greater sense of our power, it also bestows on us the responsibility for it. Many retreat from this notion as it's too much for them to own the fact that we are responsible for *everything* in our lives and that our thoughts, feelings and actions have a true impact upon the world we live in. You can see why this could be too much for many people to handle. However, being conscious of one's impact comes with great rewards."

She smiled a wide loving smile, one that Tikvah felt inside her soul.

"Speaking of reward," Moriah said, "let's celebrate your accomplishment! Let's treat ourselves. Is there anything you'd like to do that would be a fun way to mark the moment?"

Tikvah couldn't think of anything she particularly wanted beyond what she already had, so she blurted out the first thought that came to her mind.

"I'd love some of your berry compote, please!"

Moriah threw her head back and laughed. "What a delightful idea! And for that we'll need to go to the forest to collect the berries. It'll be fun!"

Tikvah's pleasure turned to uneasiness. Her several forays into the forest had been difficult and far from fun. Yet in her last trip, she had become viscerally connected to the forest. She'd spilled her rage and tears into it, and in return it had given her its peace and strength.

"We'll all go, my dear girl—you, me and the dogs. Look at it as a field trip." She handed Tikvah her woven basket and picked up a large wooden bowl. "This should be perfect to fill up."

Tikvah laced up her moccasins, and they summoned the dogs before heading behind the cabin.

They stopped to admire the geese who were sleeping with their beaks tucked into their chests while standing on one leg. Their bellies overfull, they were resting from the morning's feast in the shade of the cabin. They were tiptoeing around the geese to enter the path when Moriah said, "First let's reward our dear new friends for saving our garden and welcome them into our yard! We can make a comfortable nesting place for them below the cabin roof as their new home."

She motioned Tikvah and the dogs to follow her to the front yard and into the field beyond it. The flowers and green pasture that had covered the field a short while ago were gone, replaced by thigh-high dry grass. Moriah began cutting the grass at the base with sweeping gestures, and a moment later Tikvah followed her example and rhythm. When their arms were laden with a thick stack of fragrant yellow hay, they headed back to the geese and set it on the ground next to them, an area where they could arrange their nests. The geese were still asleep, so the six of them hurried quietly into the forest.

They walked along the trail, Moriah leading the way with her usual songs. Tikvah was familiar with the recurring melodies, so she hummed along. The dogs ran beside them, and sometimes ahead, scouting with their noses.

The forest's fragrances had awoken after the recent torrential rains. They mixed together in a pungent elixir of wet soil and leaves. The aromas sent shivers of delight into Tikvah's body. The fragrant pine carried a faint familiarity that made her feel at home. She tried to connect to this feeling, trace it back to this familiar place and hold on to it, but it escaped her grasp like a fleeting reflection of sunlight on a cloudy day.

A few minutes later, Moriah stopped at a large blackberry bush almost completely covered in black delights.

"Yum," Tikvah said, popping berries into her mouth.

Moriah warned her not to let the dogs get the blackberries. "One or two are fine, but they can make my boys sick. There are other berries that they can eat."

They quickly filled the bowl and basket as well as their bellies.

"Don't fill up your basket completely," Moriah warned. "We need other berries too."

Next she led them away from the path and into the thickness of the forest to a patch of small red balls protruding from the ground. "Wild strawberries!" exclaimed Tikvah as she threw a small handful on her tongue. They were so delicious that Tikvah struggled with getting any into the basket rather than into her mouth. A laughing Moriah let her know when she'd gathered enough and it was time to move on. "We need to leave a few to the forest animals."

When Moriah turned away to continue down the path, Tikvah snuck a couple more into her mouth, holding up her hands in surrender when Moriah glanced back at her with a knowing grin.

Next came the elderberry bushes.

"Be careful with these!" Moriah warned her. "They can be poisonous if you eat too many of them raw. Cooked, they are just fine. Actually, more than fine. They are great for the immune system."

The berries were a bit sour, so it was much easier for Tikvah to abide by Moriah's warning. Finally, their baskets full, they headed back, much to Tikvah's reluctance, as she was enjoying herself immensely.

"We'll be back before summer's end," Moriah said, consoling her. "But the sun is setting, and if you want the compote tonight, I need to make it while I still have some light."

The idea of the compote, her favorite of Moriah's dishes, lightened Tikvah's steps as she rushed ahead. She was starting to be familiar with the path that led back to the cabin, and she and a couple of the dogs—they changed places with one another every few minutes—hurried ahead.

"Look," Moriah said when they neared the geese's den. "They've already laid eggs in the nests we made for them."

She picked up an egg, admired it and handed it to Tikvah. It was warm and smooth, and so large that Tikvah had to carry it with both hands, balancing both it and her basket.

"This will be our treat for breakfast tomorrow." Moriah took the egg from Tikvah and put it into a wooden bowl when they entered the cabin. "Now for the compote!"

She brewed the berries in her miraculous cauldron with the fresh spring water they fetched that morning and raw honey that she kept in a closed pot after collecting it from hives in the trees. For a long time the berry mixture simmered over the low embers beneath the cauldron, releasing its sweet aromas into the room.

While Moriah weaved and sang, Tikvah played with Uri and Gabi by the light of the fire. Micha and Rafi were outside on guard duty. Tonight, unlike all the other nights, they really had something to guard; Moriah had asked them to protect the geese from a possible invasion by coyotes. The night was again warm, the sky filled with stars, the earth still moist from the rains, and Tikvah's heart was full for the first time. At least the first time that she could remember. She felt that she truly belonged to the land, to the cabin and forest, and to Moriah and their dog companions. Through her own involvement, she was casting her roots in this magical realm they were creating together. And the process didn't seem scary or daunting or intimidating. It felt right. Natural.

She wanted to keep creating that life.

CHAPTER FOURTEEN

The Mushrooms

THE FOLLOWING DAWN, Moriah invited Tikvah to go with her on a mushroom foraging expedition. "There's no better time to find mushrooms than after a sunny day that follows rain," Moriah told Tikvah. "Eager to express their tender presence, the mushrooms pop their heads through the canopy of moist leaves and pine needles that normally hide them from predators."

Tikvah was still slightly groggy after falling asleep with a belly full of berry compote the previous evening. Nonetheless, she was eager to return to the forest in the company of Moriah and the dogs. Their berry foraging the day before had been so much fun.

Soon after entering the forest, they strayed off the path. Moriah walked in her usual resolute step, meandering her way between trees, fallen trunks and mounds of moss-covered rocks. Since their route made no sense to Tikvah, she followed Moriah like a shadow, afraid she'd be lost in the thickness of the woods. After a short, brisk walk, Moriah stopped abruptly, bent down and gently began sifting through the ferns with a stick she'd picked up along the way. She removed a blanket of wet leaves, uncovering a bed of mushrooms underneath it, their small brown heads dotting the moist black soil.

"Ah, such wonderful little fellows," Moriah exclaimed as she carefully cut their stems with a blunt piece of rock similar to the one she used as a knife for her vegetables. She kept several by her cauldron and had brought one of the smallest with her.

"Oh yes, these will be wonderful to dry; they'll help sustain us through the winter." She handed a handful of mushrooms to Tikvah to put in her basket.

"They're called slippery jack. You can recognize them by their stringy underbelly. They're quite tasty. Study them carefully, as they can be confused with another variety, which is poisonous. Mushrooms are nourishing and medicinal, and in some cases can alter perceptions of consciousness through the brain's reaction to their chemical composition. They can also be deadly."

Tikvah stared at Moriah when she spoke nonchalantly about plants being deadly, but Moriah continued her exploration of the leaves and soil. A few steps later she clasped her hands and laughed when she discovered a cluster of white mushrooms.

"Lion's mane!" she exclaimed. "Aren't they beautiful?"

"They are." Tikvah drew one finger down what looked to be a long white waterfall. "How bright they are!"

"These have antiseptic properties. They use enzymes to fight off bacteria, which is their nutrient's competitor. They help keep the entire forest, including the bees, healthy through these properties." She gently blew on a bee that at that very moment was circling her head. "Wonderful bees. So important to the reproduction cycles of the forest ecosystem."

"Bees?" Tikvah watched as Moriah's bee joined another to buzz around a stand of flowers poking from the ground. "How are they important?"

As they continued to hunt mushrooms, Moriah explained the critical role of pollinators before returning to the topic of mushrooms.

Tikvah was amazed by the bees' importance and even more amazed that cute tiny plants sustained the entire forest.

"Not plants. They're fungi."

Tikvah dug her fingers into the earth. She'd watched Moriah plant seeds to grow vegetables, so she assumed everything that grew from the soil was a plant. As Moriah told her more about fungi, Tikvah wondered if she'd known anything at all about plants and animals and fungi before her accident. Some general knowledge had come back to her the last few days, but she didn't know much about nature and its systems. She wondered if only some people, wise women like Moriah, studied the natural world. But who wouldn't want to know all they could about the earth and the living species that lived on it? She found another mushroom and again ran a finger gently along its length. Magnificent.

"The earliest living organism, fungi have been around for over billions of years," Moriah said. "They're essential to the survival of all species. They're the smallest of all beings but have the largest network on earth."

Tikvah understood networks. But a network made up of a living organism? "What kind of network?" she asked.

Moriah plopped herself on the ground and waved both arms. "Fungi are all around us and inside of us. Trees and plants use them to feed each other and communicate among themselves through their root system in a connective web that the fungi create. This is a huge underground network of neurotransmitters sharing information through all that grows in its ecosystem."

Moriah took a deep breath while admiring the cluster of white mushrooms in her hand. For a moment, her face took on the distant gaze she wore when she saw something beyond the obviously apparent. But then she grinned and pointed a grubby finger at Tikvah.

"You'll like this, dear one. Fungi are also responsible for the decomposition of all living organisms, and thus they harmonize the cycle of death and rebirth. Their enzymes decompose dying organisms, breaking them down to nutrients for themselves and the soil, creating a complete ecosystem for the worms, the birds, the insects to feed on." She rolled a few mushrooms into her basket. "Rather magical, isn't it?"

"Fascinating." Tikvah tipped her head back and stared at the underside of the forest canopy high above her. "And yes, magical in its way. What if..."

"Wouldn't it be great if I could communicate with my beloved, wherever he might be, through this same system?" she thought. Then she wouldn't be limited by her lack of memory.

"Remote communication is possible and happens all the time, whether we're aware of it or not," Moriah said.

"What do you mean?"

"Sometimes it's enough to think of someone for the person to feel our presence and think of us in return. We can even heal others from a distance by sending healing intentions to them."

Tikvah didn't wait but concentrated, trying to conjure up an image of her beloved so she could connect with him, tell him she was alive and well and happy and that she hadn't forgotten their love.

Well, her mind might have forgotten the events, but her heart still recognized love. If she could remember something, even the tiniest detail about him, that memory might expand, and she could go to search for him. Yet no image came to her, not even in her imagination. The only face she knew was Moriah's, with its dark loving eyes set in a sea of deep wrinkles. All she had to connect her to her beloved was the hope that they were still bonded through the love that coursed through her and that somehow, somewhere, they would be united again.

Moriah nodded sympathetically when Tikvah caught her eye, obviously knowing what Tikvah had been trying to do. Knowing too that she'd failed.

They stood and resumed their hunt.

Moriah's breathing grew heavier but didn't stop her quest. She walked slowly but purposefully, her head bent forward, her torso curved toward the ground.

"All nature cooperates to sustain itself and its ecosystems. Fungi are the ultimate living example of how everything that lives is interconnected and interdependent, but it's only one part. Everything works together in harmony to maintain and recycle life. All is one."

As she said those words, she looked straight into Tikvah's eyes. Tikvah felt as though the words had been engraved on her soul.

Tikvah followed Moriah's steps while the dogs played at a distance. She was amazed that she could learn so much from the tiny mushrooms, and she was in awe of the magic that guided the cycles of the forest that buzzed with life and energy. She could *feel* all the elements interacting to sustain the magnificent creation all around them. She contemplated the lion's mane in her basket with awe, its small white heads clustered together to guard tightly their magic healing qualities until they could be shared with the world around them.

"Never underestimate a *fun guy*."

She smiled at the lame joke, certain that she'd had the same response at another time and in another place.

All things and times and places were most definitely connected. Perhaps someday in the future she could reconnect to her past.

CHAPTER FIFTEEN

The Weaver

IN THE AFTERNOON, after they feasted on a stew of mushrooms that they'd collected that morning, Tikvah approached Moriah's rocking chair and studied her rhythmic motion as she weaved. Moriah's hands worked quickly and diligently, but she seemed to be in a trancelike state as she hummed one of her beloved melodies. Tikvah had been wondering why she spent her days weaving and yet undid all her work at night. It seemed a futile activity for someone who was as industrious as Moriah was. But she never dared to question her about it, because she wasn't sure how to ask it without sounding critical.

Moriah interrupted her weaving to hold the crimson fabric up, showing its intricate design to Tikvah. "This one is particularly beautiful tonight," she whispered, as though musing to herself, before she resumed her task.

"I know you've wondered why I weave so much and then undo all my work by the start of the new day."

Tikvah nodded and drew her feet up into her own chair, leaning her cheek against her knees, eager to hear Moriah's reason for the puzzling ritual.

"You see, my dear, the essence of life is not about the result but about the process. It's in the journey that learning happens. The outcome is just a motivation, or if successful, a prize. But the real prize is how the journey shapes us, how it makes us evolve beyond what we had been when we undertook it. This shaping is the most valuable reward. All physical forms eventually dissolve; only the evolution of our consciousness remains." Her fingers flew, adding to her creation. "There will be plenty of time to complete the garment; it's not time yet. It is the working itself that is most valuable."

"But why? What does this work accomplish?" Tikvah didn't mean to be disrespectful, but she'd been waiting a long time to know why Moriah destroyed the beautiful work she created every day. She truly didn't understand the value of the act of weaving itself. Not when there was nothing to show for all that work and effort and time invested.

"I could respond in so many ways, as we are the ones who determine the value of anything we do or what we value in our lives. It's always a matter of subjective perspective where value resides. I could say that I enjoy the creative process of designing, which I do as it allows me to express my creativity. I could say that it sharpens my mind as I need to keep track of the pattern and the number and type of gestures in designing it. I could say it relaxes me and is therefore beneficial for my health. I could say it fills up the quiet evenings in the cabin when the work's day is done, so it entertains me. But the real reason is that my weaving is an act of love that helps the world."

Perplexed, Tikvah frowned. She had become accustomed to Moriah's enigmatic and mystical statements, but this one made no sense to her whatsoever.

"You see, my dear girl," Moriah continued, "through my weaving I assemble all the troubles of the day and rearrange them into patterns of love and joy so that the world may have the possibility to recreate itself anew on the following day."

That sounded good. Actually, really great. But Tikvah couldn't figure out how such an activity would have a genuine impact. "So . . . how is that working?" Tikvah's incredulity seeped through her question.

"Each day I weave back together what destructive forces tore away. Some days we avoid calamities. Some days a person's path to destruction is averted and that changes the course of an entire community. The impact can seem small but can lead to great universal changes. Thankfully, I'm not the only one redirecting the world in the direction of love and joy. There are many of us working to help the world heal itself, and there have been many more throughout the ages. Weaving a tapestry of love happens to be my special talent. Others are going about it in their own ways, such as inspiring writers, poets, musicians, or influencing people in various fields like agriculture and medicine. Although our work unfolds on the energetic realms, it helps sometimes to have a tangible focus into which to pour light and prayers. So you see, my dear, as long as there is destruction in the world, as long as one day follows the next, I must keep weaving. My work is never done."

As understanding washed through Tikvah, so much of what had happened to her began to make sense. Her miraculous healing, the marvelous dishes that energized her body and delighted her palette, the presence of the angelic dogs, even the help of the geese took on a whole new context. They were the products of Moriah's love and joy that she infused into every aspect of her existence and beyond. With this new perspective, everything that happened now appeared magical to her, an extension of Moriah's personal and sacred alchemy. She regretted that she ever dismissed Moriah's weaving as a nonsensical activity.

"Your confusion and misunderstanding of my purpose was quite normal," Moriah assured her, once again divining her thoughts. "As your consciousness grows, so does your realm of possibilities. What appeared impossible one day becomes normal the next, the more your field of awareness expands."

As with many things that Moriah taught her that Tikvah didn't quite understand, she took the information at face value. Not having anyone else to compare her to, she found Moriah's talents to be natural. She accepted them intuitively just as she accepted the growing of plants, the geese laying eggs, and the timely changes of the seasons. They were all expressions of a ceaseless and magical cycle of life moved by love and joy.

There was much that she wanted but was too timid to ask, however. Where was Moriah from and how did she become this magical woman who could daily heal the world with an intention? A swarm of unspoken questions darted through her mind, flittering shyly in the space that separated her thoughts from her speech.

"All will be revealed in time . . ." Moriah said, her hands busy. "And in the right time, you'll be ready to hear."

Tikvah closed her eyes. So when she was ready to hear, what would she be asked to do?

And would she be able to do it? Or would she fail to do her part?

CHAPTER SIXTEEN

The Garden

E MBOLDENED BY THE success of her garden rescue from the geese, Tikvah undertook the tending of the garden and the caring of the animals with gusto. Her days were delightfully filled with work by Moriah's side. Actually, their activities didn't seem like work at all to her. Caring for the garden was her labor of love. She took it upon herself to do the hardest physical chores to alleviate Moriah's burdens, even though Moriah never asked for her help or complained of the work. Nonetheless, she wanted to carry the heaviest burdens, as her work and dedication to their garden filled her with a sense of purpose and pride for her contribution to their marvelous creation.

She'd been brought to Moriah's home broken and lost, but she now possessed the strength and clarity to leave, should she choose to search for her past and her loved ones. Yet she felt bound to the garden and tethered inextricably to Moriah by an invisible cord that linked their destinies together.

At early dawn she would go to the spring well to fetch fresh water for bathing, meals, drinking and watering the garden. This required several trips with heavy wooden jugs on her back. She couldn't fathom how Moriah with her stooped body had been able to do it daily for so long.

After gathering water, she tended to the animals, cleaning manure from the geese nest, which she deposited in the compost pile. There she gathered fresh fertilizer and spread it in the many plots of the vegetable garden. A new harvest was on its way. They were now growing root vegetables in addition to the leafy ones. The work in the garden itself took several hours for weeding, watering, fertilizing and gathering plants for their meals. Tikvah's greatest joys were watching the plants grow from tiny seeds and observing their daily progress. The reward of tasting the fruits and vegetables was delightful, yet eating now seemed an integral part of a chain of pleasurable events. She came to understand that the real reward, as Moriah had said, was the process itself. The gardening brought her closer to the earth, to nature, to creation, and allowed her to feel her work as an expression of herself. *Everything* became an energetic extension of herself, reflecting her thoughts, emotions and love.

She loved to work beside Moriah, feeling their collaboration, knowing that she was contributing to Moriah's extraordinary creations. They chatted gently as they tended the garden, commenting on how well the lettuces were developing and encouraging the turnips, carrots, radishes, leaks and onions to take their time to grow and to absorb the nutrients from earth, sun and water so that they themselves would be rich in vitamins and minerals. At times Moriah would drift off into song, and Tikvah hummed along with her. The two women were in perfect harmony with each other and everything around them. Their lives flowed along the eternal cycles of nature and its seasons. The only time of which Tikvah was aware was dictated by the garden's progression. As Tikvah's involvement in the garden grew, Moriah seemed content to stand back and watch more often, these breaks growing longer over time. She would sit on the shaded bench in the front yard as Tikvah had done during her convalescence, wearing a satisfied smile as she watched Tikvah do the fertilizing or watering. The dogs gathered around her, protectively staying by her side.

Tikvah only noticed the change when one sunny day Moriah stayed inside the cabin after their midday meal. She sat in her rocking chair and weaved. Her singing sounded even fainter than usual. The next day, however, she was her usual self, and she joined Tikvah in their first harvest of the root vegetables. The feast that she made was unforgettable, amazing Tikvah by the lavish dishes concocted from a blend of turnips, yams, fennel and beets. She tasted the sweetness of the sun and the richness of the soil mix in their juicy flavors.

The days were becoming shorter and slightly cooler, the evenings chilly as the fog descended, obscuring the stars. Moriah's energy seemed fainter as well, as though the cooling of the earth drained her of her fire. Her eyes, however, remained bright and vital, and their jovial glimmer never faltered. Even though Moriah was no longer teaching her in the evenings and during the day they spoke very little, Tikvah felt strongly connected to Moriah, as though their silence, a secret language, bonded them in a private pact of mutual knowledge, understanding, trust and caring.

There were more and more days when Moriah sat on the porch watching Tikvah care for the garden and calling out instructions on how to protect the plants from the coming winds, where to use more fertilizer and which plants to harvest.

Tikvah was grateful for Moriah's presence, even from afar. She still cooked her illustrious meals for them, but she seemed to enjoy them less than before, eating only a few bites and leaving the rest to Tikvah, whose appetite became more ravenous the harder she worked.

Late one afternoon they were sitting together on the outside bench after Tikvah devoured a large plate of vegetable stew. Moriah leaned against the wall of the cabin, as though gathering the pale rays of sun that hovered on their front porch. Her eyes were closed, but she wasn't sleeping.

"Where did you come from?" Tikvah asked, piercing the silence of their day. She finally gathered the courage to ask Moriah a personal question that had been on her mind for a while.

Moriah opened her eyes and focused her tired gaze on Tikvah. "I came from my creator," she replied simply. After a long pause, she added, "I'll be returning home soon."

Tikvah's heart plummeted, as though the earth had dropped out from beneath her. She regretted that she had asked the question. "What do you mean return home?" she demanded. "I thought this was your home!" The statement burst out of her in broken shards. How could Moriah leave her and their garden? To go where? What home?

"This was my home, because I chose it and made it so." Moriah's whispered words were strung together by a thin thread. "But my true home is with my creator; that is where I must eventually return."

Tears welled in Tikvah's eyes. How could Moriah abandon her?

"Not to worry, my dear girl. I'll always be with you."

Her words were barely audible, and Tikvah decided not to ask any more questions, as Moriah clearly didn't have the strength to continue the conversation. Weighted by deep sadness, she didn't know how to pull herself out of this feeling that filled her with confusion and despair.

She gazed around, trying to collect her thoughts. Her eyes grasped at anything that could free her from the agony that gripped her heart.

Fears of the unknown future without Moriah and of loneliness rose in her, obliterating, in the swoop of a single moment and in a few words, the peace, the joy and the hope to which she'd become accustomed. Her eyes rested on the garden plots brimming with leafy growth. They seemed to be smiling at her under the dimming evening sun. They were connected to the earth, from which they drew their life and strength. Just like them, she felt planted to the earth and to the only life she'd known, her life with Moriah, their dogs, the garden and the forest. She was entwined in the love she shared with all that she knew, drawing life and strength from that love. She released her confusion and sadness to the garden, to the lush leafy greens, a tribute to Moriah's and her efforts and their love. She didn't know what her future could possibly be without Moriah, so she chose to plant her focus in the goodness that surrounded her. And Tikvah did exactly that.

With all the tasks that she now assumed, Tikvah's days were filled more than ever, but the heaviness of her workload didn't bother her. Only in the evenings would fatigue catch up with her, and she would fall quickly into sleep. She slept so deeply that none of the troubling dreams that plagued her when she first arrived ever disturbed her again.

Her only concern was Moriah. Would she be able to cure herself, as she had healed Tikvah from a much more serious condition? Her mysterious statement about returning home to her creator remained an enigma, and Tikvah never dared to bring it up, wishing that by not raising the subject it might be forgotten. Still, the uncertainty hovered, and as time wore on, Moriah said less and less.

CHAPTER SEVENTEEN

The Note

THE MORNING SUN had been bleak for days. A veil of fog nearly obliterated the surroundings, washing out all color as Tikvah emerged to begin her day's gardening. Moriah hadn't left the cabin for a while, entrusting Tikvah with all the garden procedures. She toiled intuitively. Whenever she felt uncertain, she gently touched the pinecone hanging from her neck on the red cord where Moriah had tied it, and the answers would flow to her instantly.

The fog usually dissipated by midmorning and the colors would return to the landscape—both certainties soothed Tikvah. But today the low heavy clouds hovering in the pale blue sky held the coolness in the air.

She reminded herself to choose a large egg from one of the geese nests for Moriah, hoping that it would increase her strength. Sometimes after Moriah ate, her energy would return enough that she would get up from her chair and go outside to inspect the garden or caress the dogs or pick up her loom and start weaving. Unfortunately, those moments of activity didn't last long. The energy would drain out of her a short while later, as though there was a hole in a vessel that couldn't stay filled. Tikvah's concern grew, but she stayed hopeful that Moriah would be fine eventually. Yet despite her best hopes, Moriah had grown weaker. On cold days, Moriah wouldn't get up from her chair but sat drifting in and out of sleep.

The fire underneath the cauldron was always lit, and Tikvah planned to replenish the wood when she went inside. Moriah had taught her to prepare special elixirs from the roots and herbs that hung along the walls. The elixirs provided an added boost of energy, keeping Moriah awake for a while. Tikvah would mix up an elixir and fix an egg with herbs, do something with the very small vegetables that she'd pulled from the ground, and the two of them could talk a little.

Smiling, she hurried to the back of the cabin to fetch a goose egg and saw that the geese were gone. They must have flown off to a warmer climate. Tikvah couldn't blame them.

Distraught, she walked into the cabin and to her surprise found Moriah by the cauldron preparing herbal tea with honey, which she handed to Tikvah in a cup. Tikvah felt slightly ashamed to show her the small vegetables she'd gathered. But Moriah took the tiny potatoes from her with a smile.

"Don't worry, my dear girl." She studied Tikvah with her usual gentle gaze. "The forest is full of mushrooms now. Why don't you take Gabi on a stroll to collect some?"

Tikvah was overjoyed that Moriah seemed better and picked up a basket to collect mushrooms. She called out to Gabi, who jumped to his paws and followed her to the door. As she looked back to Moriah, the golden fire illuminated her face and she seemed to glow. Her expression was bright and extremely loving. She looked so beautiful that Tikvah paused to gaze at her. Sensing her glance, Moriah smiled. Her eyes twinkled with their old joy when she said, "Go, dear. My love will go with you."

Tikvah froze, overwhelmed by Moriah's words. Although her love was always implicit, she had never said the words. Theirs was the kind of love that was never spoken but shown. "Thank you!" was all she could bring herself to mutter as she walked out of the cabin, followed by Gabi.

As evening began its descent, Tikvah burst through the cabin door full of excitement. Basket in hand, she searched for Moriah in the gloom of dusk. The only light source was the open door; the fire under the cauldron had gone out. She couldn't see Moriah anywhere. Whining, Gabi joined the other dogs on the floor by the side of the bed, and that was when Tikvah noticed that the sheet had a lump in it. As she approached and leaned over the bed, she saw that the bump was Moriah. She was lying with her eyes closed in deep sleep. Tikvah realized that she'd never seen Moriah lying down. She looked so tiny cradled by the large boat-bed. Tikvah didn't dare to disturb her. She collected logs and lit the fire, which cast its warmth and light around the room. She sat in Moriah's chair by the bed, rocking as she waited for her to wake up.

In the dim light she discerned a soft smile on Moriah's face and wondered what she might be dreaming of.

Tikvah kept rocking. She hummed the melodies of Moriah's songs, the slight creaking of the chair accompanying her for what felt like an eternity. She watched Moriah, who looked peaceful. Her body was motionless.

Tikvah saw the first star appear at the window above the bed. Although impossible, its twinkle seemed to illuminate Moriah's pale face. Tikvah decided to wake Moriah and caressed her arm. "Moriah?" It was past dinner time, and she needed Moriah's help to figure out if the mushrooms she collected were edible. She wasn't completely sure which, if any, were poisonous, even if she touched her pinecone, looking for intuition about them. Moriah would be the final judge of which were safe to eat.

When Moriah didn't respond, she shook her gently. Still no motion. Curious to see what was happening, Micha sat up and let out a squeal. The other dogs appeared to be in a deep slumber. Tikvah walked to the table, where she set down the basket with the mushrooms, and discovered a note on the other side of the table, next to the acorn surrounded by the arrangement of crystals that had been there since the evening of her first adventure in the forest.

Tikvah, my dear girl,

I love you so very much, always have and always will!

It has been my honor and joy to be your companion and teacher from the time you appeared, to help you along your healing and with your spiritual growth. Your progress has been glorious to observe and joyful to experience. I'm grateful for your trust in allowing me to guide you and for your bright and open heart. You have transformed so much since I have known you—a true miracle.

You healed yourself by making a willful life choice.

You faced your deepest fears and transformed and transcended them with your courage and hope.

You accepted yourself and your circumstances and gained the consciousness of belonging both to yourself and the world around; you and have experienced the connectivity of all in our universe.

You got connected with your hope, intuition and emotions as the sources for creating your life.

You have used your intuition to connect to nature and create sustenance. By doing so, you came to know the gifts of the journey itself.

You have understood and accepted the endless cycle of life and death.

Most importantly, you have grounded yourself in love and joy as the foundation for your life.

My darling girl, you are now ready to create a marvelous life for yourself in whatever direction your heart choses.

It's time for me to leave this body and return to the light of my creator, to the source of all love and joy.

I am with you always.

You will find me in the melodies you hum and in the whisper of the wind, and anywhere you wish to call my name, I'll be there.

Mostly you will find me in your heart.

Remember always that I love you more than you can know!

I am the one called Moriah, the Weaver Woman.

Tikvah sat motionless, the piece of paper dangling between her fingers. Her body felt paralyzed. She understood the words written in the note, but for a while her mind couldn't comprehend them. Could not take them in. Slowly the realization was dawning on her; Moriah was not going to wake up.

Paralyzed by confusion, it took a long time before Tikvah could bring herself to move. The first feeling that she acknowledged was voracious hunger. Not having prepared any food, and in her haste to eat, she absently grabbed a few mushrooms from the basket, swallowing them whole. She no longer cared if they might poison her. She didn't know how she could go on without Moriah.

Her heart was breaking, and depressing thoughts raced through her mind as she realized all that she would no longer be able to do in Moriah's company. Gone was the hope that they might soon be able to garden together again. There would be no more delicious meals from Moriah's cauldron. No more sweet conversations under the stars.

How would she go on with the garden without Moriah's counsel, especially now, with winter approaching? Panic was gripping her, mixed in with the deepest sadness she could remember feeling. Pain seemed to rise from an abyss of all pains, from memories she didn't even know, yet somehow was carrying deep in her, logged in her very cells. She rocked herself on Moriah's chair through the sadness, the pain and the despair of her loss. She hummed to deafen the thoughts of doom that drained all glimmer of her usual good spirits. Eventually she drifted to sleep, finding momentary relief.

~

Startled by the flow of sunlight on her face, she awoke in a spasm. For a fraction of a moment, it seemed like any other day, except what was she doing sleeping in Moriah's chair? In a horror of recollection, she remembered when she saw Moriah's body lying in the bed. Not knowing what to do next, she simply stood up. She peered around the room in the light of day, searching for clues or maybe instructions. Her intuition had abandoned her, drowned by a complete and utter loss. The dogs woke up and gathered around her affectionately, licking off the salty tears that had dried on her cheeks. She felt a bit less alone and petted each in turn. Then she noticed something hanging at the dark corner of the wall. As she neared it, she saw it was a crimson cloth. For once Moriah hadn't had the chance to undo her weaving. Or was this intentional? She took it off the hook. The fabric was soft, and its weave bore an intricate design. Tikvah held it up to the light; it was a long tunic. She hurried to slip it on. It fit her perfectly, loosely hugging her hips and feeling luxurious on her skin, like a light caress as she slowly swirled around the room. She ran her hands along it, feeling its silky softness. Something bulged on the right side, by her hip—a secret pocket in the inside seam. She quickly removed the garment and pulled out the piece of paper hidden in the pocket. Another note from Moriah.

My darling girl,

This robe is your present, my farewell gift to you.

Let it carry you to your magnificent future.

I have one last request:

Please place the acorn inside my mouth before returning me to the earth.

The mycelium will take care the rest.

You must now continue your journey.

My love will be with you always wherever you go.

Tikvah felt a mixture of gratitude and disappointment. She thanked Moriah for the robe from the bottom of her heart, as she knew she must have weaved it with her last bout of energy, her parting gesture of love after all that she had given Tikvah already. However, she had hoped that Moriah would have left her more guidance about what she should do without her. She had no idea how to carry on with her life. She had no memory of who she had been before the life with Moriah, and staying on in the forest cabin by herself didn't seem to be an option. Moriah had been clear that Tikvah must now carry on with her journey. But where to? How would she survive? Who might she encounter? The unknown was daunting. All she knew at that moment was that she must bury Moriah's body before doing anything else.

The gloomy mood followed her outside and was echoed by the gray sky and chilled air. The sun that woke her up had dissolved behind a thick layer of fog. Everything was grim and colorless. Listlessly she picked up a shovel and began digging a hole next to one of the garden plots. The ground was moist and soft, and it didn't take long before a gap deep enough to accommodate Moriah's small body appeared. But now she wasn't sure how she would get her out there. She leaned on the shovel before deciding to take one step at a time. She felt certain that the solution would make itself known when she touched the pinecone on her chest, since she was acting in faith.

When she bent down over Moriah's body, she was overcome by an impulse to hug her. To hold her and never let go. She'd always felt Moriah's love as a palpable extension of her body even though they rarely exchanged physical affection. Now with her gone, Tikvah needed a way to reconnect to that love. She caressed her cheek tenderly, but nothing came back to her from Moriah's still body. Moriah's smile was frozen, the spirit gone out of her. She gently pushed the large acorn that Moriah had charged with the seven crystals and which she'd saved for all those months into Moriah's slightly open mouth. A shiver raced over her, but she had to abide by Moriah's instructions for her burial. She covered Moriah's head with the simple garment she had worn before changing into the red tunic and then folded the sheet she lay on neatly around her. Now that Moriah's covered face and body looked more like an inanimate mass and less like herself, it would be easier to put her into the earth. The means of getting her out of the cabin and into the garden became obvious; she'd tie the boat that had served as her bed to the dogs, who would drag her outside and close to the hole in the ground. She could then lift one side of the bed and let the body slide out and into the hole. It seemed ironic to use the same method for moving Moriah's dead body as Moriah had done with her own barely living body so many months earlier. The parallelism, moving in and out of the cabin, struck Tikvah as symbolic of the cycle of life and death.

She concentrated all her focus on the difficult task, not wanting to be lost in sentimentality, because if she stopped to think about what she was doing, she might not be able to go through with it. She used the remainder of the red yarn to tie the boat to the dogs and Moriah to the boat.

Slowly the boat moved across the floor, as if it and its cargo was sailing to a new destiny. When it reached its destination in the garden, she untied the rope and gently tilted the side and the bed toward the hole. The sheet with Moriah's body billowed into it. Both body and cloth slid into the ground, which welcomed its burden. All that was left was to cover them with the earth she had dug up earlier. Within minutes there was no trace of the cloth or the body. Moriah was gone forever. She covered the hole, thrusting raging fistfuls of dirt into it, wishing she could disappear into the pit with the dirt. But instead of throwing herself into the hole, Tikvah did the opposite; she built a mound. She collected the largest rocks she could find, and propelled by an impulse to leave something of herself there because she couldn't leave Moriah to rot in the ground all alone, she created a small shrine a foot from the head of Moriah's grave. The shrine was a simple pile of round rocks gathered when they'd cleared the land for the garden plots. She finished off this monument to Moriah by twisting the red yarn around and around the rocks, in the hope that their souls were connected and that Moriah's path on Earth would never be forgotten. With the shrine completed, Tikvah felt complete. She was also spent from the exertion and emotions of the day.

As if the earth sapped all her strength, her knees buckled, and she fell to the ground next to the fresh plot where Moriah's body was planted. She stifled a cry, knowing that the earth would absorb her pain if she let it spill out like it had done long ago. Yet this time was different. Moriah was no longer there to welcome her with soup and a warm hug and coax her back to joy as she had done when she returned to the cabin emptied and spent. She looked down at her hands throbbing from their hard work and saw that they were coated in dirt. She wished she could climb into the earth where Moriah lay, to be cradled in its moist and soft womb and be obliterated by the mycelia and worms. To be no longer meant that she didn't have to figure out life on her own and didn't need to face an unknown future without Moriah's guidance. But the earth wouldn't take her as she lay on it, wondering what to do next. To return to the cabin, to the hollow space left by Moriah's absence would require confronting the abyss of pain that welled inside her, and she dared not look there. Being swallowed and obliterated by the earth seemed easier than confronting the tornado of emotions that churned inside her, pulling her into the abyss.

Paralyzed by confusion, she was pinned to the ground, unable to rise and take a step. Her eyes searched her surroundings, then noticed the dogs huddling at a distance by the entrance to the forest. In her despair she had forgotten about them until now. It seemed they didn't want to return to the tragic scene of Moriah's death and burial, as if instinct kept them away. Since she couldn't summon her own intuition, she would follow the instincts of the dogs, she decided. She must and she would get away, if only to save her bleeding heart from a flood of pain. She pulled herself up and dusted the dirt from her new tunic. Taking one last scan of her surroundings, she said goodbye to their garden, to the geese nest, to the green meadow, to the odd-shaped small cabin with seven sides, to all that sustained her, all that she had known and loved. All the life-affirming love and beauty she saw meant nothing now without Moriah.

There was nothing left to do in the yard and nothing to take with her on her journey. Clad in the red robe and the moccasins Moriah had given her, followed by the four wolf-dogs, she entered the forest.

PART III

Becoming

CHAPTER EIGHTEEN

Into the Woods

T HE DOGS SURROUNDED her as she followed the usual path into the depths of the woods. Shafts of light seeping between the trees licked the trail, warming her steps. She walked along listlessly, following their lead, yet quickly her survival instincts kicked in. She became alert to every sound. Anticipating possible danger, she attuned her ears to stealthy paws that might shuffle through the shrubs or step on twigs. In her concentration, her grief dissipated, giving way to total emersion with the forest. Clearing her mind of anything else, she breathed its breath and felt its heartbeat pulse under the soles of her feet. The now familiar path guided her steps, to where she didn't know, but she trusted it as she trusted the dogs' instincts. Now there was no longer an obligation to return to the cabin before nightfall, no risk of getting lost.

The company of the angelic beasts beside her was reassuring. She also knew where to find food and water in the wilderness. With nothing to constrain her leisurely stroll, she marveled at the majesty of the trees, forming families in circles out of a single sequoia trunk. She took in the aromas of the moist soil, the pines and the ferns that cascaded along the slopes of the rolling hills. When she smelled the strong pine, she stopped to inhale deeply. The smell soothed her, and she inhaled again, closing her eyes as she leaned against its bark. Layers of sounds encircled her. The *swish* of the breeze as it traveled through canopies of leaves awakened their song – thousands of tiny bells chiming before fading away. High above, birds flapped through the wind and glided on its currents. A loud chirping directly over her head made her open her eyes and look up. A squirrel perched on the branch, squealing rhythmically, hugged an acorn to its chest. Its shrill cries traveled through the evening air mixing with the distant sounds of the forest.

How could mates recognize each other's calls in such a jungle of sounds? How did birds find their way back to their nest after foraging an entire forest? Maybe these mysteries contained the clues for how she could find her mate again and return to her home. She wished she had asked Moriah these questions. Now it was too late. Her heart swelled with yearning. There was so much she still didn't know... Instinctively her hand reached to the pinecone on her neck, her fingers playing with it idly. The small gesture pacified her.

The forest was no longer a threatening cacophony, as it had been on her first encounters with it. Rather, she sensed that she was penetrating a magnificent harmonious creation where all existed in perfect equilibrium and support of each other, from the smallest elements such as the fungus networks underneath her feet to the highest and widest canopies above her head. The forest and its plants and creatures wrapped around her as if celebrating her presence with them. She laughed again, feeling silly that she'd feared the forest. There had been no need. It and its inhabitants were no threat to her.

When she resumed her trek, she was struck by the change of perception from her first expeditions and knew that Moriah's spirit and teaching were to thank for this consciousness. Moriah had opened her to an understanding of the intricacies of nature that were an integral part of herself, and she had fostered the opening of Tikvah's heart to know that nature and to love it as her own existence. Laden with deep sorrow from the task of burying her friend and mentor, she nonetheless found solace in the beauty that surrounded her and which Moriah had so loved.

She drank water from a stream and ate berries from the bushes. Ran with the dogs some more. But night was descending at a surprisingly quick speed. Soon she wouldn't be able to see her feet on the path. She chose a wide oak trunk to settle against for the night. Her furry friends gathered around her, making her resting place both comfortable and warm. It didn't take long before she fell into an abandoned sleep.

CHAPTER NINETEEN

The Road

THE LOUD CHIRPING of birds announcing the imminent arrival of sunlight burst into the air and shook Tikvah out of her slumber. The dogs stretched lazily as they got up. She greeted them with caresses and they returned their love with licks. Standing, she stretched her arms, extending them as far as she could toward the rays that peeked gingerly between the foliage. She welcomed the light to her and thanked the forest for her peaceful night's rest.

Tikvah's intuition inspired her to head toward the ocean. She'd caught a glimpse of it on one of her first escapades in the forest, when Moriah sent her to collect pinecones. The expansiveness that she saw that day was now drawing her. After her months in the meadow sheltered by the forest, she yearned to see and feel the wide horizon of the sea. Her curiosity overcoming her fear of the unknown, she tried to remember its direction. A beam of sun blinded her, and she remembered that the evening sun had headed down as she gazed toward the ocean on that evening long ago. Clearly the direction toward the ocean must be opposite the morning sun, she deduced, and turned around and followed the trail, the shifting sunlight caressing her back.

Not wanting to lose any moment of daylight, she moved swiftly. The sun followed them as they wandered through tall trees, high bushes and steep slopes and stepped lightly through twisted trunks and protruding roots. The dogs were clearly enjoying the trek, sniffing their way energetically in all directions, yet they stayed protectively close. The sounds of small animals scurrying away at their approach, the distant hoot of howls, the chirping of birds, the crackling of leaves and twigs underneath their feet, and the occasional creak of a tree swaying in the gentle wind accompanied their expedition, the noises of the forest seemingly responding to her presence.

She recalled one of Moriah's queries: "If a tree falls in the forest and there is no one there to hear or see it, did it really fall?" Her intuitive response had always been, "Of course it did!" But now she understood Moriah's riddle through the complexity of sensations that she experienced. She was the observer of her reality and her observations created this reality for her. Her presence completed the forest.

Her philosophical musings gave way to the many cherished memories of her life with Moriah. Their experiences together may not have been long, but they were a lifetime for her, the sum of all her memories. She understood implicitly that she was profoundly a different person from the time they met, even though she had no recollection of who she had been before. She knew who she was during that span of time with Moriah but had no idea who she was about to become. Still, her experiences with Moriah taught her to be comfortable with the unknown as she relied on her intuition to create a life in accordance with her truth. Her joy, love and hope would guide her way.

Deep in thought, she roamed the woods, eventually arriving at an area where the trees were younger and the forest thinning out. She climbed a mound and just barely saw the blue ocean on the horizon. It was still far away, but at least her direction was confirmed. She drank from a brook and ate a few handfuls of mushrooms and felt energized enough to continue her trek. Quickening her step, she headed toward the sea.

The sun that had been following her shifted, the pale-yellow globe diluted by the swelling fog that hung over the water ahead. Not long after, her path was intersected by a narrow road. She hesitated only briefly before turning toward it, deciding it afforded her a more expansive view than the forest path. As soon as she stepped on the road, Rafi took a turn to the north. A few minutes later Uri turned south and Micha west. Only Gabi remained faithfully by her side. She wondered why they had abandoned them but understood that they weren't comfortable in the open space away from the shelter of the trees. She knew from Moriah's stories that the archangel Rafael was the keeper of the north, Uriel of the South and Michael of the west. Perhaps like Moriah they too decided to return to where they'd come from. She wished she'd had a chance to say goodbye to her friends before they separated from the pack. "You won't abandon me, will you Gabi?" she asked quietly. Gabi looked up at her, his panting tongue hanging to the side of his open mouth. She thought she discerned a reassuring smile.

But when the woods thinned out completely and the open terrain grew rocky, Gabi stopped. Tikvah didn't say anything, waiting to see what he would do. Her eyes pleaded with him not to leave her. For a long moment he returned her gaze with his gentle eyes. A car sped by, pulling Tikvah's attention. When she turned back, Gabi was no longer there. He'd expressed his farewell before vanishing like the others.

They were all gone.

Her heart heavy, Tikvah continued down the road. Being separated from all her beloved companions in such a short period of time was a formidable loss. She was utterly alone for the first time ever. Since there was nothing she could do but persevere, head low, she continued toward the ocean.

The asphalt was hard—unyielding—under her soft moccasins, and the protective warmth of the sheltering trees had given way to a brisk ocean wind. Yet her thin tunic kept her surprisingly comfortable against the cooling air, and the moccasins felt solid despite their soft leather. Her sadness slowly transformed to gratitude for those gifts, and for the love and companionship she had experienced with Moriah and her dogs.

Turning a sharp bend, she was confronted by a vista that stopped her feet. Her breath caught. She was facing the full expanse of the ocean that stretched endlessly into a mysterious horizon. Waves crashed thunderously against huge boulders that rose from the shore below. She had never experienced such a spectacular sight. And the sound, the crashing and shushing and more roaring. It was almost too much to take in. She cautiously continued down the steep road, mesmerized by the natural forces that lay beyond it. The crashing of the waves swallowed all other sounds, only to recede rhythmically into whispers of foam before returning in an explosion against the cliffs. A loud honking made her spin briskly and jump out of the way of another car, its wheels hugging the shoulder. She understood immediately that walking on the road wasn't a good idea and negotiated her way onto a narrow rocky path that swerved between the road and the ocean. There, her advance was slowed by attempting to manage the difficult slope without falling into the abyss at her side. She felt suspended between two worlds, the solid mountain to her left and the ethereal void to her right that stretched to eternity. She tasted the salty spray in the air, smelled the ocean's pungent aromas. They reminded her of joy but also of danger, and she braced herself as she stepped around the bend on the road, carefully following the low barrier that protected her from the sharp slope of the hill and the water and rocks below.

As the sun set over the water, the pale blue sky was transformed by magical sweeps of intensifying red, orange and pink. Facing the water, one foot propped on a boulder, she gasped at the beauty—her first sight of a sunset over the ocean. *Moriah, I wish you were here. You would probably tell me how the light changes color and what the shapes of the clouds mean.* Moriah always had such fascinating explanations for everything, while she knew so little.

When the spectacle was over, dark purple strokes lingered until full darkness swallowed them as well. She stayed for a moment, allowing the magic of the beauty she had just witnessed settle into her heart. She had seen lovely pink and orange sunsets before, but none as spectacular as this one.

Under the dim light that filtered to her from beyond the horizon, she returned to the road. There was no safe place to stop and rest, so she walked on.

At the next bend a sign read: Jenner. Noting that for a place to have a name, someone must have named it, meaning that there might be someone who lived there and probably more than just one person, she expected to encounter someone at any moment. Her curiosity piqued. She detected a few lights ahead and realized that houses were hiding between trees on the land side of the road. She walked faster.

The road widened enough that there was room for stout wooden buildings on either side of it. She stopped at one that had a large terrace and collapsed onto the first of a series of wooden benches she reached on its side. Catching her breath, she tried to study her surroundings through a veil of increasing darkness. A light emanating from the adjacent building revealed a wide glass door, but since she sat to its side, she couldn't see what was inside it. It was a large structure compared to Moriah's cabin, but most of it was obscured by darkness. Beams of lights approached, blinding her. When the lights stopped in front of the building, she realized that a car had driven up and stopped.

Then she noticed the people. They poured out of the car and slammed its doors with a loud thud that shook the evening's silence. She got up, cranking her neck in their direction. The people . . . There was something peculiar about them. She stepped closer, trying to make out details in the dark. A few seemed to be children.

The children were dressed in elaborate costumes, one looking like a fairy-tale witch and one covered head to toe by a sheet. A small green fellow with a pointy red hat jumped out of the car door, cried out "wait for me" and ran to join them. They walked together beyond the building's glass door, accompanied by a man and a woman who wore masks over their mouths and noses. The woman's mask had a wolf snout complete with whiskers printed on it and the man's had a protruding brown nose that looked like a bear's snout. Tikvah inched closer and closer, watching them go inside the door where the light came from, but not daring to approach out of fear of being seen. She needed to figure out who or what these strangely dressed people were before approaching them. A short while later the witch, the ghost and a third one – a gnome, she decided – came out carrying paper bags. When they noticed her, the children raced directly at her and cried, "Trick or treat?"

She was startled. Not expecting to be discovered and having no idea what they were asking, she was mute, fighting for words, but none came.

The little witch tilted her head, studying Tikvah. Then she reached into her bag and decisively pulled out something. She handed her an apple and a bar covered in colorful paper.

"Are you Pocahontas?" she asked.

"Thank you. I'm not. I'm Tikvah." She swallowed, finding her voice, and extended the gifts, assuming the girl had mistaken her for a different person. But she and the others laughed and ran to join the adults who were waiting at the car. Ravenous after the long walk on a meal of only a few mushrooms and berries, Tikvah was grateful for the treats. She devoured the apple and unwrapped the bar that had the word *Stix* written on it. It tasted particularly good and sweet and strangely familiar. She wished the children had stayed longer. Perhaps she would have found the words to talk with them. Ask them about their outfits and where they were from. They seemed to be in such a rush to go somewhere, she wasn't fast enough, not clever enough, to engage them. They called her Pocahontas; was that her real name? Did they recognize her from another time, another life? Questions churned in her mind. She hoped they might come back or maybe someone else would show up. But soon the light turned off in the building and the area was shrouded in darkness. Shortly after the darkness arrived, a lone slender figure limped out of the building. From the dark silhouette of his back, she deciphered pointy boots and a wide-brimmed hat. *Cowboy.* The word sprang out from the recesses of her distant mind, conjuring a ghost of a memory. The man didn't turn around and got into his truck and drove away before she had a chance to call out to him.

"Hey, Cowboy!" she said out loud to the empty darkness, reeling the word closer to her, as if luring it out of an ocean of memory.

She could see her breath on the air with each exhale. Or was the fog so thick it felt as though it was a part of her? She hugged her knees to her chest to conserve heat. Perhaps there was a reason her feet led her to this place. Maybe she would finally find the answers to the questions that haunted her. The thought lifted her spirit until a distant howl of coyotes sent cold shivers down up spine. *If she survived her first night completely alone.*

CHAPTER TWENTY

The Coast

M UFFLED BY THE humidity in the air, the night's sounds drifted away. Now there was only her own breath. In the silence, the darkness engulfed Tikvah. She tipped her head back and searched for Sirius to guide her, but the sky was void of stars, completely covered in fog. The cold and damp of the air seeped into her robe, so she pulled it tighter against her body. She tried to sleep on the humid bench, but it was too cold and uncomfortable. And though she tried to ignore them, the howls of coyotes at a distance sent shivers of fright through her as she remembered her encounter with them. She hoped they wouldn't approach the building.

Alone in the darkness, there was nothing to distract her from the sadness of her losses and the despair over her situation. Her two-day journey had kept her mind occupied and her instincts on edge. Yet now there was nothing to lift from her the grief of missing Moriah and the dogs, the only friends she remembered knowing. She found herself humming one of Moriah's lullabies, raising her voice to calm her nerves. Alone and cold, she felt self-pity. She scolded herself for the folly of leaving Moriah's comfortable cabin and the only security she had known. She fumbled in her pocket for Moriah's letter. Just the feel of it would remind her of Moriah's promise to always be by her side. But she couldn't find it. She stood and searched again, then closed her eyes, picturing the last couple of days. *Where could it be?* She had probably forgotten it on the table at the cabin when she went outside.

No letter. No words of reassurance from Moriah. She *was* alone. She curled up on the bench, lying on her side. She hadn't cried much at Moriah's death, but tears can only be suppressed as long as the heart is sheltered or distracted from its pain. There was nothing to shelter and no distraction for her now. Her mother, sister, teacher and friend was gone. Even the dogs had deserted her. Heavy tears rolled on her cheeks, mixing with the moist air.

Tikvah had nothing and no one. She had no past and didn't know how to imagine a future. And the present was awful. Not bothering to wipe away the stream that gushed from her eyes, she curled into an even tighter ball. She spiraled into a dark abyss, so dark she couldn't find her way out. She stifled a sob, muting the sound of her agony. Her only hope now was that sleep would come.

~

Tikvah was startled awake by something wet and slimy dragging across her cheek. Her heart in her throat, she sat up quickly to find a dog sniffing her. It was much smaller than her dogs but tall enough to reach her, with his nose wiggling by her cheek. When she drew back, the dog jumped on the bench and settled at her feet, resting his head on his paws. His presence was comforting, and he radiated the warmth she so desperately needed. Stretching out again, she drifted back to sleep.

When she woke again, the morning was surprisingly sunny, a rare occurrence lately. She had gotten used to waking up to deep fog, which typically burned off by midday. Today, however, she was given the gift of the sun's warmth early. She glanced to her feet. The dog was gone.

In the light of day, she saw the bay that spilled inland beyond the terrace. The water glistened in the morning sun, revealing silver and gold hues gliding in the tiny waves. A small wooden boat tied to a pole by a rope bobbed in the shallow water, swaying gently in the swells. The air swooped around her in gentle caresses. Tossing off her fears, self-blame, discomfort and worries from the wretched night, she welcomed the new day and what it might bring. The sunlight brought relief, although the sadness of the night still lingered, like dawn's dew caught on the surface of leaves. But she was glad her heart had been brave enough to face its storm, allowing it to settle into the sadness without fighting it or protecting herself from it. She knew that whatever came, she could handle it. Moriah had taught her well.

The sound of a motor startled her. A few cars arrived and people appeared on the terrace, carrying paper cups and small paper bags. Tikvah sat up, inhaling sweet scents. The terrace filled with the quiet chatter of friends and murmured conversations that blended into laughter and then back into murmurs. The people were no longer clad in colorful disguises, yet they wore fabric masks concealing the lower half of their faces, pulling them down only to take bites of food. After a few moments of consideration, she assumed the masks were there to warm their noses from the brisk air. She tried to listen to conversations yet couldn't decipher much. Still, she enjoyed the presence of other people. After a short while the visitors dispersed, leaving behind morsels of unfinished meals. Tikvah slowly approached the empty deck and helped herself to leftovers, which she found herself savoring despite the unfamiliar tastes, particularly the sweet pastries.

Feeling rejuvenated, Tikvah went back down to the water to explore. She loved being where land and ocean met. The strong smells of the sea and kelp released into the cool air invigorated her. The seagulls continued their cries, seeming to have found their habitat around the terrace. She watched them dive for bites of food and carry bits of pastry in their beaks while emitting thrilling sounds. Tikvah understood how they felt. Like them, she had been delighted to discover the delicious treats left behind.

When she settled on the sand and glanced toward the water, she spotted a large rock protruding beyond the waves. It took her a moment to realize that seals populated that rock, sleeping with their bellies in the sun. From a distance they looked like boulders until one waddled toward the water. Could they be the seals that saved her from drowning? If not them, perhaps their brothers or sisters?

They turned their heads toward her, their heavy bodies twisting awkwardly to keep them balanced on the rock. Even from a distance, she could see a dozen curious black round eyes turn in her direction. Could they recognize her? Her dog companions surely would, no matter how much time elapsed since they were together. At that moment, the biggest seal let out a loud nasal bark, making her laugh out loud. She sensed he was acknowledging her presence, as there was no need for him to defend his territory since she was far away on the shore. She blew a kiss toward the seals in thanks before moving away so she wouldn't disturb their morning nap.

She walked over to explore the boat she had seen earlier moored in shallow water under the terrace. It appeared long abandoned and unused.

Kelp and all sort of debris discolored by salt and baked by the sun were scattered across the bottom. She watched the boat's lazy motion and wished she could climb inside and be cradled by the gentle movement of the sea. But the stench that it gave off prevented her.

When the sun reached the top of the sky, she heard a murmur of voices above the whispering waves. A new group of people arrived on the terrace. She hurried up, eager to see what she would find. The terrace was crowded. At the sight of so many people, she froze, unsure what to do next. Should she engage them? Would they have things to teach her? Perhaps they would know something about her loved ones. Maybe they could even help her find her home. Curiosity overcoming her shyness, she braved approaching a woman about Moriah's age sitting alone in front of a plate of food and sat on the bench next to her. The woman turned her head. Tired eyes opened above a black fabric mask that concealed most of her face. *N95* was engraved on it. *A code?* Tikvah smiled, but the eyes that met hers spat blazes in return.

"Put your mask on and stay six feet away from me!" the woman barked behind her mask. Several people nearby swung to face them.

"You should put your mask on!" a man's voice bellowed behind her, his baritone striking her ears with a distant familiar sound.

Why were they all hiding their faces even in the heat of the day? she wondered. Why were they so angry at her? She didn't have a mask but wished she could disappear behind one when the heat rushed to her cheeks. She had never known such utter loneliness until this moment. Even her first night alone had been shared by a sweet dog that warmed her to sleep. Surrounded by these strangers, she felt the cold iron rod of alienation jab into her heart. She left the terrace as quickly as she could, briskly moving down the stairs, yet controlling her steps so she wouldn't break into a run. She grasped at anything to shield her vulnerability from the eyes that burned at her back.

"When you encounter a wild beast in nature, never run from it." Moriah's words echoed in her mind. "Prey animals only attack if they're hungry or scared, and in this area, it is unlikely they're hungry. You walk around it calmly and then away slowly so you don't frighten it with sudden movements."

To escape the stares and her own anxiety and confusion, she hurried toward what she loved and what she knew loved her in return. On the beach the waves lapped softly before retreating in foamy whispers and the rustle of shell shards and tiny stones they carried back to the sea. The gentle sounds washed over her, muting the buzz from the terrace and erasing the glares of reproach. The cries of gulls hovering above the sand welcomed her. They circled around her before settling at her feet.

"You don't need me to wear a mask to get close to me," she said to the gulls, and she pulled out the slice of bread she had stashed in her pocket that morning to share with them. The feeding frenzy was brief, but the cries of their thanks could be heard over the people's chatter as the gulls lifted their yellow beaks and flew toward the high pale sun.

She walked along the beach, leaving her footprints on it, and when she turned around, she watched the oozing waves erase her steps. The beach held no memory of her passage, yet a moment later she could still feel the sand's coolness on the soles of her feet and taste the salty mist of the air. She turned to face the rolling turquoise swells; the sun was beaming straight on them from a bright blue sky. The beach might not remember her, she mused, but she could hold its beauty in her heart forever. *Forever.* She chuckled. Forever was a grand notion for someone who had no clue about her future. Still, she clung to the magnificent moment, planting it in her heart.

She immediately knew what to do next. Since she couldn't rely on the kindness of strangers, she needed to fend for herself. She headed toward the boat and pulled it out of the water. Nose pinched, she emptied its contents and piled them under the deck, setting the boat a short distance away from the risk of a rising tide. She spotted trees at the other end of the beach and collected leaves from them, finding to her delight many red and yellow ones that had fallen to the ground. She gathered them into the broken plastic bucket she brought from the boat. Back near the boat, she discovered a cardboard box that must have been tossed off the terrace by the breeze. She lay it on the bottom of the boat and covered it with the leaves, then lay another piece of cardboard, a thinner one, on top of it. Finally, she climbed into the boat and tested her bed. Not quite as comfortable as the one at Moriah's home, but it would do for now. At least it would make her next night a lot drier until she came up with a better plan.

Further down the beach was a secluded area surrounded by high grasses. Far away from the possibility of intruding stares, Tikvah removed her tunic and walked into the water. Her feet were met with such a chill that she took a few steps back, bracing herself to meet the cold water. It had been a few days since she'd bathed, and she yearned to wash off the dust of her journey and the stench of items she had removed from the boat. She waited before taking another step. Her feet were slowly acclimating to the water's temperature, or perhaps they just became numb. Step by cautious step, she immersed her body in the calm but icy water until only her head remained dry.

A strange sensation of remembrance fluttered through her, but once again it was only a twinkle of a feeling and no images came with it. She closed her eyes, but the elusive memory was completely gone.

When her body finally relaxed to its chill, the water felt wonderful, invigorating. She lingered a moment, gazing at the blue stillness glimmering in the sparkles that surrounded her, allowing it to wash away the dirt, the sadness and the pain. Leaving the water, she ran toward the boulder where she had left her tunic. Shielded from the breeze and intruders by the tall grasses, she lay out on the rock, and like a seal, she let the sun warm her body. Her skin dried, she slipped her tunic back on and sat, losing herself in the flapping waves. When the sun was about to set, she hoped to find something to eat on the terrace and to bring some nibbles to the beach to share with her seagulls. As she walked past the grasses, their quivering fluffy heads glittered in the evening sun, as though gathering the last rays of light. She caressed the flickering light gently, barely touching the reeds, and felt a tingle on her fingertips in return. A wave of gratitude washed through her for this glorious place and its bounty, for Moriah and her healing and for being alive on this beautiful day.

At sunset she settled on a round rock on the beach to watch the now familiar yet still amazing spectacle of the changing colors dancing over the water. Here the display was punctuated by the flight of gulls overhead. She recognized her friends and smiled. As the colors dimmed, stars began to appear in the dark blue sky. Cradled in her boat-bed under a canopy of stars, she felt safe and filled with peace. The anxiety of her first interaction with people had dissolved. She had learned her lesson, to stay away and to figure out things on her own from now on. She hoped she would find her beloved even without their help. Moriah had taught her that she could take care of herself, and she also showed her that she could belong wherever she chose if she was true to her emotions.

She recalled the magical night she spent outside with Moriah and the dogs gazing at the stars. The memory was a reminder of how connected she felt to be in the space between heaven and earth. Her heart was telling her that she loved this place by the ocean and that she belonged to it.

CHAPTER TWENTY-ONE

The Encounter

T HE STOUT BUILDING with all the traffic in and out turned out to be a convenience store that doubled as a deli and seemed to be a gathering spot for locals. Tikvah never went inside. She would probably have been thrown out for not wearing a mask. She settled on enjoying the plentiful leftovers that she picked through after every meal. After a few days she was accustomed to the schedule and knew to be close to the terrace when the sun first rose, when it was at its high point, and right before sunset. She was quite content with the rhythm of her days as she explored the ocean and the beaches and returned to the terrace for food, sleep and shelter. She kept her distance from people, and they seemed not to notice her. Although her days drifted along a pleasant routine, she still had no plan for how to move forward. How to find out who she was and where she had lived before her accident remained a mystery. Yet she was filled with hope that in time the way would be revealed and that she would know what to do when it was.

Her explorations afforded her the time to review the lessons Moriah had taught her. She replayed Moriah's words about the garden, the stars, the crystals, the mushrooms and the trees, hugging to her heart the lessons they brought to her about her own nature. She laughed often, thinking about their dog companions and how much fun it was to play with them and how much love they shared. Sometimes, alone in her boat, she missed their company so badly that her heart ached. She would then hum Moriah's songs, hoping the lullabies would bring her friend and mentor closer to her and help her fall asleep.

One evening, when the sky's sweep of purple dissolved into gray and the moisture in the air rose to greet the night, she got into her boat to cover herself with the leaves and cardboard. They had become less effec-

tive at shielding her from the night's coolness, which seemed to be intensifying day by day. The cold was making it difficult to stay asleep. She was
contemplating how to make her bed warmer when the dog who shared
her bench on the first night appeared. In the dimming light she could see
that it had a short dark brown coat and was a male, as her companions
had been. He searched for her with his nostrils and then leaped into the
boat, settling at her feet. Despite his damp doggie smell, she welcomed
his company and warmth into her bed. She patted his head. His fur felt
coarse, unlike her Gabi's.

"What is your name, dear friend?" she asked in a whisper. His black
eyes stared blankly at her, and he let out a short moan. "Fine, then, Mo it
is!" She realized that the name she came up with, or that her new friend
told her, reminded her of the name of her dear lost friend. But that was
fine. Moriah wouldn't mind it. Why would she? Mo was her friend and
so was she.

With Mo by her, she slept soundly for the first time since her arrival at
the beach.

~

"Ah, here you are!"

An unfamiliar male voice woke her in the morning. By the position of
the sun, she realized that she had slept later than usual. She shuffled her
way out of her blanket of leaves to look up to the balcony above her. In the
bleak morning light, she recognized the silhouette of the young man who
opened and closed the store each day. She had seen him several times on
the terrace, clearing off plates. From his slight limp, she realized that he
was also the cowboy she had seen the night of her arrival, although he'd
never again worn a cowboy hat or boots. The sun shone from behind him,
casting his face in shadows as he faced her. She smiled but remained silent.

"I brought apples from the apple tree in my yard; would you like some?
I've been wondering where you were spending your nights." He shook his
head. "Sorry, I didn't mean for that to sound like it did." He flashed a thin
smile. "I mean, I've been wondering if you had a house. You know, since I
always see you hanging out here in the morning and when I close up."

Tikvah climbed up to the balcony and accepted a small apple. "Thank
you." She bit into the apple. Mmm. Crunchy and sweet.

"I see you found my boat." He pointed bellow the terrace to Tikvah's bed. "No worries. You can use it as much as you like as long as you clean it up after you leave. The last person who 'borrowed' it was not so considerate. I haven't used it for months. Been too busy with work."

Tikvah nodded, remembering the stench of the debris she'd removed from the boat.

"I'm James." He stretched out his hand but withdrew it immediately. "I keep forgetting you're not supposed to shake hands anymore. I guess I can't shake the habit."

His grin grew wide. Only then did Tikvah realize that he wasn't wearing a mask and was standing close to her despite the fact that she wasn't wearing one either. She guessed that for whatever reason, he didn't mind. Or maybe it wasn't such a strict rule for interacting with people after all. She might have misunderstood something.

"So, what's up?"

"The sky?" Swallowing the last bite of the apple, she wondered why he would ask a question with such an obvious answer. Was it some kind of game? Obviously, she wasn't good yet at understanding people.

"Would you like some warm tea? I can get it for you."

"Sure. That would be nice."

"Coming right up. And don't worry, it's on me," he said while advancing toward the door. "Oh, would you like sugar or honey or a sugar-free sweetener?" he called out, turning toward her.

"Honey! Please." Tikvah was glad to have her first cup of warm sweet tea in what seemed like ages but wondered why it would be "on" him? What kind of way would that be to serve tea?

A few minutes later he hurried out, saying, "I brought an assortment to choose from."

He handed her an array of colorful folded papers and a paper cup.

"Careful, the water is boiling," he told her.

Perplexed, she studied the packets.

"Okay, let's see here . . ." James tapped a few of the colorful packets. "Do you prefer peppermint, chai or Earl Grey?"

"Peppermint, please." She didn't know what the other names meant.

He handed her the green bag, and when she turned it over a couple of times, trying to understand how it made tea, he opened the plastic lid of the cup, freed what she recognized as a tea bag from the green wrapping and dropped the bag into the hot water steaming in the cup.

"Here you go," he said, closing the lid again. "You're supposed to drink it from this hole, but wait a few minutes because it might still be too hot."

Tikvah took the cup from him, grateful that it warmed her frozen hands. For a moment they stayed silent, then he settled on the terrace bench next to her and looked out over the ocean. She studied his elongated profile with its high forehead. His blond curls spilled around his neck. There was something feminine in the curve of his body as he crossed his legs with his torso hunched forward, yet his exterior was rugged, as though he was covering up the tender part of himself, which he didn't want to reveal.

He eventually turned to face her, his cheeks reddening when he saw that she was watching him.

"So what's your name?"

"Tikvah."

"That's an unusual name; does it mean anything?"

"It means hope in Hebrew."

"Oh, are you Jewish?"

Tikvah thought for a moment. "I don't know. I don't think so, but I really have no way of knowing."

"Ah, I see."

He let the silence drop again between them. Tikvah drank her tea. She wished she could think of something to ask him but the words didn't come.

"So, where are you from, Tikvah?"

He enunciated her name intently, as though it was filled with meaning. She realized that besides Moriah, no one had called her by her name before. It made her feel more present with him. She grew a few inches taller, then responded.

"The forest." Tikvah pointed north.

James nodded. "You're from up north. You have family out there?"

"Only Moriah." But she didn't have Moriah anymore. "I had to put her in the ground. So, no. No family up there." Tikvah realized how miserable she sounded, so she added a smile, not wanting to expose her sadness to this stranger, no matter how nice he seemed. "I like it here," she added.

James stared at her, mouth gaping. "You put her in the ground? You mean like you buried her, right?"

Tikvah nodded, and his tense body relaxed.

"I get it. I'm from here. Born and raised right over here." He motioned to a house up on the ridge across the street. "This store used to belong to my grandfather, but he passed away this year. Covid, you know. Well, he was old, over eighty, but still . . ."

A heavy silence stretched between them, and Tikvah nodded, acknowledging his loss. Once again he turned to the water, and she hoped he drew comfort like she did from the constant motion of the waves and the steadfastness of the sky. Again she searched for words.

A few moments later he said, "So, he's gone, and now the store and deli are mine." He turned back to Tikvah. "I guess I'll spend the rest of my life here like he did. Not a bad place." He grinned. "Still, I'd like to travel someday. See the world, you know . . . At least we get a lot of visitors from everywhere, although not lately. Just the locals now. So I was kinda surprised to see you appear, but I figured you might be one of the new people who bought houses in the area. A lot of city folks have been buying houses lately, some moving in and some renting them out. Real estate is going crazy—you probably already know that. Maybe I should sell everything and move on, but I just can't imagine where else I would be happier than here. I've had to let all my staff go since there aren't enough customers anymore, only locals. The city people go only to the supermarket and back home, or they have food delivered to them. Yours is the only new face we've seen around here for a few months."

Tikvah studied him after his speech ended. She recognized the sadness he was holding inside and how he tried to distract himself from it with many words, words that hung uncomfortably in the air.

"We have something in common," she said finally. "We both recently lost someone we love."

"An unfortunate thing to have in common," James said, rubbing his face.

At that moment the first morning arrivals pulled up in front of the store, so he excused himself and told her he'd be back after the morning rush to bring her another cup of tea and some food. "Please stay." His smiling eyes pleaded for her not to leave as he rushed off.

She didn't stay to watch the morning customers or wait for their leftovers. Instead, she descended to the shore of the bay to watch the sun make its procession across the sky and illuminate the water that reflected its light. She was now familiar with the natural rhythms of the shore, the cries of seagulls that rose over the deck with the appearance of food, the arrival of the seals on the rocks to take advantage of a momentary sunbeam and the roar of the ocean beyond the bay. Her heart swelled with joy when her feet touched the sand, filling her with love for her surroundings. The intensity and rawness of the landscape had washed into her soul, burrowing deep.

Watching the steady swells, she wished she had asked James questions that could help her find her beloved, but she didn't know what to ask. Surprised by her first conversation with someone other than Moriah, she didn't know how to begin. She would take her time alone by the water to think about it. She'd be ready with her questions when he brought her more tea and food.

At midday she felt a pang of hunger and climbed back to the patio. She sat on the bench waiting for James to appear from the glass door. She was pleased to have made a friend. His shyness welcomed her through its gentleness.

A car pulled up in front of the building. The word *Sheriff* was written on its side with bold green letters. A tall burly man wearing a wide-brim hat and heavy black boots pushed out of it. A metal star was pinned to his tight-fitting black shirt.

"Hello, ma'am," he said to her, touching his hat. "May I sit down?"

He wore a black mask over his nose and mouth, like so many of the people did. When Tikvah nodded, he sat down next to her, keeping his mask on.

"What's your name?" His voice was calm and slow.

"Tikvah."

"Nice to meet you, Tikvah. I'm Sheriff Johnson. May I ask what your last name is?"

Tikvah thought for a moment. It had never occurred to her to ask Moriah for her last name. She had no idea what to say and so said nothing.

"Where are you from, Tikvah?" the sheriff asked intently.

As she had with James, she pointed north.

"Up north?" the sheriff asked.

"Yes."

"Do you have an ID?"

Tikvah went motionless, not knowing what an ID was. Then she realized he meant an idea, and she searched her mind for idea she could share with him.

"Do you have documents that show your identity?" he asked, impatience creeping into his controlled voice. She shook her head. "Tikvah, I'd like for you to come with me to the station so we can figure out who you are and where you live."

For the first time, Tikvah looked directly at his face. "My home is here, and I know who I am!" She felt flustered with his questioning and balked at his suggestion.

"I understand, Tikvah. Of course." There was that tone again, calm but firm. "But I hope we can help you figure out your full name and where you lived before coming here."

"I lived up north in the forest with Moriah."

"Where is Moriah now?" he asked.

"In the ground, where I put her."

"Please come with me, Tikvah."

Sheriff Johnson's voice was quiet but its firmness was clear; he intended for her to go with him. She hesitated while fiddling with the pinecone hanging against her dress. Touching the pinecone had become her automatic habit whenever she felt unsure of what to do next, and it always instantly brought clarity. Perhaps even though she didn't like this man, he was really trying to help her. After all, she *had* been looking for help; perhaps he was her answer. She decided to accept the sheriff's invitation despite wanting to see James again.

James hurried out of the store and called out to Tikvah as she followed the sheriff. She stopped to look back at him and thought she thought saw him mouth, "I'm sorry!" but no sound reached her. He waved slowly when the sheriff helped her into the car.

Moments later, when the car took off, she wondered why James would be sorry.

CHAPTER TWENTY-TWO

Self-Encounter

S HERIFF JOHNSON SAT behind the old computer at the even older Formica desk, focused on the report he was typing. It had been some time since he'd filled out a report, and the prospect energized him. He poured all his attention into the task, scarcely acknowledging the woman who sat across the desk from him. He could barely see her at the angle he was sitting at, anyway.

November 5, 2021. Caucasian female about thirty years of age. Approx. 5'4" 110 lbs. Found on the deck of Spinnaker at 1:35 p.m. Wearing a red dress and tan leather moccasins. She appears disoriented. She identifies herself as Tikvah. No last name. No domicile. Possible homicide. Possible amnesia.

"Tikvah." He twisted on his swirling chair to face her. "I'm contacting someone from social services who will come here to help you. They'll take you to a place where you can live more comfortably. And help you with any health or other issues you might be experiencing."

He picked up his desk phone and dialed. Tikvah stood and glided toward the window. The sheriff's gaze followed her when she bent down and peered through the bars. Her demeanor—calm, composed and graceful—caught his attention. Her poise indicated that she was in complete possession of herself. She displayed none of the characteristics he would expect from someone on the run from the law or suffering from mental trauma. In fact, her presence was quite commendable in a quiet way.

He shifted in the chair when it occurred to him that she might be someone important and that he might be making a mistake by turning her over to social services. He might have been too quick to judge her based on her external appearance, he thought. He hung up the phone and pushed back on his chair, observing her as she gazed out the window. She turned around and smiled at him. Something about her smile kindled a memory; it looked strangely familiar. Like he'd seen her, maybe on a screen, but didn't know her personally. Maybe she was a movie actress who had escaped the set and was still deep in character? He closed his eyes when she turned back to the window, his mind quickly rushing through images.

A moment later there it was—Joyce Woodland smiling from a photograph. He opened his eyes. Could she be the missing woman they'd written off for dead months ago? The one who disappeared on that cold and foggy February morning?

Her husband had combed the surrounding shore and forest in his search during the months that followed, gathering hundreds of volunteers and even hiring a search crew that scoured miles of surrounding area for her, 24/7, to no avail. They'd finally concluded that she must have drowned and been carried off by the ocean. He turned around and began typing quickly. He'd closed that file a few months ago and buried the details in the recesses of his memory. It was hopeful thinking by a long shot that the woman standing in front of him might be her, since the woman who disappeared was in her forties and this one seemed barely thirty years old. Still, there was something about that smile . . .

He studied the screen and looked back at her and at the screen again. Could it be? He didn't want to raise false hopes and seem foolish in case he was mistaken. But still . . . Clearing his throat, he turned to her.

"Does the name Joyce Woodland mean anything to you?" he asked, his heart pounding. Hope sank quickly when she shook her head. "How about Willson Woodland?" Another head shake followed. His courage dwindled. He was concerned about what to do next but decided to take a leap of faith. Or rather, one of hope. After all, she was about the height of the missing woman. Yet as he compared the image to Tikvah, his hope waned. The wild-haired disheveled waif in front of him bore no resemblance to the composed sharp-eyed executive on his computer screen. Despite his misgivings, and at the risk of being humiliated, he decided to take a far-fetched gamble. It wasn't like he'd never made a boneheaded move before. He dialed a phone number from the missing woman's file.

"This is Will."

Will Woodland sounded brusque. Tense. Maybe even officious. The sheriff and he had spent many hours together, and the sheriff recognized fear and maybe panic in the other man's tone.

"Hello, Will, This is Sheriff Johnson." He tried to match Will's official tone, but gave up his pretense instantly, his concern for Will taking over. "I don't want you to get too hopeful, but we've had a possible development here." He proceeded cautiously, leaving himself room to back away from his supposition in case he was mistaken. "There's a woman here at the station who might fit the description of your wife. But..."

"I'll be right there!" Will said without hesitation before Sheriff Johnson had a chance to backpedal his statement, as he'd intended. "Give me an hour."

In the course of searching for Joyce, the sheriff had become accustomed to Will Woodland traveling from San Francisco to Jenner on the helicopter he purchased for that purpose. He'd even gotten his pilot's license, but he hadn't been to the station since the summer. Will would be there in no time, and Johnson worried that he didn't have much time to prepare the woman for his arrival and to figure out their next steps.

While he was on the phone, Tikvah wandered into the hall. She moved quickly toward the door in the back, but it wouldn't open for her.

Johnson hung up and headed in her direction. She obviously didn't know her way around a police station; otherwise, she would have known the outside door would be locked.

He followed her down the hall. They found themselves face-to-face when Tikvah turned around. She stepped back, obviously startled.

"Tikvah." Johnson gentled his tone as he also stepped back, not wanting to scare or crowd her. "How would you like some tea or coffee and donuts? We've got some right there in the reception area." He motioned her to follow him.

God, he hoped he'd done the right thing by calling Woodland before they had more information. If not, he'd have a few very upset people on his hands.

~

The room Tikvah entered was somewhat more specious and inviting than the office. A half-open cardboard box revealed a couple of donuts in one corner.

"They make them right here in town." The sheriff opened the box and tilted it toward her. "The best I've ever had." He smiled broadly. "Why don't you wait here for a moment, and I'll get my wife to come over to keep you company. We live right back there." He pointed toward the oak tree that Tikvah had been studying. She accepted one of the pastries and sank her teeth into its soft sweetness. She'd been feeling hungry and was grateful for the treat.

A few moments later a round rosy-cheeked woman arrived carrying a kettle and offering to make tea. She introduced herself as Mary-Joe Johnson, the sheriff's wife. She was so sweet, she made Tikvah feel welcome. She chatted away about the weather and about her two teenage boys who were at home doing nothing but playing computer games and watching TV. She described how hard her life had been since the lockdown began, cooking and cleaning all day, every day, for her men but not getting to visit with her friends. TV? Computer games? And why was she locked down? Tikvah had no idea what she was talking about but sensed the woman's distress and nodded sympathetically.

"No time for myself, dear. Not even to take a walk along the ocean; did you ever expect anything like this?" She waved both hands. "I'm tired of wearing masks everywhere, aren't you? So I prefer to stay home where at least we're safe, since none of us except for my husband ventures out. At any rate, there haven't been many cases in our community . . ."

Tikvah listened as she sipped the dark bitter tea. She felt relieved that Mrs. Johnson never interrupted her excited monologue to ask her personal questions like the two men had done. When her speech ended, she patted Tikvah's hand and said, "Could you use a trip to the bathroom, dear?"

Tikvah wasn't sure, so she decided not to offend the woman, who seemed very hospitable. Mary-Joe showed her the way to the woman's restroom and waited outside.

"Don't worry, it's clean," she called through the door. "No one ever uses the ladies. There are only men in this station, my husband and his assistant."

The pale green room was very clean. Someone glanced at her from a window over the basin, startling her. She didn't expect to see anyone else there. It took a moment for her to realize that it wasn't a window, but a reflective surface. Tikvah was looking at herself. She'd seen only vague reflections of herself in the glass door of the store but had never seen her face clearly. The woman staring back at her was such a surprise that she took a step back. She then approached the mirror cautiously, studying parts of her face one at a time. The unexpected moment of self-discovery felt overwhelming. She leaned forward until her nose nearly touched the glass. Bony cheekbones; she poked at one. Her brown skin was drawn tightly around them. She tugged at the fluff of wild hair that hung around her head and descended her shoulders like a wolf's mane. The skin above her eyes held thin transparent lines. Her lips were cracked and flaking; she picked off the dry skin.

She stared into her eyes and they stared back at her, curious and filled with light. She again pushed close to the mirror, recognizing Moriah's eyes in her own face and felt satisfied by what she saw. She didn't know if hers was an attractive face, but she was pleased with it. She looked around. Behind her was another small room, its door slightly ajar. It had a basin on the floor filled with water. She dipped her fingers into it and splashed the refreshing water on her face. Maybe that was what Marie-Joe meant when she invited her to use the bathroom. Mission accomplished, she turned to leave.

CHAPTER TWENTY-THREE

The Reunion

Will dashed into the station and was immediately greeted by Sheriff Johnson, who told him to temper his expectations before taking him to meet the woman who'd introduced herself as Tikvah. Eager to see for himself, Will brushed aside the sheriff's warnings.

His heart leaped when he entered the reception room and saw the back of a woman's thin frame clad in a red garment. Her face was turned partially away from the door as she gazed out the window while the sheriff's wife chattered away. He nodded to Mary-Joe. As if she was sensing him—or maybe just hearing his footsteps—the woman turned her head toward the door. Will was confronted with the sweet face of a woman he didn't recognize. Her disheveled long hair extended in all directions, a wild dark mane which crowned her tiny face. Her skin was tanned a deep brown, and she had an exotic look unlike any he'd ever seen before. Unexpectedly Will stepped back, uncertain.

She returned his gaze head-on. And then she smiled.

It was the smile that stopped Will's retreat, pulling his hope back to him as it connected to a memory deep within his soul. Hope tugged at his heart. He walked toward her. When she didn't shy away, he sat on the couch by her side.

"Joyce?" He tried to say her name softly, but his voice was hoarse.

Her expression didn't change as she gazed at him, yet a tiny twitch of her head caused his heart to plummet again. His hunch had misled him, and he couldn't bring himself to continue. The conversation that he'd been practicing on the trip to the police station and which he'd prepared during many months of fantasizing about the moment he'd come face to face with Joyce now failed him. He didn't know what to think or what to believe. Was this woman Joyce? It seemed improbable. Impossible.

He found himself uncharacteristically paralyzed by an encounter with this woman he didn't recognize, yet who somehow felt distantly familiar.

Tikvah lay one hand on the couch, her palm open. He took it instinctively. A jolt of a distant echo shot through his arm and into his heart. He continued staring, trying to find the woman he loved in the woman whose hand his was holding.

"Joyce, do you recognize me?" he finally brought himself to ask. Once again, she shook her head, but only slightly. In spite of his misgivings, he couldn't let go of the hand, which felt strangely familiar despite being coarse, filled with calluses and darkened by earth and sun. He was willing to take the chance to find out who this woman was, even if she wasn't Joyce.

He considered his words carefully before asking, "What's your name?" He wanted to hear her speak.

"Tikvah. What's yours?"

There was that smile again that pulled at the strings of his heart. He couldn't figure out this feeling of attraction, so he dismissed it as the roller coaster of emotions that had surged through him for the past hour.

Disappointment struck hard. How could she not recognize him, not know his name?

If that was Joyce, what had happened to her?

"Tikvah, I'm Will. I'd like for you to come with me to a place where you'll be cared for. *I'd* like to take care of you. Will you come?" His heart was racing. He needed her to say yes.

This time Tikvah nodded.

Will turned to Sheriff Johnson, who was standing a short distance away and carefully observing the exchange. "So, what are the formalities? Is there paperwork I need to fill out?"

"There is indeed. Please come with me."

The sheriff turned toward his office. He printed a document from his computer while Will shifted from foot to foot, eager to be out of there and talking again with Tikvah. *Who might be Joyce.* He sighed loudly and paced across the room and back, wondering how he couldn't recognize his wife *or* conclusively declare that she wasn't his wife. Regardless, now that he told the sheriff he'd take care of her, he needed a plan, but had no clue what to do next. Surprised to remember a conversation that he'd had with Joyce about her work, he had an idea, and without losing a beat he stepped outside to the corridor to make the call that could possibly determine their next steps. Back in the office, the sheriff frowned intently at him before handing him several sheets of paper. Johnson opened his mouth, perhaps to voice an objection, but ultimately said nothing and focused on the tile floor.

If Johnson changed his mind about Will taking her, Will didn't know what he would do. Without a positive identification, would the sheriff's department even have the authority to let her go with him?

"I just need your signature acknowledging that this person is your wife, Joyce Woodland, and that I'm releasing her to your care."

Johnson spoke uncharacteristically quickly. Maybe he didn't want Will to change his mind.

But no fear of that. Not when there was a chance the woman was Joyce. And yet . . .

If this was Joyce, why couldn't *he* identify her? Did that mean that she wasn't Joyce?

He closed his eyes. No, it didn't mean that. The woman had obviously been through some trauma or illness; she was much too thin. And she'd definitely been exposed to the elements for some time. It wouldn't be unusual for her to look different to those who knew her.

He opened his eyes, acknowledging the delaying tactic.

Taking a deep breath, he reached for the pen extended to him, and yet he hesitated with the pen held over the final page. Was he doing the right thing by taking this chance? He could always make sure that she was settled somewhere safe if she wasn't Joyce. But if there was any chance that the wild-haired woman *was* Joyce, he'd never forgive himself for not taking care of her immediately when he had the chance.

Setting his doubts aside, he took the plunge and signed the paper. Sheriff Johnson breathed a sigh of relief.

"I brought some clothes for you to change into," Will said when he was facing Tikvah again. He opened Joyce's black Vuitton bag and pulled out a gray cashmere sweatsuit and pink Nikes. "I thought you'd like to get into your favorite comfort clothes as soon as possible."

She stroked the soft cashmere, held it to her face and thanked him.

"Would you like to go to the bathroom to change?" Mary-Joe asked, interrupting the silence.

"No thank you," said Tikvah politely as she smiled at Will. He put the clothes back in the bag.

"Okay, let's go, then."

Will extended his free hand. Tikvah took it without hesitation and let him guide her out of the station. A chauffeured car waited for them outside.

"Back to the heliport, please!" Will said to the driver, and turning to Tikvah, he asked, "Have you been in a helicopter before?"

"I don't know."

He hadn't anticipated that response. If she was Joyce, she would have answered yes.

"Well, if you haven't, you're in for an adventure," he said, determined to stay positive. There'd been enough surprises for one day, so he decided to accept whatever came at him from now on and suspend his judgment. When they reached the heliport, he gave her a hand into the helicopter and hopped into the seat next to her. "We're flying south to San Diego."

He'd yelled over the propeller noise, but he couldn't be sure she heard him. He leaned over her to put the noise-canceling headset on her ears and help her buckle up. He lifted off as soon as he was strapped in too.

His didn't know what to think, but at least this was progress of some kind. He shifted against the seat and angled his head so he could watch Tikvah and see out the windshield.

Tikvah. He'd have to find out where that name had come from. Maybe that line of questioning would produce results.

~

The view was dizzying. Tikvah wished she could return to the ground where she belonged, where she was safe, but it was too late. She was strapped into a seat, and the good-looking kind man from the station was operating the loud metal machine that whisked them through the sky and clouds. Being suspended in midair reminded her of something dreadful. She had no idea what it was, but she hated the sensation. She sensed an imminent danger of falling, of disappearing, and panic engulfed her.

Suddenly Will's hand was on hers. She opened her palm, allowing his warm gentle hold to tighten. She couldn't understand what he was saying, but she felt his assurance that everything would be okay, so she let go of her worry and melted her back into the seat.

Within moments she was leaning to the side and then to the front, searching the ground and trying to identify what she saw there. The houses below grew smaller and smaller until they appeared tiny, nothing like buildings at all, and the horizon grew wider and larger. The thick forest was disappearing behind them, taken over by the expanse of the blue of the ocean. So thrilling was the view that she was lost to the moment.

Goodbye, Mo; goodbye, James; goodbye, Moriah, Gabi, Uri, Rafi and Micha.

The forest, her home with Moriah and the dogs, was drifting farther and farther behind, until it completely disappeared from view.

But Tikvah was continuing the journey that Moriah had wished her to take.

While the past disappeared, the future approached.

And she couldn't wait to discover the wonders it held.

CHAPTER TWENTY-FOUR

The Clinic

"**D**O YOU RECOGNIZE where we are?" Will asked, immediately regretting the question that was met by another silent head shake, his question again answered in the negative. His heart sank. He so needed something positive to hold on to.

The copper plaque at the entrance gate announced Neurotronics Clinic. Joyce had founded the clinic as a memory research center that also accepted a small number of patients for observational studies. He had called from the police station to make sure they could accommodate her, given the possibility that if it was Joyce, she might have suffered from mental confusion, or worse, amnesia. The response from the head doctor had been a resolute yes! Will concocted the plan at the station, hoping that returning to a place she had known might jog her memory and that she would magically transform back into her old self, *if* she was Joyce. Wishful thinking, he knew, but he kept hoping.

The automatic gate opened, and the car descended onto a wide road that wound downhill. Large cypress trees stood tall on either side of it, casting shadows. But the dappled effect was upbeat rather than dark or gloomy. The road led to a colonial Spanish–style mansion set on a large lawn and to a view of the ocean.

"I'll take you around the property after you get settled in," Will told Tikvah as he opened the car door for her. At the entrance they were greeted by a middle-aged woman wearing a white coat. "This is Dr. Gladwell. She'll take care of you while you're here."

The doctor shook Tikvah's hand while studying her intently. Her generous figure filled the entrance door, and she stepped inside to let them in. Excusing herself, she walked away into a wide corridor.

They entered into a spacious wood-paneled room with enormous windows that framed the blue expanse of ocean and sky that dominated the room. Will was glad for the brightness; he understood how light was necessary for a positive outlook. Plus, Joyce had loved the ocean view from their vacation house.

A young man strolled into the reception room and introduced himself as Jerry, the staff nurse. He invited them to follow him down the same corridor with many closed doors that the doctor had hurried into. The space felt grand despite its length because of the high rounded ceiling and the skylights that punctuated it. Jerry opened the door to a simple room, rather small relative to the scale of the public areas, but well-lit by a large window that overlooked the ocean. It contained a full-size bed covered with crisp white sheets and a fluffy duvet, and a wooden desk by the window with a white mesh office chair in front of it. On the wall across from the bed hung an abstract painting of blue, green and gray hues, melted together to evoke the motion of rolling water.

Will turned to Tikvah. "How do you like your room?"

Eyes wide, she stared at him. Her fingers stroked the duvet.

"Is there anything else you'd like, anything you need?" Jerry's voice and frown declared that he was evaluating Tikvah. Will thought he was being too obvious, but maybe he was showing his concern. "We can set up a comfortable club chair for you so you can sit and look out at the view." He exited the room before she had a chance to reply.

"Is this really my home?" Tikvah turned to Will, smile wide. Her joy was clear.

"Yes, all yours. Would that be okay for a little while?"

She flashed her brilliant smile, and relief washed over him, relaxing his body for the first time in hours. Dr. Gladwell appeared at the door with a younger woman, and he and Tikvah both turned to the newcomer.

"This is Gina. She's here to help you settle in and wash up."

Gina gave Tikvah a quick smile, and Tikvah followed her to the adjacent bathroom. Gina turned on the shower and stuck her arm in, checking the water temperature.

"How warm do you like it?" she asked. Tikvah shook her head and looked to Will.

"On the hotter side is always nice," he said.

"Soap and shampoo for your hair," Gina said, pointing to bottles attached to the shower wall. That was his cue to leave.

"I'll let you shower in peace," he said. "Then I'll be back to check on you."

"See you later!" said Gina, still watching Tikvah as she shooed Will out and closed the door.

Will stared at it, sighed and then laughed. Well, Joyce had always loved a great shower.

He turned and headed back down the hall to Dr. Gladwell's office.

He hesitated by the door which announced her name. Should he knock? "Please come in, Will." Dr. Gladwell responded to his knock. He assumed there were cameras everywhere. How else would she know it was him?

Dr. Gladwell sat behind a wide mahogany desk covered with books and notebooks. She seemed to be studying a particular thin book but she looked up at him when he came in.

"Are you sure it's her?" Gladwell asked. She was looking through a Neurogentics annual report, and Will recognized Joyce's official company photo smiling at him when she pointed to it. He had to admit that she looked nothing like the woman he'd brought there.

"To be honest, no, not really, but there's something very familiar about her." He drummed his fingers on her desk. "I can't explain—it's more a feeling than anything else. I thought I recognized her smile. But I can't be sure. The feeling is fleeting. One moment I think it's her, and the next I think it can't possibly be. If she's Joyce, how could she look and feel so different from how I remember her?"

Uncertainty filled the silence. Will tried to read Gladwell's face, yet she wasn't revealing anything.

"Well, I don't recognize her at all," the doctor said, "but I haven't seen her in person for several years."

She rocked back in her chair, and Will tried to mimic her ease. But he felt unsettled.

Unsettled? Hell, he was having trouble hiding the fact that he was jumping out of his skin with worries and doubts. He didn't want the doctor to focus on him.

"She's clearly suffering from severe amnesia and disorientation. Obviously, she's been through a lot. Whatever it was could have had an effect on her physical appearance. We'll let her rest tonight and examine her tomorrow. You mustn't lose hope, though. Do you have anything at home that could conclusively identify her? Fingerprint records or dental X-rays? Anything of that nature could help. If you don't, we can run a check on her fingerprints with the California DMV tomorrow morning, but it might take a little while to get their response."

Will reflected for a moment and almost immediately an idea came to him. Her old cell phone used Joyce's fingerprints for identification. There should also be a panoramic mouth X-ray somewhere in her home office from a dental procedure she had had a few years back. He had looked through all her office drawers and shelves searching for clues to her disappearance and seemed to remember stumbling on the X-rays. "I'll see what I can find," he told the doctor without elaborating. Fatigue was descending on him, and he still had to fly back home that evening to get anything that might help confirm whether or not the woman he picked up in Jenner was his wife. "Thank you so much, doctor. I must get going."

"And get some rest yourself, Will. She'll be fine here; you know we'll take good care of her." She stood and extended her hand to him. "If this is Joyce, she needs you safe and rested. Don't stay up all night searching for stuff, okay?"

So he hadn't fooled her. He shook her hand, thanked her and hurried out. Doctors and researchers were trained to notice, but he still was bothered that he'd been unable to conceal his uncertainty and worry.

On his way out he stopped by Joyce's room to check on her, say goodbye and tell her he'd be back the next day. Did it mean anything that he was thinking of her as Joyce? No. His choice of name was wishful thinking combined with ease—Tikvah was an unusual name.

He knocked and opened the door. She was curled up on top of the sheets in the fetal position fast asleep. With her hair slicked back and still wet and her relaxed features, she seemed peaceful, serene and vulnerable all at the same time. He searched again for Joyce in the small figure lying there and felt a bit more hopeful. It might be her after all. But what if it wasn't?

CHAPTER TWENTY-FIVE

Re-Joyce

WILL SPOTTED HER from a distance as he stepped onto the wide lawn in front of the clinic. She wore the soft jogging suit and sneakers he had brought. He had a flashback to the moment he first met Joyce—on the campus museum's stairs. She looked very much like the slender young woman she appeared to be now from a distance. He stopped and studied her, spellbound by the memory, and then realized that he had "seen" her many times since her disappearance.

She would suddenly emerge from a crowd as he walked down a busy street or appear in a supermarket aisle when he shopped, and he would always feel the pinch of disappointment when he approached, only to find an entirely different woman. His wishful mind played tricks on him, he knew, so he was careful not to let himself to get too carried away by this mysterious stranger who from a distance resembled his wife.

She was sitting by a giant acacia tree, eyes closed. As she leaned on its thick trunk in the midst of the sprawling lawn, the leaves and branches cast gentle shadows on her serene face. A slight smile hovered on her full lips. Was she sleeping? He stepped quietly, not wanting to disturb her. She opened her eyes the moment he stood in front of her as though she felt his presence and sat up. Her welcoming smile sent ripples of another long-ago memory through his heart and her twinkling eyes met his. He sat next to her.

"How are you feeling?" he asked after a brief hesitation. "Did you get a good rest?"

"I'm feeling wonderful, thank you. This is a blessed place. Thank you for bringing me here."

"You're most welcome, darling. Or should I call you Tikvah?" Needing her to remember, he again tested the boundary of her memory.

"You can call me anything you'd like as long as it's nice," she replied mischievously.

Will smiled awkwardly, not knowing how to respond. She was still foreign to him, different enough from Joyce to cast doubt on her identity. "I'd like you to do something for me," he said as he drew an iPhone out of his pocket.

"Sure thing!"

There was that smile again, playful and warm, mysterious yet familiar. "Could you please put your right thumb here?" He placed his own thumb on the circular button on the lower edge of the phone to show her. She took the iPhone with curiosity and examined it from every direction, then placed her thumb on the prompt button. In a flash the phone turned on and a photo of Beau as a puppy appeared on its screen. She threw her head back in laughter when she saw it.

"That's a neat trick."

Will was speechless. Unless she was a magician, she had just proven that she was Joyce. Excitement and relief overwhelmed him as the realization began to sink in.

"Tikvah, I mean Joyce, it's really you! He wanted to take her in his arms and hug her but restrained himself when he read her astonished stare. He sensed immediately that he mustn't be hasty. "Darling," he blurted. "Please wait here while I go speak with the doctor. I won't be long."

He raced toward the clinic entrance, no longer holding on to restraint.

"Is Dr. Gladwell available?" He tried to muster calm as he approached the day nurse at the reception desk, but he was out of breath despite the short distance, and his heart felt like it was exploding. Head down, he held on to the counter to steady himself. Oh God, *it was Joyce*. Where had she been all this time? What had happened to change her so much? He whirled around, needing to get back to her. *Joyce was outside sitting under a tree*. He knew he needed to contain his excitement and keep focused, but all that could wait.

"Hi, Will. What's going on?" The doctor's voice had him switching direction.

"Did you see the X-rays that I left with Gina when I got here?" The question leaped from his mouth before he could slow himself down for the usual polite exchange of greetings.

"I have," she responded with a smile. "They appear to be a match. Please come to my office; I'll show you."

Two sets of dental panoramic X-rays had been stuck to the light box on the wall.

"This is the set we took this morning," she said, taking one off the box and placing it on top of the second image, the one he'd brought with him that morning. "As you can see, they fit each other all the way down to the missing wisdom teeth at the bottom. We examined them carefully, and they appear to be a perfect match."

"She opened her cell phone with her thumb print." He leaned against the wall. The X-rays wavered, and he rubbed his eyes wiping away his tears. "She's Joyce. And she's back. So why don't I recognize her?"

Will sank into a chair. The weight he'd carried for months lifted in a fraction of an instant, and he felt faint.

He lowered his head to clear the dizziness before asking, "Does she know?"

"Not yet. She's suffering from severe amnesia and possible delusion. We haven't gotten the results from the brain scan we did this morning, so we don't have a complete diagnosis yet. We don't know if the condition is psychological or physiological. If it's physiological—such as a tumor, for example—the memory deterioration may be permanent. If psychological, our research has shown that it could take a patient months, sometimes even years, to regain their full memory, if they do recover." Dr. Gladwell bent forward and looked at Will intently. "She may be experiencing dissociation, where her identity got replaced with a fictitious one as a result of a traumatic event, which would explain the memory loss. We need to proceed carefully to keep from adding to the trauma or confusing the brain further. She's found a fragile equilibrium that needs support. We need to be careful not to do or say anything that could shock her. At any rate, for the moment she seems peaceful and pain free, but we need to conduct further tests to know how to proceed with her treatment."

Will nodded his understanding, although he knew he wasn't considering the implications of the doctor's words. The knowledge that Joyce was alive and seemingly well was in itself the greatest of miraculous gifts.

"For the moment, we should continue referring to her as Tikvah so as to not upset her present mental state." The doctor tapped a pen rhythmically against the papers on her desk. "After all, although we know that she's Joyce, she doesn't. We'll start our psychological evaluation as soon as we determine the cause of her memory loss."

Will exhaled a long breath. She was saying that he would need to be patient. That he couldn't claim her as his wife. He hunched forward, wanting to argue with the doctor. But that was what *he* needed. And right now, he had to do what would be best for Joyce.

Nothing in his daydreams about their reunion has prepared him for this moment. He would need to adapt to the new realities, most still unknown.

"Very well," he said after a moment of consideration. "Tikvah it is. So how then do I present myself to her? How should I act?" *Please don't ask me to stay away.*

"Initially it'll be best that you don't reveal to her your or her identity; we want to minimize confusion. I suggest you spend limited time with her and instead allow her to adjust to her new circumstances, find safety and comfort in her new situation and become familiar with her surroundings and the people here." She paused and fixed him with her gaze. "So let's limit the interactions to about half an hour twice a day and see how it goes."

Will jumped up and found himself at the window. Her suggestion didn't sit well with him. He finally got his wife back, and now he had to limit his time with her? How would she remember him if he wasn't there all the time?

He strained to see her, but the window's placement didn't allow him to see Joyce or the tree where she'd been sitting. He closed his eyes.

Twenty minutes earlier, he'd been so happy. No, not happy. Ecstatic. And now he'd been thrust back into despair.

He knew, however, that he must relinquish his desires to the medical knowledge to which he'd entrusted her healing. He was convinced that he was doing the best for her by handing over her recovery to the most advanced research center in neuroscience, the center that she herself had created. She had always told him that science knew best; he would trust her judgment.

"Very well. I'll go spend my first half hour with her now."

When he returned to the tree and sat by her side, Tikvah studied him.

"You look anxious," she said.

"Tired," he said. And worried again and frustrated and yet excited and—

"Why don't you lie down with me under the tree."

She extended one hand to him. Even her hand had changed. He knew her hands, her face, her body. But she was different. What had happened to his Joyce? He lay down next to her, the sides of their heads just touching, as were the backs of their hands. He felt strangely at peace, like he hadn't felt for ages.

"Take your shoes and socks off."

He followed her suggestion and placed his large bare feet next to her small ones on the lawn.

"Draw the energy of the grass into your feet," she told him quietly.

In the silence that followed he heard the hissing of the leaves overhead and the waves of the ocean in the distance. Deep serenity overcame him. Their soft breathing in unison mixed with the soft breeze as they drifted into sleep.

CHAPTER TWENTY-SIX

Regeneration

ILL WAS STARTLED awake, and for a split second was panicked that finding Joyce had been a dream.

She'd come to him in his sleep before. Those dreams had been rare respite from the nightmares that usually filled his nights. But their sweetness had always been met with the stark contrast of reality when he opened his eyes and found himself alone. This awakening was no different, until he saw her. When he opened his eyes, her soft eyes met his. As his consciousness focused, so did the realization that she was really there, sitting next to him. He took her hand, wanting to make her presence that much more real.

He had no idea how long he'd been sleeping. Judging by the sunlight hugging the horizon, it must have been a few hours.

"They came looking for you, but I asked that they let you sleep." Her sweet voice seemed to come from a distance as his mind was slow to emerge from the deep slumber. "A friend of yours is here to see you."

"Really?" He wondered who could possibly know that he was there. "I'll go see." He kissed the back of her hand before getting up. "Maybe I'll see you again soon?" His face heated when he realized that he sounded like a bashful suitor.

"I'd like that very much," she said, her smile generous.

As Will entered the reception area—finger-combing his hair out of his face—a man he didn't recognize got up from a leather club chair and walked toward him.

"Ah, Will!" he said. "Finally! It's great to see you."

Will took the wide hand extended toward him, but he still felt no recognition. An absurd thought struck—Did the isolation of the pandemic erase his ability to identify friends and acquaintances?

"Hmm . . . I guess you don't remember me. Ravi Varadkar from Neurogenics."

The man kept his hand, as if demanding a response before freeing it.

"Of course!" Will exclaimed. "I'm so sorry . . . It's been a few years." His hand now free, he indicated two of the chairs, and they sat. "I'm surprised to see you here."

"Franka—Dr. Gladwell—called me this morning. You may not remember, but the three of us—Joyce, Franka and I—were in undergrad science courses together at Stanford."

Will was already nodding, recalling that the two of them had been Joyce's study buddies, which was the reason she later hired them for their respective positions in the company.

"Yes, of course I remember," Will said. "I'm just waking from a nap, and I guess I'm still a little out of it." He ran a hand through his hair again.

"Not a problem," Ravi said. "We were told not to disturb you." Ravi nodded his head toward the window and toward where Joyce waited outside. "As always, she calls the shots," he added with a chuckle.

"Did you see her?" Will hoped for Ravi's impressions both personal and professional.

"Only from a distance. The two of you seemed pretty chummy out there, so I didn't want to disturb. Just like in college." He winked.

Will relaxed, welcoming a friendly presence in the midst of upheaval. He had completely forgotten that Dr. Gladwell was Franka, Joyce's study friend in college, and felt a wave of relief as he realized what that meant: Their common past and current working relationships could be instrumental in bringing Joyce's memory back.

"Dr. Gladwell contacted me on a hunch that I might have some useful information, since I've been running the Neurogenics lab and she knows that Joyce and I saw each other once in a while. And she told me she can't remember who she is." He paused to give Will a sympathetic glance and then continued. "So she was hoping I might have some medical records that could definitively identify Joyce. And as a matter of fact, I did. Speaking with Franka reminded me that Joyce had come to me for a brain scan right before she disappeared."

"What? Why would she have done that?" Will was shocked, but almost immediately he wondered if this brain scan had something to do with Joyce's disappearance and her memory loss.

"Please come with me so you can see for yourself." Ravi motioned Will to follow him, letting the suspense accompany them down the hall.

They entered Dr. Gladwell's office, and Ravi pointed to the light box on the wall. He turned it on to illuminate two brain scans. One had an ominous black blotch the size of a golf ball in the middle of it. Will's breath caught.

Did Joyce know there was something wrong with her brain? And was that nasty mass what was impairing brain function and causing the memory loss? Panic raced through his mind at lightning speed. As he moved closer to the images, a completely different reality than what he had assumed reflected itself. The X-ray with the black spot in the middle of the brain was dated *the day of her disappearance*. The other showed today's date.

"How can this be?" He turned to Ravi. Dr. Gladwell entered the room at that moment. "Could this mean that it's not her after all?" he asked. He didn't know what to think anymore.

"We studied both MRIs closely before showing them to you, and the two brains are identical in every aspect in terms of size and proportions except in two ways," Dr. Gladwell told him. "The absence of the tumor is obvious. And there is another difference, very minute, but which was deciphered in the diagram calculations of the mapping of the different areas of the brain. The pineal gland, which has a normal size of about a third of an inch in the earlier scan, is slightly larger in the scan we took today. The pineal is responsible for hormonal balance, particularly the secretion of melatonin. However, despite the enlargement, the blood tests we took this morning display no hormonal abnormalities. Furthermore, the scan shows that her hippocampus is normal, as are the synapses between brain cells, indicating normal memory function."

Completely lost, Will shook his head.

"Forgive me," Dr. Gladwell said. "And let's sit. I am so used to speaking with scientists here at the lab, I forget not everyone is familiar with our terms."

They moved to her desk. Will looked over his shoulder at the scans, but they made no more sense at a distance.

Dr. Gladwell pulled a model of the brain from the bookcase behind her. "The hippocampus is where memory is generated and stored in the brain and where the neurons responsible for the creation of memory are generated. There is no indication of any physical abnormality there. We also checked on the synapses which provide the connections between brain cells, and the synaptic plasticity appears normal. In fact, all our tests show that she is as healthy as can be. The things we cannot understand are the absence of the tumor and the enlargement of the pineal."

Will was more concerned about the disappearance of the tumor than about the pineal, which meant nothing to him. "Why didn't you tell me?" He turned to Ravi, unable to contain the anger mixed with helplessness and confusion he felt after being left ignorant of important information. "And how could that possibly be . . . the same person?"

Ravi sighed deeply. "She swore me to secrecy." He bowed his head apologetically. "In truth, when the Wave detected the blood flow block-age and then when I saw the MRI, I actually didn't expect her to live out the year, and so I figured that the abnormality might have led to her dis-appearance and I wanted to respect her wishes. I feel ridiculous about it now, but back then it seemed like the honorable thing to do, to respect the last request of a dear friend whom I thought I'd never see again." He looked down at his hands, and when he looked up again, his eyes bore a miserable expression. "Will, I am sorry, truly I am, but I never thought she'd make it . . ." His words choked his usual good humor.

Will accepted Ravi's explanation. He understood the honor and loy-alty it took to abide by Joyce's wishes. A small part of him was relieved that Ravi hadn't shown him the X-ray after her disappearance. If he had, Will would probably have lost all hope for finding her and might not have accepted the possibility that the thin but very healthy Tikvah was Joyce. He went lightheaded imagining himself calling off the search. He might have notified the sheriff that she was probably dead, and Sheriff Johnson might have considered not telling him about the vagabond he'd found in Jenner. Joyce would be alive but lost to him forever. A shudder ran through him and he gasped, thankful that he hadn't known.

Needing to put the fear of what could have happened but hadn't behind him, Will had to ask the obvious question. "So how is it possible that the tumor is no longer there?"

Dr. Gladwell tapped at the model brain, but she looked at Will. "Sometimes tumors go into spontaneous remission without logical expla-nation, particularly when they are lethal. The medical establishment has not yet arrived at a scientific explanation for this. Psychology, however, has found a correlation to a dissociative process. In very rare cases when the person's psyche severs their identification with the illness through a traumatic occurrence such as near-death experience, the tumor simply disappears."

"Did Joyce know about the tumor?" Will asked. He needed to understand if Joyce's disappearance had been intentional. He remembered that she'd been suffering from migraines for several months and blamed them on the pressures of the company's international expansion and the incessant travel.

"I never got the chance to tell her about it," Ravi said. "If she knew anything, it wasn't from my lab work."

Dr. Gladwell pulled out another X-ray, one that showed the upper portion of the skull, and she pointed to a slightly darker shadow at its center. "The rest of Joyce's new imaging shows a possible fracture of the top of the skull. Here we can see a slight discoloration, which may suggest scarring in this area although the skull is complete and perfectly aligned. The scar tissue may point to a possible trauma or even fracture of this area. But to be honest, we cannot figure out how it healed so perfectly. The most talented surgeon could hardly have done such a perfect job. A fracture right at the top of the skull where the scar tissue appears could have only resulted from a vertical fall or something falling straight on her head and smashing it. This kind of trauma may explain her memory loss. She has a perfect possession of language, it seems, so the cognitive part of the brain that processes language and new information has not been damaged. However, she does not recognize most of the basic things of daily life, such as showers or phones, leading us to assume that her mind erased entirely whatever memories comprised her subconscious cognition prior to the accident. Her only cognitive knowledge seems to be made up of what she learned afterward. We have not had a chance to interview her yet to begin to ascertain her emotions and mental balance and connection to reality. We thought to give her a day to rest and get her bearings here. She seems quite happy and comfortable and is friendly with everyone. The great news is that she is in perfect health in every way we could possibly test."

The doctor's report was a lot for Will to take in. But it *was* good news compared to what he had been preparing himself to hear. His head was whirling with the information, and he felt inundated by it. Questions chased one another through his mind. There was so much mystery to uncover. Where had Joyce been all this time? How was she able to heal so well from her tumor and head injury? And if she was so healthy, why was she so bony thin? But the question that burned most was would she ever get back to being herself and be his wife again? He decided to hold back his inquiries for the time being and allow the answers to unfold in their own time.

CHAPTER TWENTY-SEVEN

Recollection

D<small>R.</small> F<small>RANKA</small> G<small>LADWELL</small> was deep in thought, devising a strategy
for the woman who had once been her friend, then her boss, and
was now her patient and study subject, a woman she'd admired for half
her life. Her role as head of the clinical research center was to gather data
for the company that financed the institution through the treatment of
the extreme and severe cases that they studied. However, Joyce was not
just another case. Franka's concern was that she wouldn't be able to
approach this situation with complete objectivity, and she wanted to
make sure that she maintained her integrity as a doctor and researcher
throughout the process.

Her personal knowledge of her patient could actually be an asset
rather than hindrance, she concluded. Recalling Joyce's quick and brilliant mind, her ability to focus for long periods of time and retain huge
amounts of information at once, Franka opted to begin treatment
through a psychological route. There would be time for drug treatments if
the psychological approach failed; they'd had some success with them in
treating seemingly incurable psychosis and dementia. For now, she determined not to interfere with the beautiful mind that she hoped was still
active inside Joyce.

For the first interview, she decided to meet Joyce at the place where
she seemed most comfortable, by the acacia tree. Ten minutes later, they
were seated under the shade of its extensive canopy that cocooned them
from the vast surrounding lawn and the ocean beyond, as though guarding their privacy within its protective branches. It was a compelling site as
well as a comfortable one, and she could understand why Joyce felt at ease
there.

"What is this?" she asked Joyce, pointing to the tiny pinecone that hung from her neck by a red thread.

"This pinecone is a talisman, a symbol of intuition." Joyce held the pinecone out to give Franka a closer view. "It helps me connect to my innermost truth at moments when I'm undecided and can't see clearly. By touching it and connecting to my heart, the answers flow to me easily. It's very helpful. I'd be happy to show you how to use it."

"Why a small pinecone?" Franka continued her questioning, grateful to hear the elaborate and clear explanation. For the first time, Joyce was expressing herself eloquently beyond the polite, short responses to the practical questions addressed to her.

"The pinecone resembles the pineal gland in shape and form. This gland is in the middle of our brain between the two hemispheres. Some believe it to be the source of intuition beyond its role of regulating hormonal functions. Many spiritual practices throughout the ages and around the world have considered it to be the seat of the soul, or the third eye, as it was called by Eastern spiritual traditions."

Franka was amazed at the detailed and thorough explanation. Her friend's mind was still sharp. "How do you know this?" Franka asked, probed.

Joyce took a deep breath before continuing and pressed the pinecone close to her heart.

She told Franka about Moriah, her friend and mentor who saved and healed her and taught her everything she knew. Told her about a time Moriah sent her to the forest to find her hope, a hope symbolized by the acorn, and then explained to her intuition, symbolized by the pinecone. Joyce described their four wolf-like dogs and their angelic names and her rescue by Gabi who had pulled her out of the ocean after seals had kept her afloat. She explained in detail their vegetable garden and how they tended it and enjoyed its harvest. She recounted a tale about geese and adventures in a forest filled with mushrooms and berries. She shared the magic of a clear night's sky after a storm when Joyce discovered how she belonged to the earth and to the cosmos. Through it all she shared how Moriah had guided her to create her personal foundation of love, joy and belonging.

The sun was setting when she concluded her story. A deep crimson and orange sky hovered over them, reflecting its golden light on Joyce's serene face. No, on *Tikvah's* face. The woman was Joyce Woodland without doubt, but Franka had spent the afternoon coming to know Tikvah. Franka had been enthralled by the tale. She hadn't taken notes but had recorded the session on her phone in its entirety.

"Amazing!" she said when Tikvah finally fell silent and drained her second water bottle. Franka drank too before saying, "Thank you for sharing your story with me. You must be tired and hungry. Shall we go inside and have some dinner?"

"I'd love to."

Tikvah's smile illuminated the dimming dusk air. When they stood, Franka had the impulse to hug her but restrained herself. She didn't completely believe all the details of the story—some were too fantastic for her mind to accept—yet the story moved her so deeply that for the first time since she could remember, she felt deeply peaceful and not alone, as though she was viscerally connected to a vaster source of intelligence than she had ever known. The universe, perhaps?

Franka was eager to begin the standard psychological evaluation that would help her determine how to proceed with Joyce's memory loss treatment. There was a lot at stake. If Joyce wasn't in a stable state when confronted with the realities of her past, the disconnect could create deeper psychological damage, even psychosis. A thorough assessment was the first essential step, which she scheduled for early the next morning. They relaxed in the dining room, and Franka observed her friend as she ate calmly, not saying much. Franka couldn't have wished for a more successful first day.

The next morning Joyce arrived at her office at 7 a.m. precisely, as they'd agreed the previous evening. She looked fresh and full of energy and seemed excited to participate in the study that Franka had detailed to her over dinner.

Franka studied her carefully, peeking over her reading glasses as Joyce moved around the room examining her photographs, diplomas and bookcases. She tried to recognize her friend, whom she had known since college, in the exotic woman who flowed from one wall to the next, delighting in the objects and reminders of Franka's professional life.

Joyce's hair, now combed, cascaded down her shoulders in a frizzy auburn mane quite different from the slick dark bob Joyce had always worn. Her face was deep brown, and aside from a couple of very thin lines on her forehead, she appeared much younger than her age.

The loose workout clothes she wore made her look even smaller as they hung shapelessly on her diminished body.

Franka suddenly felt self-conscious about her own figure, realizing how much she had changed since Joyce and she first met. Would Joyce be able to recognize her if she remembered who she was? Franka smoothed one hand over her own cheek. Time had definitely left its mark. Not a bad one, but Franka was no longer the young adult she'd imagined herself for so long.

She shook off the thought and turned back to her patient.

Joyce's smiling face was slender, like the rest of her, but something about her presence seemed bigger than her body. It wasn't a commanding presence, yet she occupied the space of the room as though it was a natural extension of herself. After studying the last of Franka's photographs, she took the chair that Franka gestured to with unconscious grace and leaned back casually. Franka waited to see how Joyce initiated their conversation.

Joyce focused on her, and for an instant Franka felt naked under her stare, as if Joyce could see through her as no one ever had. She crossed her arms and smiled back awkwardly.

Then recognizing what she'd done, she dropped her arms to her desk.

"I know we've just met," Joyce finally said, "but I feel like I've known you for a long time and that you care for my well-being as I do yours."

Franka leaned back into her chair and took off her glasses to return Joyce's gaze straight on. Did Joyce actually remember her? When Joyce said nothing else, Franka chose to proceed with the evaluation protocol and not broach the subject, since Joyce didn't show other signs of actually remembering who she was.

"Let's play a game," she said, gathering a bunch of 8 by 10 cards from her desk drawer.

Joyce's face lit up and she sat forward, looking eager to begin.

"I'm going to show you images on these cards, and I would like you to tell me what you see in them. Like this one, for instance—what do you see here?"

She held up a Rorschach image. A playful smile appeared on Joyce's face. "I see a garden filled with butterflies and flowers, and there is a river that runs through the middle."

Franka held up another card, and Joyce's response came just as quickly and enthusiastically.

"A young girl is sitting on the grass admiring the tree casting shade above her."

And so it went for drawing after drawing—the images were all nature inspired, vivid and joyful. To reveal more of Joyce's subconscious, Franka switched gears to word associations.

"Please say the first word that comes to mind after the word I tell you. Ready?"

Joyce nodded.

"Sun."

"Warmth."

"Night."

"Darkness."

"Forest."

"Life."

"Road."

"Journey."

"Pinecone."

"Intuition."

"Acorn."

"Hope and courage." Joyce laughed. "But those were easy since we already talked about those."

Franka smiled and nodded. She'd already noted the consistency, one trait that she was evaluating. "Ready for more? Mushrooms."

"Connectivity."

"Belonging."

"Presence."

"Sadness."

"Loss."

"Happiness."

"Connection."

"Will."

"Kindness."

"Will."

"To live."

The word pairs flew at lightning speed, filling the room, swirling faster and faster, accelerating, until they seemed to be connected by invisible threads. Where one thread began, another attached to it, weaving the two women into a dance of reciprocity, creating an energetic vortex between them that they lost themselves in until they erupted in simultaneous laughter.

Franka checked the time. The session had gone on for three hours and twenty-three minutes, much longer than she'd intended.

"Thank you," Franka said.

"You're welcome!"

Joyce's response was so quick that Franka thought she might think they were still engaged in the game. "You have been a most gracious participant," she said to break the spell.

"That was fun!" Joyce said, her eyes shining. "I enjoyed our connection."

"How so?" Franka recognized an opportunity to find out more about what Joyce might remember about knowing each other in the past. Perhaps their connection could be the conduit to open Joyce's memory.

"Beyond the words, we connected energetically and telepathically. Joyce responded brightly. "I love that feeling. The words led us to it, but our connection with each other was the best part of this game."

Their word exercise reminded Franka of their college debates, when Joyce could outsmart and outshine any opponent. Joyce's quick and sharp mind had given her the ability to think ahead and calculate myriads of underlying meanings and possible outcomes before most people had a chance to parse the issue.

Franka admitted that the possible loss of that mind was one of her greatest fears. She didn't yet have an answer, but Joyce certainly didn't seem to have brain damage, certainly not in the usual sense.

On the other hand, this was not the Joyce she had known, by any stretch. She felt the truth of that in her gut, as a clear and unobstructed sense of calm and joy emanated from Joyce. In college there'd always been an undercurrent of angst about her, as though everything she strived for flowed out of a fear deep in her that kept a tight grip on her psyche. Joyce was a master at hiding her anxiety, however. It was so subtle that people who interacted with her were quickly seduced and distracted by her determined charm, so no one could nail down the anxiety and call her on it.

Yet those closest to her sensed it, as she must have known it herself, a stench that clings to a dead body no matter how well you clean and dress it. Joyce's skills had been carefully honed out of a determination to overcome the inner turmoil and from the existential need to hide it from herself and the world. Franka knew that she had to push her skills and experience to make sure she wasn't being misled by her now. Despite her misgivings, she couldn't deny that Joyce was expressing herself truly from her essence.

When recording her notes after the session, she still wondered what had brought on the change in Joyce. Surely, she'd made up the story of a magic woman in the forest and the wolf-like angels, so what was the reality lurking underneath? She was determined to uncover the hidden truth, no matter what it took.

When Will arrived in the afternoon, Franka was eager to share her assessment that Joyce's emotional state was balanced, perhaps even more than before her disappearance.

Will sighed his relief and relaxed back into his chair.

"There is one glitch, though," she added carefully.

"What is it?"

She hated to cast doubt after her positive report, but Will needed to know what she was thinking.

"The story of her experience is uncanny. She is most likely suffering from a delusional response to her accident. This happens sometimes when the trauma is so great, the brain cannot process it. The mind replaces the actual events with a made-up story in order to survive the experience. We see this sometimes with people who've experienced years of torture or molestation. Their recollection of the traumatic experiences is erased and replaced by an imaginary story, and they can remain in the delusional state all their lives and appear to function well despite the horrific experience. The trouble is that the actual experiences continue to live in their subconscious and could create a threat to their lives as time goes on, often in the form of uncontrolled and unconscious addictive behavior that leads to an eventual breakdown. There is a definite risk in exposing the traumatic events too quickly, as the additional trauma could cause a permanent personality split, so we must tread gently."

"Dr. Gladwell . . . Franka. What can I do to help?"

Before she could answer, Will pounded both fists on her desk. "Why can't it just be simple? Why can't we fix it quickly and move on?"

"Will . . ."

He waved her off with one hand. "I know, I know. And I'm sorry. I'm certainly not blaming you for any of this."

"It's okay. I'd be worried about you if you *didn't* have that kind of response."

He laughed, but the sound wasn't happy.

"No fear of that. If emotional and physical responses are the sign of a healthy reaction, I'm clearly very healthy."

Once again, he waved a hand, this time adding, "Please go on."

"For the moment, we will maintain the status quo of her beliefs and encourage her to express them as much as possible to hopefully exorcise the story from her mind. At the same time we can slowly introduce elements from her past so that her mind can begin acclimating to reality. The hope is that the more exposure she receives from her normal previous life, the more memories will emerge related to it. Eventually her real-life memories could dissolve the contrived ones as she integrates herself into reality. As I said, it's a process and we need to be gentle about it. And patient. I'd like to try this before resorting to psychotic drugs that might affect her mind in the long term. So, what you can do is encourage her to talk about the experiences she remembers, while slowly exposing her to the conditions and environment of her life before. After all, what are memories but the collections of stories that we tell ourselves?"

~

Will was prepared do anything to bring his wife back to him mentally and emotionally now that he had her back physically. He was up for the challenge—he had to be. However, the uncertainty of Joyce's psychological condition weighed heavily on his heart. After everything he'd gone through, he braced himself for the worst.

CHAPTER TWENTY-EIGHT

Husband and Wife

I T WAS AN unusually brisk day for Southern California when Will pulled up in front of the clinic's large lawn in his convertible Porsche. Autumn could be felt even there, announcing the approach of the Thanksgiving holidays. He spotted Joyce where she often sat under the acacia tree. She was facing the entrance of the building rather than the ocean as she usually did, likely anticipating his arrival.

Will opened the back door and out running came Beau, who at four years old *still* acted like a puppy more often than not. Beau leaped directly toward Joyce, his strides a blur. He jumped on her and licked her face while letting out his squeaky excited yelps, just like he had when Joyce would return home after being away for several days. He knocked her to the grass with his large paws, and she played with him and laughed. Her joy augmented Beau's excitement, and he was pouncing and racing around her uncontrollably. Will hurried to put a stop to it, but before he could yell out, he heard Joyce say, "Beau, settle down!" Will stopped, astounded. Had he called out to Beau when they arrived, and if so, loud enough that she might have heard his name? He searched back. Nope. He had no recollection of doing that.

"Good morning." He was now standing over them, Beau lying next to Joyce, panting, his tongue spilling to one side of his smiling face.

"How did you know his name is Beau?" he asked, curious for her answer. This could be the breakthrough they'd been searching for.

"I don't know, I just did," was her simple reply.

Will sat down next to them. She couldn't explain her knowledge, but this was wonderful progress nonetheless, which he hadn't anticipated to happen so soon. After his last visit to the clinic, he felt despair with the situation and disappointment at Joyce's inability to recognize him. He yearned for her to acknowledge him as her husband, but he knew that she wasn't capable of that yet. Still, he was frustrated at not being allowed to tell her who he was by the doctor, who warned him to tread lightly in reminding her of who she had been before becoming the woman she now believed herself to be.

He'd returned home to San Francisco to reflect, planning to return in a week, but he hadn't been able to stay away for so long. He yearned to be near her no matter who she believed herself to be or who she thought he was to her. Needing to be even closer, he rented a small cottage in San Diego by the ocean so he could be with her daily throughout her recovery. It actually didn't occur to him that Beau would jog her memory, as he'd assumed that just like she couldn't remember him, her own husband, she wouldn't remember her dog. Why would she, since Beau looked like any other goldendoodle and there were so many of them around? And he had grown and changed so much in the last year since she had last seen him. The unexpected recognition between Beau and Joyce raised mixed feelings in him that he now struggled to digest. A jolt of jealousy, as surprising as it was irrational, swept through him as he watched Joyce and Beau play together. Of course he was elated at this first sign of a memory of her past, so he was astonished to feel sad as well. Why was she able to recognize Beau and not him? And how had Beau known her instantly, whereas he'd needed proof? He picked up a few pods of the acacia tree from the ground and crushed them between his fingers.

He realized that he was still pining for her, just as he had for all those months before her disappearance. Both then and now, he wanted his wife to want him the way he wanted her.

Joyce smiled, her generous welcoming smile, and his apprehension melted.

"That's wonderful that you recognize Beau. He was your dog for three years. You got him when he was just a puppy." He reached out to Beau and caressed his head. Beau in turn licked his hand. "He was always very protective of you," he added with a smirk. "When you were around, he had eyes for only you."

Joyce looked down at Beau lovingly and began playing with the curls on his neck. Their fingers met and then separated immediately. Will studied her face; was she remembering their connection as well?

"I feel our connection, mine and Beau's. Perhaps . . ."

"Perhaps what?"

She leaned over Beau and kissed him. "I think he could be the bridge to my past."

Beau but not him? Before Will let himself be carried away by frustration and disappointment, he reminded himself that he wanted Joyce healed by any means necessary. He shouldn't fuss that a dog was the key to her recovery.

"Could you tell me about the past year of your life? Where have you been?" Will asked with hesitation, remembering the doctor's warning not to push her too abruptly because of her fragility.

"Of course! I told Dr. Gladwell about it already, and I'd love to talk about Moriah and her dogs and her forest home with you."

She pushed at Beau and he rolled to his back, allowing her to rub his belly.

"I had a serious accident," she said, speaking slowly.

Will knew she had no trouble with words, so he had to assume she was looking for the right way to tell him, maybe the best place to begin.

"I'm not sure what happened, what kind of accident. I may have fallen into the ocean, because that's where they found me, Moriah and her dogs. They pulled me out of the water and took me home to Moriah's cabin in the forest. Moriah took care of me until I got better. She taught me many things and healed my body and my soul."

Who was this Moriah person and where was she now? Why hadn't she taken Joyce to a hospital? Why did Joyce leave her? Questions were coursing through his mind, yet he held back, not wanting to overwhelm her.

After a short pause to stroke Beau's paws, she continued.

"When I woke up in Moriah's cabin, I was very confused and extremely weak. It was a long time before I got out of bed, and then I could only walk as far as the bench outside the door, where I sat to watch the dogs play and Moriah work in her garden. I had no idea where I was or how I got there. To make things worse, I had no idea *who* I was. But I felt safe there, so I accepted her kindness." She laughed. "I couldn't do anything else. Her wonderful food that she grew herself was amazing and it helped me heal and regain my strength. When I had more energy, when I could sit up longer or take more steps without growing lightheaded, Moriah started to teach me. I learned about the properties of the healing plants and crystals that had helped my body mend. When I was well enough to get around, she sent me on errands to the forest. I didn't know until afterwards that the errands were lessons for my soul."

"What do you mean, lessons for your soul?"

"The first lesson she taught me was about hope and its importance as the foundation of my life. I didn't know I had hope ingrained in me until Moriah unveiled it to me and named me Tikvah, which is the word for hope in the Old Testament. In its original form, Hope isn't just yearning for the realization of a desire, it's a covenant between our present beliefs and the forming future."

She played with Beau's fur, wrapping and unwrapping the curls around her slim fingers. Will recognized the action; Joyce's fingers were always occupied.

"She then taught me how to connect to my intuition, which guides me toward my hopes and the actions I need to take to realize them. That lesson helped a lot because I felt so disoriented until then, feeling that I didn't have the knowledge from my previous life experiences that I could rely on to guide my way. I had forgotten everything before my accident, you see, so I thought I didn't have much understanding of the world I lived in or of anything that could help me with making choices. Moriah showed me that I belonged to myself and to the world I inhabit, that my presence is integral to it and impacts everything. After a while, when I started helping her with the vegetable garden, I learned that it is my love that connects me to all that I do and come in contact with."

She peered up at him, both eyes and soul wide open. "I became happy."

Marveling, he didn't know what to say. She was even more extraordinary to him now than she had been before. He didn't see a mentally wounded person, as he had been led to believe she was. Instead, he saw a powerful woman who overcame great obstacles and was transformed by the process in the most beautiful way.

"Do you know who you are now?" He was hungry to hear more.

"I know my feelings. I recognize them, acknowledge them, interact with them. I am in dominion of them, which is not the same as domination. In other words, I let them guide me through my experiences instead of being controlled by them. I feel connected to my surroundings, particularly to nature and the people I interact with, and of course the animals." She passed her gentle hand over Beau's head. He licked it. "I feel my intuition most of the time, I feel love much of the time, especially when

I'm in nature or around animals." She looked down at Beau with a smile, and then back to Will's eyes. "And I always have hope. So, yes, I feel like I know myself for the most part."

"What is your hope?"

"To be healthy and joyful and know who I am and where I belong."

"Haven't you already got that, at least most of it?"

"I suppose in many ways I do. But the hope is always there, a beacon keeping me focused on my path."

Will was silent. He didn't know where he belonged on her path. Perhaps she didn't need him after all; she had it all so well figured out on her own. She'd already achieved all that she'd strived for.

Something in him was grasping, not willing to let go of her or the love he felt for her and his need to protect her. For a long, desperate time, their love had been lost; then he found her again and the spark was rekindled. Now he felt it slipping from him once again. Their hands met briefly, connected for a moment and disentangled.

"It is true that I feel like I belong to myself most of the time . . . but . . . Her eyes lingered on his as though she searched for words.

"I always had a feeling that I left loved ones behind, and now that I've reunited with Beau, I'm more sure of that than ever. Perhaps he could lead me to them." Her face brightened, as if she came up with an idea or a realization. "Or perhaps you could help me find my loved ones just as you found Beau?"

He swallowed hard when once again his hope yielded disappointment. Unsure of what to say next, remembering the doctor's warning, he was silenced by fear. Yet pushing aside his despair, he took a leap of faith. "Do you know that before your fall, we were married? I'm your husband. You're my wife."

She gazed at him for what felt like a lifetime. Finally she took his hand in her small palm and squeezed. Relief washed over him, cleansing him inside and out. She didn't remember who he had been to her, or their life together, but she knew him and trusted him. It felt right.

"May I call you Joyce?"

"I told you already, you can call me anything you like as long as it's nice." She giggled and leaned into him, resting her weight against his side.

He smiled. Her memory was remarkable for someone who had supposedly lost it.

CHAPTER TWENTY-NINE

The Treatment

J OYCE BURST INTO the library eager to begin her memory training. After Will told her that he was her husband and her real name, she wanted to claim it. She wanted to be Mrs. Joyce Woodland with all her heart. She loved Will from the moment she saw him at the police station but didn't dare say anything because she wasn't sure who he was. Even though he was kind and attentive to her, she couldn't jump to any conclusions until she assessed her new situation at the clinic.

She was the only patient at the research center at that time, so they had the whole place to themselves for as long as necessary to dive into her past and retrieve the memories she had lost. Dr. Gladwell informed her that she believed her psychological state was sound enough to encounter whatever she might uncover. She was bursting with curiosity over what she might learn about herself and her life before her accident. She already knew Beau and Will, and that was a lot of love and goodness to hold onto, but who knew what other marvels would be found in her previous life.

It was like going berry and mushroom foraging and uncovering treasures much more personal than lion's mane or wild strawberries. She was on a search for precious memories, one-of-a-kind treasures that existed in only one place—her mind.

She wasn't sure if she'd ever realized this before—that every individual was a treasure house for unique memories. But not only memories. Each individual was the keeper of thoughts and dreams that no other human possessed. How precious and rare each person truly was.

Dr. Gladwell sat in front of a huge dark screen and a smaller screen lay propped in her lap. She invited Joyce to sit in the comfortable leather lounge chair in front of the big screen.

"Please watch the screen. It will display in quick sequences images we collected from your life. I want you to say the feeling that comes to you when you see them. Your emotional memory is still strong, so we will try to awaken your episodic memory of the things that actually happened through association with your emotions." She straightened the screen in her lap and asked, "Would you like to ask me any questions before we begin?"

Joyce had no questions for the moment and was on the edge of her seat, eager to see the images of her life. She waved one hand.

"Ready? Let's go."

A second later, an image of a room full of people Joyce didn't recognize filled the large screen. The men were all dressed in dark suits. She was the only woman there and she sat at the head of a large conference table. She was wearing a dark suit as well and a pale cream top. Her body immediately tensed.

"Nervous," she blurted.

Another image flashed as soon as she spoke. This one showed her from the back walking on the beach. She assumed that the thin figure in a blue bathing suit was her even though her hair was darker and straighter; she sensed herself in the erect posture and the wave of her hand to someone outside the image.

"Relaxed," she said.

A close-up of Beau jumping appeared next. He was much smaller than he was now and seemed to be jumping abnormally high for his small body in order to reach a ball in the air.

"Joy," she said, almost without thinking.

The images kept churning, each one opening a window to a new world, stretching her imagination of what was possible for her and expanding her self-image. She couldn't get enough of them. Her emotions exploded in all directions whether she understood what she saw or not. Without fail, she always felt a visceral reaction to each image.

"That's enough for today!" Dr. Gladwell called out from behind her. To her dismay, the screen turned black. "We'll continue again tomorrow. And I have more fun exercises in store for you."

Only then did Joyce realize how exhausted she felt. But she was determined to go on. She enjoyed the process of discovery, plus she was certain that the games and exercises would produce a breakthrough. "Will you tell me what's actually in the images?" She was hoping to get more information about the life of which she'd only perceived glimpses today.

"That will be up to you to tell me!" Dr. Gladwell said.

Joyce wondered how she could possibly do that, as she had no idea what the images meant aside from her emotional reaction to them.

"I'll explain tomorrow. But for now, it would be good to rest your mind and allow it to absorb all that you saw today. You don't need to make sense of it yet. The hope is that the memories wills start seeping in on their own because we're stirring up the emotions associated with them. That might happen in your dreams as your subconscious takes over. We will put a notepad and pen by your bed tonight, and I want you to record anything that you remember from your dreams."

Filled with curiosity over what the night might bring, Joyce couldn't wait to go to sleep. But her excitement only prevented her from sleeping. As the images of that day's exercise flowed through her mind, her frustration grew when she couldn't decipher them. They were shards of memories plucked out of a data bank of images of her past and reassembled into a fragmented story only loosely woven together by her emotional recollections. None of it made sense.

She joined the doctor for their session the following morning with obvious disappointment.

"I guess you had a hard time sleeping," Dr. Gladwell said sympathetically. "That's to be expected under the circumstances. There was so much that was stirred up in you in our first session, we might need to step it down for a little while."

"No. Please." That was the last thing Joyce wanted to hear.

Seeing her dismay, the doctor added, "Don't worry. Today we will dig much deeper into these memories, and it's very likely that you will connect to them more from the exercises we are about to do."

The prospect filled Joyce with hope again and she perked up.

"Today we will go back to some of the images that you were shown quickly yesterday, only they will remain on the screen for five minutes. During this time you can write down what you think is happening in the image."

Joyce felt bewildered, as she had no idea what the images she saw yesterday were about. She was expecting an explanation from the doctor of what they were, so she could finally begin piecing her life together.

"Don't worry, whatever you write is fine," Dr. Gladwell said. "We're not looking for what you already know but what's hiding beneath the surface. Just use your intuition."

That was something Joyce knew how to do, and she intuitively reached for the pinecone hanging on her chest underneath her sweatshirt.

An image of a beach house surrounded by pine trees appeared on the large screen.

"That must be my house!" Joyce exclaimed, studying the doctor for signs of agreement. But Dr. Gladwell's face remained blank and she motioned to Joyce's notebook. Joyce picked up the pen.

I lived in a small wood house on the beach with my husband Will and our dog Beau. I loved this place. It smelled of ocean and pine trees. I loved to roam along the coast, maybe that's where I fell into the ocean . . . She had no idea if what she was writing was correct, but she let the words flow. She handed the page to the doctor after a few minutes, and a new image flashed on the screen. This one was more perplexing. It displayed a lab much like the one in the center where she now lived.

"Did I work in a lab?" she asked. Again she received no reaction. She sighed and picked up the pen. "This is going to be a long day," she murmured.

It was. As were all the days that followed.

Joyce didn't know if the kind doctor finally took pity on her desperate attempt to describe events connected to images, because after a week of those exercises, Dr. Gladwell told her that at the next stage of her treatment she would be told about major of events from her past.

"Did I fail so miserably at describing the images that you're giving up on my coming up with the memories on my own?" she asked.

"Quite the contrary," Dr. Gladwell said, much to her surprise. "You described the scenes and their relationship to you so well that we are ready to move on to the next stage much quicker than expected."

Joyce pulled her legs up into the chair and rested her chin on her knees. She needed to confess that she had made it all up. That she had no idea what the scenes were when she wrote about them. However, she bit her tongue, not wanting to jeopardize her chance at moving on to the next level, where her curiosity about what she had seen up until now might finally be satisfied.

The next day's meeting took place in Dr. Gladwell's office. There was no TV screen. Instead, a light box was lit with two images of a vaguely oval shape filled with different colors. The images looked identical, with the exception that one had a large dark blotch in the middle of it.

"This is an MRI image of your brain as it is now." Dr. Gladwell pointed to the image with many colors swirling around the circular sphere. "And here it is as it was on the day of your accident." She indicated the one with the large misshapen blob in the middle of it.

"What does this mean?" A wave of fear shuddered through Joyce. Was the large amorphous shape an image of the place where memories had completely disappeared from her brain? Were her memories erased forever, just as she had feared after she failed to remember what any of the images represented? She swallowed her concerns, chewed on a thumbnail and waited for the doctor's explanation.

Dr. Gladwell pointed at the blob scan.

"The large dark area here shows you had a brain tumor on the day you disappeared. Now, however, the MRI scan of your brain shows that the tumor is gone. And I have no explanation for how that happened. Do you?"

An image of crystals by her head after she awakened in Moriah's cabin flashed through Joyce's mind. She saw the rainbow of lights that danced around her reflected by the crystal that hung from the ceiling above her. But how could she explain that to the doctor? She sensed the doctor's skepticism whenever she spoke to her of Moriah, so she had decided not to mention her anymore. Besides, she had no certainty that it was this light that had cured her, no more than the wet, warm algae that Moriah applied to her head.

Dr. Gladwell waited—the woman had infinite patience—and Joyce eventually found the words that summed up what she felt at her core about her healing.

"I believe it was divine light that cured me, that and the magic healing remedies of Moriah, the Weaver Woman." She sensed a shadow of disappointment cross the doctor's face. It was barely noticeable, but she knew she had given the wrong answer.

"Actually, I really don't know how it happened." She attempted to cover up the memories of Moriah that were rising in her. Right now, all she wanted was to recover the memory of everything that happened before she even met Moriah, and she felt that talking about Moriah to the helpful doctor wasn't going to advance her cause.

Later that evening, when she was alone in her room, Joyce allowed herself to explore memories of Moriah and attempt to distill any sense out of them about the stunning information Dr. Gladwell had shared about her miraculous recovery. One of Moriah's enigmatic statements floated to her mind. Moriah had told Joyce that what had happened to her might have saved her from what could have been a worse fate, and that it was the best course that she herself had chosen for her growth. At the time the statement seemed unfathomable, as she couldn't possibly have imagined anything worse than the obliteration of her entire life. But now she understood Moriah's meaning.

The course she was on before her accident had quite literally been leading her head-on toward catastrophe. Her accident, while horrific, had saved her from imminent severe illness, an unrecoverable doom. A warm wave of gratitude washed over Joyce, and she added recognition of this truth to the chain of thanks she owed to Moriah.

All will be revealed in time. Moriah's words echoed in her mind, and with them Joyce felt the peaceful assurance that she didn't have to recall all her memories in the next days as if her very life and future depended on it.

Her next recall sessions were more serene, thanks to the awareness she gained that evening. *All will be revealed in time* became her motto, to be pulled out and repeated whenever she felt flustered or at a loss. Dr. Gladwell began informing her of what really had happened. She presented the information to her day by day, building up slowly to the people and events that defined her life. Joyce allowed herself to absorb the new events of her life without feeling the rush to assimilate as much as possible in a short period of time. Some of the information did prove traumatic and required deeper and slower reflection. Learning of her father's deadly accident and her mother's illness, which led to her death, were difficult to confront, yet she absorbed those events of her life with an awareness that they were integral to her particular growth journey toward the person she had now become.

"I feel like I'm getting to relive my life as a review," she told Will on one of their meetings under the acacia tree. "Except that this time I can adjust my reaction to an event so that I'm not swallowed by the emotions the event caused. I have a different perspective now, which allows me to choose my feelings and reactions, as horrible or as moving as the event might have been."

"How do you feel about your parents' deaths now?" Will asked. "You'd tell me if the memories were too upsetting, wouldn't you?"

"I needed to know that I did everything I could to help my mom throughout her illness. She went so slowly, and I was so young when it happened, I don't know how I possibly could have handled it. I guess you were there for some of it."

"Just at the very end. She was already living in the nursing home when we met. It was a very sad time, but you soldiered through it bravely, like you always do. You were so determined to do the best you could for her." He wrapped one arm around her slender shoulder, needing to touch her and loving the way she smiled when he did. "And you've been able to talk about it all so calmly. So that's good, right?"

"I'm sure that I was able to get through it the first time because I had a lot of support from you." She raised her eyes to him, hoping he felt her gratitude. "And now we're doing it together again."

"I did what I could to support you, but at the end, the struggle of losing a parent is a lonesome road. No one can take away the pain."

"It's never about avoiding the pain. I know that now. It's about accepting that we do the best we can under the circumstances. And besides, if we didn't feel pain, that would mean that we didn't love. And never loving would be so much worse than hurting because we lost the person we loved." After a long charged pause, she added, "I always had this feeling in me, even before I got here, and I didn't know what it was about until I found out about what happened to my mother. Maybe you can help me figure it out."

"What is it?"

"I've had a sense that I'm supposed to do something, like a mission I need to accomplish. I believe the mission came into being when my mom passed away; I wanted to keep other people from suffering like we did. Is that true? Is that the reason I decided to go into the medical field?"

"That's right! You had such a strong sense of mission from that point on." Will squeezed her hand and then continued to hold it. "And you're right to call it a mission. You took to the medical field and your specialty with enthusiasm and zeal, determined to succeed."

What a relief that she'd been on the right track. "Then you probably won't be surprised that I still have that same eagerness to pursue my mission, but I have no idea how I can go about accomplishing it in my current state . . ." She shifted to face him, but she didn't want him to see the despair in her eyes, so she stared at their joined hands. "It's so very hard, Will."

"You'll figure it out, darling. You always have." He pulled her toward him and hugged her, his hands warm on her back. "I'm sorry," he added.

"What for?" She pushed herself free so she could search his eyes.

"Sorry that it's been so difficult. But to be honest, I'm relieved that you're asking for my help again."

She didn't know precisely what he meant, but she understood implicitly that at some point he hadn't felt she needed him. And he needed to be needed.

"It must have been hard for you too. I'm sorry for that." She settled back into his arms.

She was glad that they'd talked, but all that mattered in that next moment was how good it felt to be held by him. She felt more than comfortable with Will; she didn't even have to question his motives or goals or whether he supported her; she still didn't remember their past, but she *knew* this man. And she trusted him with her present, her past and her future.

"C'mon, let's take a walk while it's still light."

Will stood up and extended his hand to help her up. She didn't really need his help but took his hand gladly.

While they strolled around the garden, he told her jokes and funny stories about Beau until Dr. Gladwell called her inside for another session.

"You're the best part of my days," she told him as they walked to his car. He'd helped her so much, she was ready to do the same in return. And so she added the words he needed to hear. "I need you in my life. I need you in the little things and in the big. I don't mean that I can't live without you—that is the romantic but inaccurate drama of young love. It sounds wonderful at first, but it's not part of reality. I choose to need you because I want to."

They stopped at his car. His eyes were wet with unshed tears. She stood on tiptoe and kissed his cheek. "I need you because we complement one another. Because we support one another. Because you stand for me and . . . I love you."

She walked slowly into the center, turning once to wave and blow him a kiss. He stood unmoving, but he was smiling. And his tears rolled freely down his face.

~

Alone again in her room after another session and dinner and a long shower, Joyce remembered Moriah's story about the girl who cared for her mother and then lost her. "How did she know?" Images of her reaction to Moriah's story raced through her—her furious foray into the forest where she spilled her rage and tears while exorcising the emotions that had been lodged in her without knowing their causes.

She sat on her bed to comb her hair and replayed the events of those days.

Using the peace she'd felt following that cathartic explosion in the woods, she'd been able to accept Moriah's explanation that the story was just one scenario out of many possibilities. She learned that she could rewrite her emotional reactions to her past and the beliefs that emerged from them, just as she could create her future out of new emotions and beliefs. The broken girl mired in grief over her mother's illness and death and her father's sudden accident and over the feeling of being abandoned by her parents—the girl trying desperately to right the wrongs of her childhood—could be reinvented. She had erased the events of the past from her cognitive memory, so she could now adjust her responses from her new perspective, as she uncovered them by connecting and rewriting her emotional responses.

Unburdened from the story she had created through her own recollections, Joyce was freed to make a choice in that instant to accept her life and all that she learned about it as her own creation. There were myriad possibilities of how her life could have unfolded. She now recognized that she was the gardener who had planted the seeds and tended the garden that had been her life. She could see the unfolding of events—the tragedies, the triumphs, the joys and losses—and how they connected to each other to form a life that was as dear as it was perfect. *Her* life. And how that life had led her to the person she was at that instant.

She realized at that moment how strongly she wanted to return to the life she once had, to pick up the pieces where she left them and reclaim her past life that was snatched from her by her accident. Thrill and anxiety rose in equal measures at the prospect. She wasn't sure how much would ever be possible because of how much she had changed and how little she knew, yet the drive and desire were strong. The hope too. But would she be able to do it?

Wanting to feel again the reassurance of the all-knowing, unconditional love and acceptance of Moriah, she went to the closet for her red tunic. She yearned to touch it, reconnect through it with Moriah's healing wisdom. Then she remembered that they had taken it to be cleaned. At first she'd been reluctant to let go of Moriah's gift that she weaved for her with her last breath. But they convinced her that they would return it to her in better condition, so she relented. It had been a few weeks already, so she wondered about when she might get it back. For some reason she kept forgetting to ask Gina about it.

But she wouldn't forget any longer. Today had been a day for decisions and for stepping out boldly. She meant to go on that way from now on.

CHAPTER THIRTY

The Void

AFTER SEVERAL SUCCESSFUL weeks during which Joyce digested huge amounts of information about her life, it was time to face the event that *no one* knew anything about. If Joyce never remembered anything about her accident, no one would ever know the details. The cause of her disappearance and memory loss would forever remain unknown, a dark and gnawing mystery.

But Dr. Gladwell had an idea to bring the unknown to light; the search for the memories surrounding Joyce's accident would be tackled through psychiatric hypnosis. A specialist was engaged, a doctor who specialized in taking his patients back in time, sometimes even to the prenatal state, to recreate possible traumas they had endured and couldn't remember and yet which still affected their lives.

In his mid-fifties, Dr. Karl was an experienced therapist who had treated patients in all sorts of unusual situations, so Joyce's condition didn't faze him. He invited her to lie on a leather recliner as he counted slowly from seven to one in a soft voice, perfected to help his patients feel safe and comfortable so that they could slide into the hypnotic state with ease.

"Joyce, are you comfortable?"

"Yes."

"Wonderful. I'm going to ask you some questions. Could you tell me what happened on February 5, 2021, the day after you came back from London?" His voice was smooth, a gentle wind caressing warm dunes.

"I'm home. I feel good. I needed to see a friend to get an exam. I feel like something might be wrong with me."

"Please take your time," the doctor said calmly.

"I'm inside a big machine that makes a lot of noise. It's over now. I'm driving a red car. It's a beautiful day. I get to a small house on a cliff by the water. No one is there, so I go for a drive. I stop so I can run and run along the coast. I see rocks rolling toward me. I can't stop. I fall down the cliff toward the water. I keep falling. I can't stop falling." Joyce's head rolled side to side and perspiration covered her brow.

"You're safe, Joyce," Dr. Karl said. "You're alive. You're not falling. I'm going to count to five and when you open your eyes on five, you'll be here in the room. You will remember your vision. You will feel calm and safe and well. One . . . two . . . three . . . Coming closer now. Four. Almost out . . . Five. You can open your eyes, feel your body, look around the room and take a deep breath. That's right. You're safe."

Joyce came out of the hypnosis visibly shaken. She assured both doctors that she was fine, but for the rest of the day she stayed in her room digesting what had happened to her all over again. She couldn't shake the feeling of dread.

When she didn't join Franka for their evening meal as she normally did, the doctor came to her room.

"Are you all right, Joyce?" she asked. "That session was intense."

"I'm okay, thank you. I just need some time. And yes, what I saw and felt was extremely intense. Overwhelming." She paced the few steps to the wall and then returned. "I'm not sure I have words to describe it. The only thing that comes to mind is a feeling of total obliteration. I don't know how to deal with what I saw and what I felt—what I'm still feeling. It's like the feeling, a smothering void, is lodged in me." Joyce's fist thumped her chest.

"Would you like some medication to help you calm down?" Franka asked, concerned.

"I'll be all right. I need to stay clear to digest this . . . She rubbed her chest again. "Maybe sleep can help."

"Oh, Joyce . . ." Franka sat on the bed, pulled Joyce down next to her and wrapped an arm around her. They were quiet for a long time before Dr. Gladwell encouraged Joyce to slip under the sheet. She sat by the bed, holding Joyce's hand until she fell asleep.

~

Franka hadn't forgotten that she was Joyce's therapist, yet compassion had told her to put her medical objectivity aside. She'd seen her friend, just her friend, in front of her, and her friend had been in dire need of comfort. But she was determined not to reveal to Joyce how she felt yet and retain their patient-doctor relationship at least as far as Joyce was concerned. She had to maintain her authority for the sake of the integrity of the treatment.

"I'm concerned about continuing the hypnosis sessions," she told Dr. Karl the following morning when they met in her office for a debriefing. "Joyce was very shaken up afterwards. She had a feeling of obliteration. That is the actual word she used." She closed her eyes briefly remembering her friend's anguish, but not wanting to show her own emotional reaction to what happened, she immediately reverted to her doctor role, putting on her matter-of-fact expression.

"On the one hand, it is valuable to bring the patient back to the moment of trauma so that they can exorcise its emotion from the subconscious mind and so as not be ruled by it for the rest of their lives. On the other hand, bringing that trauma to the surface too quickly could set her back in her recovery. She's doing well in reconstructing her past, but I'm not altogether sure how much of it she remembers episodically and how much comes out of her intuition. So I'm concerned about jeopardizing any progress – even the smallest - that we've made."

Dr. Karl put down his coffee mug and nodded. "I understand that yesterday's regression was particularly difficult. We never really know what to expect. I suggest we give her a few days to recover and monitor her closely and then ask her if she wants to continue. We don't know what her true memories of the following nine months of her disappearance could be, and the only way to access them might be through hypnosis."

His observation and suggestion made sense to Franka. Ultimately Joyce would decide to continue or not, based on how she felt. The resource of hypnosis was too valuable to discard because of a difficult session.

"I will keep a close eye on her and let you know in a few days if we will continue." Franka hedged with the therapist, but she already guessed that Joyce's eagerness to uncover the truth meant that she would want to go on.

And she was right. Joyce bravely agreed to continue the hypnosis protocol in the hope of regaining her full memory of what happened after her fall. Yet Franka was admittedly surprised by Joyce's revelations.

During the next sessions, Joyce described in detail a magical realm in a meadow surrounded by a forest, a fantasy home inhabited by a healing weaver woman and her angelic wolf-like creatures. Franka didn't know what to make of the information revealed consistently in Joyce's conscious recollections *and* through her subconscious mind via hypnosis. Perhaps her theory that actual memories were replaced by hallucinations was not correct? However, nothing in her training and years of practice could rationalize for her the fantastic experiences that Joyce described.

Franka had read about cases where victims of near-death experiences had visions or hallucinations of other realms while in a coma and came back to life completely healed. She knew about the case of Dr. Eben Alexander, the renowned neurologist who had described in his book *Proof of Heaven* an altered-state experience that had happened to him. Not having the measuring devices to analyze this mystery, Franka left the ambiguity of Joyce's memories as that—an ambiguity. She didn't know any other way to account for the nine months that elapsed between Joyce's fall until her reappearance; Moriah, the meadow, the cottage and the angel wolfdogs were the recollections Joyce had offered, whether she was conscious or under hypnosis.

Besides, Joyce's long-term memory was hardly showing signs of improvement, despite Joyce having painstakingly recreated what she could. She experienced no spontaneous memories, and even photographs elicited no related memories or links from one event or moment to another.

She hated to admit defeat, but Franka had to accept what would be best for Joyce. She recognized that Joyce's days at the clinic were drawing to an end. Unless there was a dramatic breakthrough, Joyce should soon return to her real life.

Perhaps daily life experienced in her own home, with Will and their dog, would be the key to unlock Joyce's memories. Perhaps the artificial environment of the research center needed to give way to the natural setting of the home.

After all, weren't people their most natural selves in their own homes? Loose and relaxed and free to say—and think—anything they wanted?

Franka pulled her tablet close and began preliminary notes for the protocols for Joyce's return home.

CHAPTER THIRTY-ONE

Connection

WILL WATCHED JOYCE playing with her cell phone as they chatted under the acacia tree. She kept placing her finger on the prompt button, and the image of Beau appeared, making her laugh each time. Annoyed at the obsessive habit, he said, "You know, that's not the only thing it does."

"What do you mean?"

Will hesitated, concerned about revealing too much too fast.

"Show me what else it can do!"

He laughed. She hadn't lost her insistent nature with her memories.

He took the phone from her and showed her that the slide of a finger accessed the app icons. He opened the photo library, and Joyce scrolled through the photos.

She didn't recognize the people or the locations, but Will admitted that he didn't know some of the people or the locations either.

"But this is my phone, right? So you might be in some of the photos, but you wouldn't have been with me everywhere." She held the phone up. "These are people and places and events that *I* thought were important, that I chose to record for some purpose. Maybe these moments and people mattered to me for some reason, or maybe I needed to record something for memory. Or maybe—"

"Or maybe you just like the color of a flower or you couldn't get quite the right angle on a photo." Will pointed out six shots in a row of the same rose.

She snatched the phone back. "Okay, that may be true. But still, isn't this an insight into my past? Don't these photos, objects and people I chose to record in a permanent way reveal something about me? Maybe lots of things." She drew in a deep breath.

She was as excited as a child at the discovery, and Will couldn't help but feel amused by her enthusiasm for her cell phone.

"If I looked at your phone, wouldn't I see what you considered important or noteworthy or— I don' t know. Special?"

"Of course. I was just kiddin'. You're right." He watched her scroll the images a few minutes longer, then he checked to make sure they were alone before leaning forward and accessing the internet.

"Okay, while the photos reveal you, *this* reveals the opinions and behavior of everyone else in the world. You can find news articles, TV programs, chat rooms, ads, wise advice and whacked-out kooks. Anything goes on the internet, so you need to be careful to not let the competing information confuse you." He settled back into his watchful posture again. "There's a lot of information on there that isn't true. You must be discerning about it."

She frowned but was nodding when she lifted her head. "You're saying that this contains, what, the realms of all knowledge?"

"A good way to put it. Or call it the knowledge of all the realms."

"Hmm . . ." She returned to the phone, easily swiping and scrolling and reading.

"And by the way, you've seen the computers here and Dr. Gladwell's tablet; you can access the internet on those too. And since the screens are bigger, you can see a lot more."

"I love it," she said. "It's like the mycelium underground system that connects all living things in the forest. But it's even better because it connects all humans through its invisible web."

Will was astounded. He had no idea what mycelium was, but his wife, who had a sketchy memory of her past, certainly knew how to use her brain. She was sounding more and more like the Joyce from before the accident.

Needing to touch her, he leaned over and pulled her toward him.

He hugged her against his chest, listening to her heart as it slowed. And he thanked God again for bringing her back to him.

The last year had been hell for both of them, but the future was bright. They could forget the past and move on.

"Oh God."

"What?" Joyce said, leaning back.

"It doesn't matter. Pay no attention to the silly man with the grass stains on his pants."

"Those wash easily. Tell me what you were thinking."

He gently dropped his forehead to hers. "I was thinking that even though the past year was crappy, we could soon forget the past and just focus on moving forward. Ridiculous, huh?"

"Yeah, let's not encourage any more forgetting. It's not a practice that I'd recommend."

"I know. I'm sorry. I wouldn't wish that on anyone."

"Me either. And though I don't know what I forgot, I do know that there are reasons for our memories." She ran both hands through her hair, fluffing it, before pressing her hands to the top of her head, as if holding her new memories in. She winced.

"Joyce . . ."

"I don't hurt, Will. Not physically. But I feel the absence of something that should be here. Something . . . The me from before is gone. You have all of yourself and so does Dr. Gladwell. So does everyone here. So I see what's missing in me, how memories help you cope and thrive and dream and plan. And I have memories from my time with Moriah and the weeks since then; I know that I should be an integrated whole. But I don't know yet how to make that integration happen or if it will ever happen."

She sighed. "I can live without memories—I've done so for almost a year. But I haven't forgotten that I should have memories, that I do have a past. So while the loss doesn't hurt, because I can't miss what I don't remember, I do sense the loss. And I mourn that loss." She smiled softly and stroked his face. "It's a strange feeling . . . Like missing something that isn't there, even though I don't remember having it."

Will pulled Joyce close again, and she wrapped both arms around him. He wished he knew medicine so he could heal her. Then he prayed for a miracle. And then he simply held her.

~

When Franka found out that Joyce had access to the internet, she was furious. She even threatened to take the phone away, as information she didn't control could jeopardize the entire treatment plan that she'd so carefully constructed under laboratory methods. She'd expected Will to balk, but in a surprising stance, Joyce was the one who refused to give up her newfound access to information.

"I can learn so much about brain functions and use this information to help my brain!" she'd argued. "I'm certain that it can help me with my recovery."

They'd moved the heated argument to Franka's office, Franka already regretting letting her temper get away from her. Now she hesitated over her response. Knowing Joyce's inquisitive and adaptive mind, Joyce's proposal made sense.

Maybe the internet could also open new avenues for treatment. Franka had been despairing that up to now, her methods were hardly scratching the surface. She'd consulted a few colleagues, but she was open to experiment too.

"Okay, keep it and use it," she said, relenting. "On the condition that you spend no more than one hour a day surfing the net and that you discuss with me any pertinent information you find. What sounds reasonable might be wrong or might contain bad recommendations. Practicing medicine on the inter—"

"Deal!" Joyce said, beaming.

The next day when they met under acacia tree, or what was now referred to as Joyce's office, Franka immediately noticed the excitement in Joyce's eyes.

"What do you know about mirror neurons?" Joyce spat out the question without bothering with a greeting.

The groundbreaking discovery by Italian scientists had been circulating since the 1990s and had been the subject of much debate in Franka's medical circles. It was a well-known discovery in the neuroscience community, and Joyce had obviously known about it before her accident, but to Franka's knowledge, she'd never focused on it, as it didn't have immediate applications for helping people suffering from degenerative memory loss from diseases such as dementia, which was the focus of their company's research program. Franka was surprised that Joyce would bring it up with such enthusiasm, considering the extensive information on the brain now available to her. She hesitated in responding to Joyce's question, not wanting to lead her but needing to find out why she wanted to discuss mirror neurons. Did she recognize in them a possibility to help in her own healing?

She could offer a textbook definition and see where that took Joyce.

"Mirror neurons are found primarily in the premotor cortex area. They fire when a person or an animal performs a specific action, as well as when they observe the same action performed by another person or animal."

"That's magnificent, don't you think?" Joyce exclaimed, eyes glittering and looking intently at Franka, as if expecting her to share her enthusiasm.

Franka understood that for Joyce it was as if she were discovering the information for the first time, yet she still didn't understand the fuss. She again contemplated the best response.

"It is a subject that could explain much of human evolution, but how do you feel it pertains to you?"

"It pertains to me as it pertains to all humans. Through our neurons we're connected to each other and to the entire world that surrounds us. We're not only conscious observers of what's around us, but we also experience what *all* living things experience through empathic observation."

Joyce was sounding more like a spiritual guru than a scientist. Franka chose to steer the conversation into a more observational direction.

"So as an example, what specifically do you think the benefits of mirror neurons are for you?"

Joyce bit her lip, yet she took only an instant to gather her thoughts.

"Don't you see? Here we are talking together, but it seems like we're speaking different languages. You're asking for practical application, whereas I'm speaking of scientific evidence of essential human experience of a sense of connection. Yet basically we're talking about the same thing. Isn't that what science is all about, uncovering the mysteries of nature through observation? The mirror neurons allow us to focus our observations and draw conclusions based on our unique personal sense of phenomenon which is seemingly outside of ourselves."

What Joyce said touched a chord in Franka, and she hurried to correct her. "The way we arrive at conclusions in science is through empirical observation, not through subjective feelings of empathy."

She regretted her response as soon as she said it. This was not one of their college debate sessions. Her role was to help her patient heal, so the relevance of the discovery was only important in the ways it pertained to her patient's current mental state. Her duty was to observe, not to respond. Or was it? She was losing her footing.

"Absolutely," Joyce said. "Like in the experiments with phantom limbs."

Franka's curiosity was piqued, yet she didn't see the relevance to what Joyce was saying. She gestured for Joyce to continue.

"The same neurons are fired whether we reach for something ourselves or see someone else reach for it, and yet our brains comprehend—through the interference signals sent from the nerves in our skin—that it isn't us doing the action. In the case of the phantom limb, where there is no actual arm and therefore no skin, the interference is removed, and the brain feels the action as though it was conducted by the person observing it. So at the end, what stands in the way of our complete connectivity is our skin and its nerve endings. Our sense of separation from everything in our world is skin deep. In our brains we are all connected!"

Joyce's conclusion seemed quite a far reach, although it was based on a logic that Franka could not refute, but she still needed to understand the personal relevance to Joyce.

"How does that make you feel?" She made a feeble attempt to redirect the conversation that had gotten away from her.

"We're wired to feel connection not only to actions done by other people but with everything we observe. I can feel leaves rustling when the wind blows through them, the flow of a river over pebbles or the hawk soaring in flight. As humans we connect our feelings and consciousness to all that we see and experience, and the mirror neurons grant us the ability to feel the world as we can feel our own selves."

The idea was marvelously poetic. Franka relaxed into the conversation as she eased back into her chair. She would let Joyce continue expressing her train of thought instead of prompting her to give up the information Franka was seeking. After all, Joyce had lost memories, not the other proficiencies of her brain. The woman had always been a skilled researcher. Maybe she'd continued that work all along, even after her accident. Maybe her mind was doing what it always did, exploring connections revealed by piecemeal information.

"Anyway, this helps me," Joyce said. "Understanding how and why I feel so connected to people and to nature and how these connections give me a sense of belonging. Knowing how mirror image neurons function makes me value the present moment that is filled with all these connections."

Franka felt unsettled. This whole time they'd been aiming to help Joyce regain her memories of the past through neuroscience, and effectively what Joyce was telling her was that she had found an explanation for her equilibrium beyond her memories. Maybe the entire focus of the healing protocol was off.

At this stage of the treatment, Franka feared it was quite probable that the memory neurons damaged by Joyce's accident would never be reactivated, no matter how hard they tried to reconnect to them. Still, she had not been ready to acknowledge her conclusion, not willing to admit defeat as a doctor and that she had failed her friend.

As she watched Joyce, it occurred to her that perhaps this was Joyce's way of telling her that it was all right, that their treatment wasn't a failure. Could it be her subtle way of showing them that she was well enough to go home, despite the fact that her memories had not fully returned?

Franka banished the thought just as quickly as it had surfaced. She always preferred hard fact to speculation.

She tuned back into Joyce's words. And hoped to find a possible direction for her treatment that she might have overlooked.

CHAPTER THIRTY-TWO

Thanksgiving

F ROM THE MOMENT Will told Joyce that they were married, they'd become inseparable. As in their college days, they wanted to spend every moment they could in each other's company. The gardens at the clinic provided them the refuge they needed to reconnect away from the distractions of the world. Like new lovers, they created their own complete world out of their intimacy.

Will was now allowed unlimited visitations. The medical team *finally* acknowledged what he had known—hoped—all along: that his presence helped Joyce a great deal and didn't harm her at all. She still didn't remember the events of the past on her own, but she was eager to learn about them and embrace them. And Will was excited to talk about their past, his own memories coming alive as he dramatically narrated humorous or meaningful moments from their lives, trying to include both her reactions as well as his own. He'd been tempted to skip their arguments, but he figured that was a form of lying. And he wanted Joyce to know how they'd overcome their differences and used their unique qualities to create a stronger bond, with the two able to accomplish more, and go farther, than either could alone.

He recognized that he was transferring his own memories to her and didn't want them to be shaded by his own emotional recollections. Yet despite his best intentions, separating himself from his memories was impossible.

She enjoyed listening to stories about their college years, especially his recollection of how they first met and recognized each other in a glance on the campus museum steps; she asked him to tell her the story often. It was as if they were meeting for the first time and falling in love all over again.

Will had brought a suitcase full of her old comfort clothes and sneakers, her favorite books and their photo albums. Together they explored the memories through the photos and the many videos on his phone. He'd uploaded their earlier photographs from college, adding them to the thousands of photos on his phone library from their travels, homes, outings and the life they shared from their twenties onward.

Joyce's clothes began to fit better when she put on pounds thanks to the hearty clinic food. Thank God. He hadn't told her, but he'd been worried about how thin she'd been when he'd first seen her. She was healthy, so that wasn't the problem. But so skinny . . .

In her soft, loose clothes of neutral colors, with her shoulder-length hair almost always in a ponytail and her skin rejuvenated, she seemed more and more like herself to Will every day. A softer, more relaxed version of herself, maybe. She was perfect to him, and he adored her.

They still weren't allowed to spend the night together, but their days were filled with walks in the garden, picnic lunches, naps under the vast shade of the acacia and playing with Beau. Will felt like a teenager, rushing to see Joyce every day, and she was just as eager, meeting him at the gate most days. She'd get in the Porsche, and they'd go for a ride along the clinic's two drives, top down on most days, sometimes speeding along with the wind in their hair, other times meandering slowly, the *whoosh* of the tires soothing them as they talked. He encouraged her to go running with him, as she had loved to do, but she seemed to prefer the more leisurely strolls, chatting enthusiastically about her new discoveries.

Joyce told Will how she scoured the internet for information on the brain. Thinking about the brain's structure and functions helped her to connect to her own brain, she said. She routinely visualized the brain's components and imagined creating new neurological pathways that connected her present to her past.

Will was in awe. More than once he asked her to talk through the process she used to forge new connections to the past, picking up clues for how he could help.

They were both shocked the moment she said that his stories of their past were seeping into her consciousness and becoming her own. "It's like I can no longer sense the boundary between your stories and my imagined memories."

The admission had led to a conversation with Dr. Gladwell and her team, and then to a private celebration dinner Will arranged with the clinic's chef.

After a couple of weeks, they were allowed to leave the clinic and expand the scope of their explorations. Their love of nature guided them to long walks along the ocean and through the nearby meadow. At times they walked in silence, hand in hand, absorbing the sensations prompted by the elements. The softness of California's autumn air and just being together felt wonderful.

It was almost Thanksgiving, and Will wanted to share a home-cooked holiday celebration with Joyce. Dr. Gladwell agreed, and Will, feeling almost giddy, invited Joyce to the beach house he was renting.

Instead of the traditional turkey, Will decided to cook her favorite dish, boeuf bourguignon. Perhaps subconsciously he wanted to turn back time and make her the meal they never got to have together ten months before.

Or maybe there was nothing subconscious about it. *He* wanted the meal that they'd missed. He couldn't get those months back, but he could have one moment.

He picked her up Thanksgiving morning, and once in the beach cottage, she explored the bright space, a simple one-story modern structure decorated with boho-style furniture. It didn't match his taste, but there were a lot of white accents and a generous white linen love seat, so he'd been comfortable there. Beau finally plopped down by the bay window after giving Joyce an overwhelming welcome. Will loved the bay window, and that was where Joyce ended up too, watching the torrid sea through a soft rain that had begun dripping lightly. Will stood behind her to watch the rain wash off layers of dust and ocean spray that clung to the window. It felt like a brand-new day. He dropped a kiss to Joyce's head, rewarded when she leaned back against him.

"It's beautiful, Will. A perfect day."

"Not for those who want to play outside or who'll need to work off their holiday meals, but yes, I agree."

"It's only rain."

He couldn't argue with that. And he refused to follow the rabbit hole that opened before him, the one that wanted him to worry about where Joyce had spent the months they'd been apart. Had she shivered in the cold and rain? Had she— No. He couldn't change the past.

He lit the small living room fireplace, which added its own fragrance to the mouth-watering smells filling the cottage. He had begun cooking the beef early that morning after it had marinated in tomatoes, wine and herbs for a couple of hours, and it already smelled like heaven. He headed to the kitchen, turned on one of their favorite playlists and got back to work. Beau followed him and stared at him intently as he cooked, patiently hoping for some tasty bit to land on the floor. Joyce remained by the window. The glass of Merlot he had given her still breathed on the coffee table, but she hadn't touched it.

The cascading notes of Glenn Gould playing Bach's Goldberg Variations poured out of the speakers. Joyce sat up, turning toward Will, her moving fingers accompanying the notes. Her mouth opened, but no sound came. A long minute later—fingers still in motion, body swaying -she said, "Will, I love this music!" she finally released the words. "I think I know it too. It feels like I can anticipate the notes before I hear them. Did I used to listen to this music?"

Will nodded while lifting a spoon to his lips to taste the sauce. Satisfied with the way the flavor was developing, he put the spoon down and smiled. "Yes, darling. It was one of your favorites. Particularly on the drive to Jenner." He began chopping the vegetables.

"What ever happened to our house near Jenner?"

Will lifted his head. Joyce had turned toward the kitchen, the angle leaving half her face in shadow.

"You know, the one with the huge bay window and the tiny cozy bedroom."

He dropped the knife he'd been using to cut potatoes.

"We had to drive through the woods to get to it. I used to love that house . . . I had come home that day, you know, but you weren't there . . ."

Of course he knew. He'd found her overnight bag in the bedroom.

He was stunned beyond words. Her words—*her memory*—touched a deep wound that had been steadily bleeding for months without his awareness of it. There was a hint of an apology there, as though she felt bad about abandoning him. He didn't have the heart to tell her that he had sold the Jenner house when he couldn't bear to go there without her.

Instead, he walked to the living room and drew her to him, his fingers on her waist pressing gently into her cashmere sweater, as if she might crumble. Their lips met, lightly at first, and then the kiss spread, their tongues connecting and exploring with rising intensity.

A few minutes later, the heated moment melted away—perhaps it had been just a dream.

No. It had been real. For the first time in so long, that connection had been real, not something they were striving to recreate. Not something he dreamed about at night.

Did Joyce feel the same?

"Did you feel that?" he asked, almost not wanting to know. His heart would shatter if that kiss, that reforging of their bond, had meant nothing to her.

"We touched." She traced her bottom lip with a single finger.

"Yes."

"Our souls touched."

"Yes." Thank God. The connection went both ways.

"Was it always like that?"

He smiled. "Always. From that first moment on those campus steps."

"Wow."

Wow indeed. He wrapped his arms around her and wiped a tear with his sleeve.

"I've got something for you," he said when he could finally let go.

"What is it?" She clasped her hands, curious, excited.

He took a long red box from the bookshelf and handed it to her.

She opened the box to discover an old-fashioned gold watch.

"Is this really for me?" She grinned, and then her smile dropped.

"I'm sorry, Will, I don't have a present for you, I didn't know . . . "

Will raised his hand to stop her, and then took the watch from her and put it around her wrist, adjusting the old-fashioned clasp that fit her perfectly.

"This isn't a gift, darling! It's your mother's watch. Your watch. You always wore it except when you went running. You left it on the bedside table that day . . ." He stopped, his words choking him. The memory of that day, of finding the watch in the empty house, still haunted him. She understood and stroked his arm.

"Thank you for bringing it here. It must have meant a lot to me. My mother's watch..." She glared at it as if trying to extract memories out of the once-familiar object that used to be so charged with meaning and emotion, or maybe she was staring at its face, trying to turn back time. "I wish I could go back to feeling what I did then, to knowing why this pretty watch is so dear to me. But I can't. All I can do now is make it my precious possession again." She brought it to her ear, listening to the tick-tock of time moving forward, the endless ticktock of time . . .

"Speaking of time!" Will interrupted the loaded silence. "I think it's time for dinner!" He filled up two plates and carried them over to the table that was set with white linen and flowers. "This used to be your favorite dish! I hope you still like it." She swallowed a spoonful, her eyes glowing. "Mmm. Thank you for all this, Will. You've done so much to make me feel at home here. Even though I don't remember the other ones, I do believe that this is the best Thanksgiving ever!"

"It is indeed, darling. We truly have so much to be thankful for!"

Their first dinner alone together couldn't have gone better. And Joyce even showed signs of regaining her memory on her own. His heart soared. He couldn't wait for them to finally go home.

CHAPTER THIRTY-THREE

The Vows

I T HAD BEEN the worst and best year of their lives, and it was nearing its end, an occasion with special meaning because Dr. Gladwell was sending Joyce home in time for New Year's Eve, with the promise she'd return if anything didn't feel right. She'd insisted on keeping Joyce in the clinic until she was absolutely sure that there was no more she could do through therapy to regain her memory. Joyce's recollection of the past was still sparse, however, so her doctor finally had to admit that her recovery would take much longer than she hoped, and that going home was the best way to foster that recovery.

As the day approached, Joyce was filled with excited anticipation to start living her old life again. Will greeted her with a huge bouquet of flowers as she hurried down the corridor of the clinic, rolling her small suitcase.

"Your favorites, white lilies and roses."

She took the bouquet from him and inhaled the magnificent scent. "Thank you, Will." She kissed his cheek, laughing and kissing his lips when he pretended to pout. She then hugged the staff, who had become her friends, and Franka, who she now knew had been a friend from college. "Come visit us in San Francisco, and happy New Year!" she called as she floated out the large front door.

Will's helicopter was parked on the clinic's front lawn, and she climbed in while Will loaded her luggage, although she had only a few items, since he had taken most of her things home already. She held her flowers and greeted Beau, who sat tightly secured between the seats. But his harness and leash couldn't restrain his kisses, and Joyce was wiping dog love from her face when Will joined her.

The weather was mild despite the time of year, and the day clear and bright. She was wearing her old shearling jacket, and Will matched her in a newer version. He looked quite the dashing aviator with his sunglasses and breeze-tossed hair. She tightened her ponytail and gave him a thumbs-up.

"I can't wait to be with you in our house," he said, watching her for a long moment before he started pushing buttons and warming up the helicopter. Every movement was smooth, assured, and he paused more than once to send her a grin.

A few minutes later they were off and soaring high above their beloved California coast.

It took just under three hours to get to their apartment, where she hadn't been in for almost a year.

"I didn't change anything," Will said. "But Marta was here today. She cooked a few meals, and I asked her to put flowers in every room."

"It smells great and looks beautiful." She laid her large bouquet on the credenza by the door. "But maybe you went a little overboard with the flowers."

"I couldn't help myself. They demanded to be here when you arrived."

Will picked up her bouquet and her coat as she kicked her sneakers off, and she stood at the entrance of their living space and took a long look around, inhaling the room and all it represented, needing to make them part of herself again. Then she eased into the beige leather couch by the fireplace and put her feet up on the matching ottoman. Will handed her a glass of Merlot.

"So how does it feel to be here?" he asked, grinning.

"Like home!"

"And that's *my* homecoming present. You couldn't have said anything better to make this the best day ever."

They clinked glasses, and Will stretched out on the couch next to Joyce.

Beau jumped on the couch between them and began digging exuberantly behind the pillows until he retrieved a chewed-up sock that he laid on Joyce's lap before taking off to the front door. Will laughed when she examined the sock with a puzzled look.

"For months he carried that thing around. It's one of yours that he stole out of the hamper. He would bury it in the pillows on the couch so I wouldn't find it and take it away from him, but of course I didn't have the heart to take it from him, so it became his sock."

She laughed, but her joy was mixed with a pang of pain at the realization of how much her dog missed her.

"The other one is still in your drawer." Will smiled and looked over to the other side of the apartment, as if he'd just remembered the second sock.

"Now the pair can be reunited. Although this one's been through a lot." He took the sock from her, examining it with a mixture of laugher and disgust before kissing her.

Not a minute later Beau came racing in, dragging his leash. He dropped it at Will's feet.

"Again? You just went."

Beau barked and twirled in a circle before racing to the front door.

"Stop that laughing," Will said. "Or I'll make *you* take him."

"I can't help it," Joyce said. "You looked so comfortable." She tipped her head and peered out the window. "And it's raining only a little bit."

He set his wine aside before grabbing one of Joyce's feet.

"No, Will. Don't you dare." She couldn't free her foot, and her objection was delivered with laughter, so Will ignored her and tickled her foot until Beau came roaring back in and jumped on the couch with her to ad his own contribution to the tickles.

"I'll get you for that," she said when both her boys turned toward the door.

Will waved over his shoulder. "I know you will. And I'm looking forward to every moment of it."

She was too.

She laid her head back and relaxed.

The last year had been filled with memories, with losing them and trying to regain them. But the new year would be filled with the making of new memories.

And living her life, doing what she was meant to do and sharing her days and nights with Will, she couldn't ask for more. On doctor's orders she'd had to delay her return to a work life or to any kind of service, but she was strong and healthy and determined to get started.

She lifted her wine glass and said, "To you, Moriah. Thank you. Thank you for all you were, for all you did for me and by extension, for Will. Thank you for your selflessness and your wisdom." She sipped the wine.

"I don't know where you are, but you were where I needed you to be when I needed you to do what I couldn't do for myself. I am blessed to have known you." She closed her eyes. "I hope I'll make you proud."

~

They were getting ready for the New Year's celebration that evening. Will ordered oysters from the oyster bar down the street and chilled a bottle of Dom Perignon. Joyce wore an elegant silky black dress with a big shawl over it. The Bay air was cool, and the evening was foggy. Between the weather and Covid regulations, fireworks had been canceled. They didn't mind the cold and moist weather, and they certainly didn't need fireworks; they were finally home together.

They sat on the balcony overlooking the bay and toasted their reunion, their love and the future. Truly alone for the first time in months, they savored every moment. Each word and touch.

The coolness of the evening air eventually sent them back into the house. With a flick of a switch, Will ignited the fireplace, which cast its amber glow around the room. Then he lit a few groupings of candles. Their light flickered, dancing with the shadows. Without a word he handed her a small box of chocolate truffles, just big enough for a truffle or two. Eager for a bite of dessert, she opened the box excitedly, but then stared back, mouth and eyes wide. Neither of them said anything. She reached into the box and pulled out the ring nestled into a stack of candy wrappers. Its clear oval diamond sparkled rainbows as she turned it around and around to examine it.

"Put it on," he said gently. "It's yours. Your engagement ring. Like your watch, you left it on the side table before you left on your run. I've been waiting for this day for so long. To finally see it back on your finger."

She slipped it on and once again admired the sparkly tiny rainbows it harbored. *Like Moriah's healing crystal*, she thought.

"The first time I gave it to you, you pulled it out of a chocolate box just like this one. We were on the plane on our way back from a vacation in Hawaii. And the look on your face then was just like the one you have now."

He smiled playfully and took another ring out of his pocket. This one was a simple gold band. Looking deeply into her eyes, into her soul, he slipped it on her ring finger.

"And with this ring, I thee wed."

Her eyes were filled with tears, but she smiled and kissed him deeply. He was recreating the most touching moments from their life before. She knew it and loved him for it. She hadn't regained her past completely yet, but he was there to make sure that the precious moments were not lost to her forever.

In their bed they rediscovered the feel of each other's bodies, caressing, touching and kissing in the intimacy of darkness.

"I love you," she whispered as she lay in Will's arms. He held her tightly to him, whispering his love in return. They fell asleep entwined in each other, with no idea of what the future would bring, but knowing deep in their hearts that they would never let go of each other again for as long as they lived.

That was enough. More than enough.

CHAPTER THIRTY-FOUR

The City

JOYCE WAS DETERMINED to resume her morning jog. Even though she had just returned home, she felt it was important to pick up her old habits that Will had told her about. Will offered to go with her the first morning, but she wanted to forge out on her own with only Beau as her guide.

She ran lightly, feeling uncertain. She hadn't regained her stride, and she knew her body wasn't ready for a full workout. But that wasn't the only problem. The city seemed paler and grimmer than she had expected. She didn't recognize any of the streets and faces she encountered. Her face mask made taking deep breaths difficult, so she slowed her pace even more.

The faces that came toward her, all clad in masks, wore severe gazes. The eyes she encountered briefly turned away, as though the people were afraid to establish any form of connection, even momentarily. There was a heaviness in the atmosphere, unlike anything she had ever experienced. Even Beau didn't want to linger on the cold and unwelcoming streets, and as soon as he did his business, he turned back home.

Will looked up from his laptop when she got through the door, his face displaying concern. "That was quick. Are you okay?"

"I'm fine. Well, sort of. I don't know. This place feels so different from what I expected. I saw people wearing masks in Jenner, and I understand about the pandemic, but in this city no one even looks at you. I could smell the dread in the street. It's very disturbing." She shivered and moved to the fireplace.

Will nodded. "I haven't gone out much since mid-March, when the WHO declared the pandemic and we went into lockdown. It's been so grim around here. You were only gone about a month when this started.

And everything changed so suddenly after that. People became so afraid of Covid that they hardly dared to look at a stranger on the street, let alone breathe around them. That sounds crazy, but that's what happened. It was so hard to be alone here without you. Thank God for Beau, or I might have gone insane. Remember Don from my office and his wife Meg?" He paused for a moment allowing space for her recollection.

But she shook her head.

"We were really close before the pandemic. They used to live up the street, but they moved outside the city, like so many of our friends. This city has changed so much since you've been gone. I hope it can come back to itself." Deep frown lines appeared on his brow, and he added, "I hope we all can."

The despair on his face and in his voice tore at her heart. She felt terrible that she had left him at a time when he would feel more alone than ever, without the company of friends for support.

"I'm so sorry!" she said, his loneliness reaching out to her across the room and across the months. She tasted the bitterness of his grief.

"Gail, my sister, came to stay with us for a couple of weeks in the beginning. I was so despondent then, I could hardly take care of myself and Beau while running back and forth to Jenner, so she came to help. But then when the lockdown began, she had to go back home because they closed the schools and there was no one to stay home with the kids."

The realization of the pain he had experienced seeped into her.

"I'm so sorry!" She repeated the only words she could find, knowing in her heart that they didn't come close to reflecting how terrible she felt for what he had gone through.

"We're not out of the woods yet, but at least I've got you now!" He beamed at her and reached for her hand. She stepped closer to him and hugged his shoulders.

Maybe a change of scenery was what they both needed. A place with open spaces where they could be in nature together.

"What about our house by the sea? Could we go there sometime soon?" she asked.

"Honey, I didn't have the heart to tell you this while you were at the clinic, but after you were gone, I couldn't bring myself to go back there. Whenever I went to the area to search for you, I stayed at the inn in Jenner if it was too late to fly home. The house sat there empty and uncared for.

It took months before I could bring myself to let it go, but the real estate market was going crazy, so I finally sold it with everything in it to this really nice couple who kinda' reminded me of us. I can contact them and see if we could buy it back if you want. I'll offer them a large premium. They might go for that."

She felt numb as the sorrow of loss overcame her. She couldn't understand why she was feeling the loss so intensely. After all, she didn't really remember the house and had no recollection of their life there. Yet she felt viscerally connected to it. It was as if a part of her that she loved was being ripped off. It *was* a part of her, just one she didn't know, and now she could never reconnect to it. She searched for words to respond to Will's generous suggestion, and when they didn't come, she finally said, "We'll see."

Will didn't wait for her to say more. He closed his computer and said, "I'm done working for the day. Let's go for a walk, since you didn't get a decent run."

She was grateful for the invitation, for a chance to change her mood.

"I'd love that." She hurried to the front closet to fetch her duffle coat.

As soon as the elevator began its descent, she went dizzy and off balance. Her breath hitched and then caught. Panting, she grabbed Will's arm, her fingers digging into the soft wool of his coat sleeve. God, she was falling and falling.

"Honey, what's wrong?"

Her muffled cry was lost in his cheek. He held her tightly, her shudders shaking them both. Finally the elevator doors opened and daylight flooded in.

Will pulled her outside, pushed her hair behind her ears. "What happened? Do you need water? A doctor?"

She was still glued to him. She searched his face. His concern and his familiar features began to ease her panic.

"I don't know! I felt like I was falling into a void and didn't know if it would ever stop. If I would ever stop falling."

Her body started to let go of its tension even as she spoke. She released her grip as they eased closer to the outer door, but Will hadn't let go of her.

"I'm okay now. Promise." She loosened his hands and held them in her own. "It was just the most helpless sensation, falling and falling without being able to control what was happening."

"Okay."

He didn't sound convinced that she was all right, but the sensation had completely passed. She couldn't even recapture the fear.

"I'll let Franka know, okay?"

"That's good, but you didn't see your face. I've never seen you so white. You might have been having a flashback from your fall or maybe a panic attack."

She pulled him along the sidewalk, determined to convince him with action that she was fine.

They strolled in the nearly empty inner neighborhood streets, away from the homeless encampments and the boarded-up storefronts. He held one arm around her shoulder protectively as they walked.

Their explorations took them to the deserted Fort Mason building.

"Do you remember the theater that was here and that tiny coffee shop with the huge globe and all the old instruments?" Will asked.

She shook her head, but of course he knew that she didn't remember. The old army barracks that had housed some of their favorite venues stood abandoned, looking lonely against the stunning views of the Marina and its boats, no hint of their previous liveliness remaining.

They huddled together for protection from the piercing cold winds as they crossed the road and continued along the Marina. Boats swayed lazily in their moorings, all neatly arranged according to size in their respective slots. San Francisco offered such beauty in its natural surroundings, yet some of its people weren't always as blessed. Will had steered them around the destitute and the homeless, but she'd heard the news and read internet reports. Their hometown was a blend of plenty and want, of richness and lack. She peppered Will with questions about the dichotomy. They hadn't solved the problem by the time they reached the Palace of Fine Arts, which stood majestically undisturbed in its Beaux-Arts grandeur, a testament to times long gone.

"It's been here since the Panama-Pacific Expo in 1915," Will said. "And it'll probably be here after we're gone. At least some things don't change." They stood protected from the wind by the building's thick curving walls and watched the willows by the lake dip their branches endlessly into its water.

The calm beauty of the surroundings, and of the large willows stirred a deep chord of memory in Joyce. She recalled the moment she finally found peace nestled in the canopy of the oak tree. The feeling of utter safety and contentment. Looking out into the distance, she had known that there was someone out there she loved and who loved her in return. It was a knowing more than a longing. And now she stood here with him next to her as they looked onto the same landscape. A wave of gratitude washed over her.

She loved the idea of the building's permanence, a place that spanned beyond their lifetimes and would hold the memories of bygone cultures into perpetuity. But then she remembered Moriah's words, that no physical structures would last forever, that only the experiences remained. That and the impact they had upon the world.

"Will," she said slowly.

"Yes, darling?"

She searched for the right words.

"Do you ever feel that you must do something? Something that would impact other people? The world?"

Will's lips parted in a smile, but his eyes remained serious.

"You're sounding like your old self again," he said.

"Really?"

He nodded and looked lost in his thoughts for a moment.

"Before you were gone, all I wanted was to make money so we could have a good life. I guess the taste of making money caught up with me, because it felt like it was never enough. I became so focused on financial success that I started to lose track of a lot of other things that were important. Like you. Like us." He took her hand and brought it to his heart.

"*You* were the one with a mission." He squeezed her hand.

"I was frustrated because nothing ever seemed like it was enough, not even our love and our relationship." Visibly choked up, he glanced down, letting their hands drop, and shook his head. It was a moment before he could speak again.

"Then when you were gone, all I wanted was for things to go back to the way they were, to find you and get you back. So right now, I just want to love you. Ultimately that's all I've ever wanted." He pulled her to him and kissed her tenderly right there under the willow flopping its branches around them in the wind.

"I love you too!" she said, looking into his eyes when their bodies separated. "You know, I never stopped loving you. Not even when I didn't know your name. Not even when I didn't remember your face."

He hugged her to him, her cheek pressed against his chest.

She pulled back and leaned out slightly, her hands still around his waist.

"I think it's love. The one permanent thing. It's love that remains when all else is gone," she said. His familiar face smiled back at her, eyes twinkling with tears.

"I wonder if our love ripples around to the world, affecting those we come in contact with. I feel the expanse of our love everywhere," she added watching the light and shadows of the ripples of the pond.

They kissed again and then joined hands as they walked home. The wind blowing at their backs carried their words away.

She had no idea what her future endeavors would be, what they would look like or how she'd fulfill the certainty that she could be of help to others, but she knew that love would show her the way.

Holding Will's hand, head lifted as she watched people and cars and clouds rush by, she mused about the possibilities as they strolled in silence.

CHAPTER THIRTY-FIVE

The Invention

J OYCE WAS ADAPTING to daily life rather well. Still, regular idiosyncrasies crept into her routine, reminding Will that she was not quite herself yet. Like the time he walked into the bathroom in the middle of the day to find her standing in her bra and using the electric toothbrush on her back.

"Whatcha doing there?" he asked, his smile partly amused and partly concealing concern.

"Just scratching an itch," she replied nonchalantly.

Will didn't say anything. He allowed her the space for exploration. But her new idiosyncrasies sometimes unsettled him.

She took to drenching herself in her mother's favorite perfume, Chanel No. 5, the one she had used only on special occasions and sparingly before her accident. Now it became her signature scent that trailed her everywhere, leaving clouds of her presence when she left the room. Although he teased her about them lovingly, Will understood that the eccentricities were her creative ways to reintegrate the things she'd forgotten back into her life. As though drenching herself with the perfume could imbue her mother's memory into her skin. Or maybe she just liked the scent and was rediscovering it. Regardless, he accepted that her reintegration into daily life would be a process. One that required patience. But secretly he also enjoyed watching some of the funny ways she reinvented the uses of everyday objects and giving them new life. *Her life.*

~

Their slow-paced days allowed Joyce time to relearn what had been erased from mind. In fact, life seemed rather simple and easy with Will and Beau by her side. The memories of Moriah started to fade. Her recollections began to seem unreal against the backdrop of real people and real places that constantly provided tangible proof of their existence. Moriah and her magical wolves and the garden started to blur and dissolve. The images were still there, but they were tempered by the daydreams of her imagination, until her experience with Moriah felt more like a fairy tale than events she'd actually lived. As time passed, their crispness paled, and she drew on them less and less to find her bearings in the world she now occupied.

When Neurogenics, the company where she'd worked prior to her disappearance, learned of her return, Joyce was invited to join the director's Zoom meetings. A new CEO, Scott Stewart, had been hired quickly when she didn't come back, and he had brought in a number of new board members and recruited a few executives to help him run the fast-growing enterprise.

She couldn't recognize any of the faces on her first Zoom experience and had no idea who was new and who wasn't. She gracefully accepted the congratulations and accolades shared by a few of the participants but remained silent throughout the meeting, learning of the company's progress and their plans.

She continued joining the executive Zoom call every Monday morning. For the rest of the week, she read up on the latest neuroscience research and the technological advances that the company had produced. She found her studies to be intellectually engaging, but for the most part she felt like an outsider unable to penetrate this specialized world with its specific language and codes. Her associates had grown accustomed to her silence—a far cry from her previous dynamic leadership—since for some time the company had been following the vision of their new CEO.

After the successful public offering that she'd initiated and helped launch, the company acquired its new leader, a man directed by a public board and answerable to the shareholders. The change brought a different approach to the company's vision and created a sweeping international expansion.

Scott Stewart was the newest wunderkind of the tech industry, having taken both a tech and a biotech company to soaring heights before joining Neurogenics. His high stock share and keen focus on expansion had been the constant motivators that paved his way to multiple successes. Joyce liked him. The company was in great hands.

Even though she felt she had little to contribute, Joyce was given an advisory position on the board, and she was determined to live up to her new responsibilities. Her mind felt sharp despite or because of everything she'd experienced, and she was able to digest a lot of information. A part of her had slowed down, however. She wasn't in a rush, as she had been before, to accomplishment anything tangible. The pressure to constantly achieve was turned off, freeing her to contemplate possibilities. What she lost in motivation, she gained in presence, and her intuition was keen. She realized that with her particular vision, she could possibly contribute in a way that stirred the company to a broader positive direction. Not only for the shareholders, but for humanity.

After her miraculous healing, she wanted to discover or develop ways to help others benefit from what she had learned, and she searched for methods to share that knowledge. She believed that her position in a neurological research company afforded her the best place to develop a system or a method or even some kind of technology, yet she was at a total loss concerning what she could do.

One evening as she sat by the fireplace, she absently picked up a book from the coffee table, her attention captured by the drawing on its cover. Leonardo da Vinci and his flying machines. She flipped through the pages.

The meticulousness with which he drew lines depicting flight felt accurate and real, as though he'd connected them—or been connected himself—to actual flight, which he had no way of experiencing during his lifetime. Had this knowledge come out of his mirror neurons' observation of the flight of birds, allowing him to not only deduce their mechanisms for flight, but also to sense it in himself?

She sat back in the chaise, eyes closed. The possibilities for mirror neurons in the biomimicry field would be endless, she thought, if human brains could connect to living organisms and emulate their functions.

Ever since she'd rediscovered mirror neurons, she hadn't been able to stop thinking about them. She sensed that just as they could have contributed to spikes in human progress in prehistoric times—in the use of tools and languages, for instance, when suddenly many individuals across the planet grasped the same revolutionary idea in a short span of time, seemingly contradicting the slower Darwinian evolutionary theory—so they could hold a key to the progress of healing practices today.

She was particularly intrigued by the phantom limb research of Dr. Ramachandran, a neurologist from the University of California (UCSD), who observed that sufferers could experience relief in a phantom limb by watching someone else massage their own arm. Thanks to the mirror neurons, the person with the missing arm perceived the action of another person's arm as his own. Since there were no nerve endings of the missing arm to indicate otherwise, the sense of separation between one person and another was gone.

"So maybe this kind of experience could be replicated through virtual reality technology, giving relief to patients who lost motor abilities due to strokes or accidents that affected their neurons' motor connections."

She opened her eyes when Beau woofed at her.

"Sorry, baby. I was talking out loud."

He went back to sleep, and she returned to her thoughts.

Paralysis caused by neurological damage could potentially be healed by recreating new neuron pathways in the patient's brain. But they'd have to trick their brains to connect the mirror neurons perceiving the action through VR to their own bodies and motor functions.

Hmm . . .

She opened her tablet and furiously wrote out possibilities and complications and impossibilities and solutions. When her hands cramped, she stopped. Then an idea came to her. Isolation tanks created an environment of sensory deprivation. VR imaging technology could be used in an isolation tank!

The possibility filled her with excitement, although it was only a hypothesis. If nothing else, such a technology could at least allow motion-challenged individuals to re-experience their bodies in carefree ways and engage in activities they'd been unable to enjoy, which in themselves were healing experiences.

Wow, was that the answer? Exploring ways of fostering the brain's capacity to regenerate itself was definitely worthwhile. And Joyce sensed that engaging mirror neurons was the way to do it.

Despite her rising excitement, she was cautious, knowing that her idea would need to be thoroughly researched, but what better company to conduct the neurological research than her own. Right time, right place, right researcher. Maybe *this* was her mission. She couldn't wait to tell Will.

If she could use her experience, her knowledge and the company's resources to help people, the suffering that she and Will had endured would have been meaningful not just for them but for others as well.

And she needed to talk with Ravi. They'd kept in touch throughout her recovery, and she'd come to know him as her dear and longtime loyal friend.

She didn't wait but picked up her phone.

"Look at you!" Ravi said after she described the potential invention to him. "Just recovered, and you're already at it, trying to figure out how to save humanity!"

Was he making fun of her? No, that didn't sound—

"It's a brilliant idea!"

She let out a sigh of relief.

"Let's get busy designing the research protocols and setting up the clinical studies program. I want to help! I'd love to be involved with this, as it can open up so many possibilities in researching the brain's role in how to heal the body in general. Once again, my friend, you are in the vanguard of scientific possibilities!"

She grew even more excited at seeing his excitement.

"Once we put together the R&D proposal, you can discuss it with Stewart. He's a stickler for figures, so we'll need to be thorough, but he also loves innovation, so he'll probably go for it if it's thoroughly studied and well presented. And he knows he can trust you to take the lead on this!"

Ravi's enthusiasm and assurance were contagious. In a couple of weeks they'd completed their initial proposal presentation.

Joyce arranged a Zoom meeting. Scott Stewart's now-familiar face filled her screen, showing little expression, as usual, while she laid out her plan.

She had prepared intently, coached by Ravi about the research methodology and its practical applications, as well as the processes and costs of moving the product from the R&D stage to market. Her presentation had to be clear and succinct, as Stewart had only fifteen minutes to accommodate her.

He listened attentively, not saying anything until she concluded. Then without skipping a beat, he said, "Joyce, I have been an admirer of yours for many years, watching how you were growing this fantastic company to what it was when I took over. To be honest, I was even envious of you, of your creative leadership, which is not my forte. I like numbers and facts, and I can't afford to stray from the vision that I outlined for this company and my responsibility to the shareholders and the public. We're a data-driven company; we're not in the healing business. I appreciate your innovation, but it doesn't fit our current vision."

Joyce was shocked. She so strongly believed in her idea that not for a second had she entertained the possibility that he might turn it down. Dumbstruck, she didn't know what to say.

"Thank you for your time," she finally murmured.

She continued to attend the management meetings but wondered what she was doing there. The pragmatic conversations about profits and bottom lines washed over her without landing. Her heart was no longer in her position. She kept showing up because it was one of the activities that connected her to her previous life, but she realized that both she and the company had changed so dramatically, the connection was no longer there.

Will shook his head when she told him about Stewart's rejection. "I miss the days when you were calling the shots at that company. Although I admit I don't miss missing you all the time because of how hard you worked. Still, this isn't right!"

She patted his arms as though he was the one who needed consoling, while it was *she* who felt the deep pang of disappointment.

Ravi was angry.

"We have the means to do it, to fund this research. I know, because I run the lab. That . . . *Stewart*. He has no vision. Not like you did!"

All that knowledge and vision, all the intuition to help her bring healing to those in dire need of it, and yet she couldn't do anything with it. No company but the one which she helped create would take a risk on her, given her current mental state, and it didn't do it. Wouldn't do it. And she remembered nothing of medical school; would she need to get a new degree? Start all over again? Regretfully, she had to admit that if she was the one running the company, she probably wouldn't have trusted herself either. Not to run a multi-million-dollar research project with her memory the way it was.

She felt lost. The love she had with Will was dear to her and she savored the extensive time they now had together. However, she wanted

more engagement with her world. She wanted to make a positive difference.

She found herself yearning for Moriah. She hadn't thought much
about her since her early days at the clinic. She'd even begun to wonder
whether Moriah had been a figment of her imagination. Perhaps in her
confused state she had hallucinated the magical weaver woman. After all,
the story of her amazing rescue seemed quite impossible now, so Moriah's
existence could have been a fable she'd concocted in order to survive the
months of isolation when she was lost. That belief had been planted during her time in the clinic and reinforced by the guidance from her devoted
doctor and friend. All that mattered at that time was that she would
regain mental stability, skills and possibly some memories so she could
comfortably return to her life.

But now something was missing. Confusion and doubt rose in her,
and she began questioning her very existence. She felt that she was living
her life as though it was an image she had to step into, like an actress
rehearsing a role, but one that her heart had had no connection to for
quite a while. If it weren't for Will and Beau, she didn't know if she
would want to keep on living. She still wore the pinecone necklace that
she touched from time to time when seeking guidance, but it no longer
brought her the solace it once did.

Something had to change.

CHAPTER THIRTY-SIX

The Dream

T HE NIGHTMARES RETURNED, hellish processions coming one on top of the other, making Joyce terrified to sleep. The worst one was of her falling endlessly into a bottomless pit and becoming engulfed in darkness that surrounded her until she no longer saw or felt herself. She woke from the dreams choking on tears. Will held her tightly, soothing her until she drifted back to sleep.

One night she dreamed that she was standing on the edge of a high jagged cliff overlooking the ocean, a strong wind swirling around her, and she was losing her balance and was about to be pushed off into the abyss. At that very moment someone grabbed her from behind by her waist. When she turned around, she saw a young woman who looked just like her staring deeply at her with her own bottomless eyes. Yet even though the woman looked just like her, Joyce recognized her as Moriah.

Something strong and invigorating stirred in her after she woke from that dream. It was as though she regained a sense of who she had been during the time with Moriah. She yearned to reconnect with that part of herself, the part that knew her truth and that felt joy, love and a connection to everything. She hadn't been able to find that connection in the life she was currently living.

Without hesitating, she walked into her closet and pulled out the red tunic that she'd brought home from the clinic. It still hung from the dry-cleaning hanger and under a thin plastic wrap, the way it was returned to her from the cleaners. She had even forgotten it was there until one day it emerged from its suffocating confinement between two winter coats when she removed one of them. Now she unwrapped it and stroked its smooth, silky fabric. The crimson color was as bright, its weaving pattern as vivid, as on the day she found it hanging in Moriah's cabin. As she ran her fingertips along it, images sprang from the recesses of her mind. Moriah's dear face encrusted with wrinkles, her eyes gleaming and her gnarled hands spread out in invitation. Moriah in her garden crouching over a leafy patch, murmuring and singing.

Joyce's troubled heart filled with yearning, and she knew that she had only one path forward: She must find her way back to Moriah or die trying. She didn't belong in the place she now occupied, and the only way back to her true self was through Moriah's open arms. She had buried Moriah in their garden, but her spirit must still be there, and now it was beckoning her to return.

Standing in a hot shower while devising a plan, she concluded that she must eliminate the biggest hurdle to her happiness. She could no longer continue pretending to be a part of Neurogenics, even though it had been practically her whole life before her fall. Over breakfast she lost no time to inform Will of her decision. He told her he'd support anything that made her happy.

She then called for a meeting, an in-person meeting, with the people who'd worked closely with her prior to the company's changes. Most of them lived in San Francisco and the Bay Area, so it wasn't difficult to gather eleven of her closest collaborators, including Ravi, the following week. The meeting was set for the conference room of their headquarters in the financial district; no one had been there for months. They gathered around the long table on the top floor in a room typically used for board meetings.

The floor-to-ceiling windows overlooked the Salesforce Tower that dominated the surrounding skyscrapers and the expanse of the Bay beyond. The conference table had been designed to sit thirty people comfortably, so they spread out to keep the proper social distance.

Everyone wore masks. The first thing Joyce did was to take her mask off. She wanted to face her colleagues truly and completely. A few followed her example. Their bright smiles encouraged her.

"Thank you so very much for coming today, despite the restrictions. I invited you out of deep respect for who you are and a thankfulness for who we've been for each other. I value you! Our journey together in building this company into the magnificent success it is now was an uphill battle and a hell of a lot of fun. I owe each of you my gratitude for your trust in me and for all your creativity and hard work that made this dream possible, for it *wouldn't* have been possible without you."

She met the eye of each person present and acknowledged each with a smile.

"I also want to thank you for welcoming me back, even though so much had changed in the time I'd been away. I will never forget your support and loyalty. I love you and have loved this company for over twenty years." Looking to Ravi, she took a deep breath. "However, my path is now taking me in a different direction. I don't know what that direction is yet, but I need to take the time to figure it out, and that would not be possible if I stayed here. I wish all of you success and joy on your journeys." She looked around the room that had filled with a heavy silence. Too heavy. Had she been out of line calling this meeting? A moment later Ravi stood and began clapping. The others joined him. Unshed tears burning her eyes, she thanked them and exited quickly, leaving them the freedom to speak among themselves.

An hour later, she was already home when she received an email from the company's new CFO, who had learned of her exit. Her resignation had been delivered both to Stewart and the head of the board. "On behalf of Mr. Stewart and the board of directors, we would like to state that although we regret to see you leave Neurogenics, we understand under the current circumstances your decision to pursue other endeavors. Your stock options are now released to be utilized as you wish, but we strongly encourage you to retain them, considering the prospects of our future expansion."

Joyce had forgotten that she had a one-percent share of the company's value in stock. Her share had been diluted during the public offering, but nonetheless it should now be worth considerably more.

She looked up the company's current valuation: $4.73 billion. That meant that her share was worth approximately forty-seven million three hundred thousand dollars. That was great news indeed, and it lifted the heaviness of having to let go of her attachment to the company and her colleagues. It allowed Joyce to envision a future full of possibilities, even though she didn't know yet what they would be. She could utilize this fortune to advance her mission to helping humanity. Maybe she could even fund the mirror neuron research herself if she could find a lab to partner with her.

She decided to share the great news with Will *after* she had figured out what she wanted to create next.

Wanting to clear her head, she changed her clothes and took off for a jog.

For the first ten minutes she paid attention to the run—to her form and where she was going and how fast she was breathing. But once she was comfortable with her movements, thoughts came lining up, freight cars running by, one after another.

She replayed her goodbye to her friends from the company. She revisited the hours she'd spend on research over mirror neurons and neurological disfunction. She sped through the sessions at the clinic and the days with Will.

When she stopped to walk, hands on hips and sweat sliding down her back, thoughts of Moriah and the forest filled her mind.

Moriah. From the moment Moriah, or what seemed like her spirit, appeared to her in her dream, Joyce had become obsessed with finding a way back to her. She needed to reconnect to her all-knowing wisdom and the sense of peace and joy she gained from it. But she was again doubting whether the events in those memories really happened or were figments of her imagination. After all, she was able to imagine her past before her fall and recreate events from it. She didn't remember them—she created the past in her mind based on what others said had happened and from videos and pictures. So it could be possible that she imagined a life with Moriah. She stopped walking. Was that what had happened?

A group of runners flowed around her, reminding Joyce where she was. She jogged down to an empty bench on the lawn of the Marina and stood behind it, stretching absent-mindedly.

Was her imagination that good?

The red tunic was tangible proof of what she might have experienced, but it wasn't proof enough, as she could have gotten the tunic in a variety of ways, juxtaposing the tale of Moriah's weaving of it over the truth.

And Franka had never believed her stories about Moriah. Her friend had tried to hide her doubts, but she'd never been completely successful, and Joyce had looked for telltale signs of disbelief.

She replayed what she could recall of her life with Moriah—the small heptagonal cabin in the meadow, the four majestic wolf-like dogs who played with her and protected her, Moriah's wonderful meals, their marvelous vegetable garden, and the mysterious adjacent forest. She hoped that the memories would bring back the feelings she'd experienced too, the joy, peace and love. But the more she tried to force the feelings to return, the more they escaped her, making her doubt even more that she had ever felt so immersed in them.

She finally concluded that the only way to reassure herself of her experience would be to return to the forest near Jenner. So that was what she needed to do. But before that, she needed to go home.

She took a shorter path back home, wondering how to bring up her plan to Will, who remained concerned every time she left their apartment on her own. She felt suffocated under his vigilance about her safety, but she was trying to give him the time he needed. He'd refused to see a therapist, teasing that *his* memories were fine. But they both recognized that he hadn't worked through her disappearance completely yet. And he wouldn't want her being too far away from him. Too far from where he could get to her quickly if she needed him.

Hmm. So how to tell him . . .

~

A day later, she decided to broach the subject over dinner that she'd prepared for this occasion.

"Will," she began softly. "I've been thinking about something very important."

Will lowered his roll and butter knife and stared at her intently.

So much for trying to approach the topic obliquely. The man had extra sensory perception where she was concerned.

"I've told you about the woman who saved me, Moriah. She didn't only save me, she also taught me how to connect to my true essence."

"I remember."

"I love you so much," she continued, sensing the anxiety in his stare. "Don't ever doubt that. But there's something that I must do to regain the sense of myself, to go back to who I was before you found me. I need to go back there and see for myself if it was real."

"Go back where?"

Once again she sensed his controlled fear. But before she could reassure him, he pushed his plate away.

"I thought we'd concluded that Moriah and all that was part fantasy, a hallucination. We talked about you being helped by an old woman until you were well enough to leave, but all the other stuff was your mind coping with your body's injuries."

"Yes, we talked about that. And I let Franka sway my thinking since she's the expert. But I *need* to go back to the place where I was healed, find the cabin where we lived, to see for myself if it was real or my imagination."

Now that she was able to express what was weighing on her for the past few weeks, she wasn't going to let anything stand in her way. She crossed her arms and waited for his next objection.

"Is this because that jerk Stewart turned down your proposal? Are you feeling insecure about your abilities? About your"—he gestured with both arms—"your thought processes? Should we call Franka and—"

"My thought processes are just fine, thank you. And besides, that has nothing to do with it! I can't believe y—"

"I'm sorry, I'm sorry—that was uncalled for and nasty." He picked up his roll again, but only to pick it into pieces. "It's not an excuse, but I don't want you to be hurt again. And when I think of you being hurt, I lash out. I also don't want you to ever doubt yourself and what you can do. I admit that any time you seem hesitant, I worry for you. Worry what's happening in that head of yours."

He looked down, saw the shredded roll and dropped the remaining pieces.

"And I don't mean I wonder what you're thinking. I worry that maybe the doctors missed something and that you're having a relapse or a reversal. I worry—"

She captured one of his hands and pinned it to the table. When he lifted his head, she said, "Please don't worry. And don't smother me. Will, that puts too much strain on us. I don't lie to you—I'd tell you if there was a problem. But in the meantime, you have to let me live. You have to let me venture out and even make mistakes."

She squeezed his hand, relaxing when he squeezed back.

"I want to live, Will! You want that for me, right? Lots of wonderful, beautiful life?"

He nodded.

"As I want for you. In all its messiness and glory and power."

He studied her face and then flipped his hand, threading his fingers through hers. "Okay," he said. "We'll take the helicopter and circle the area where you think you were to see if we can find the cabin."

"No, you don't understand." Why wasn't anything simple? Not even a conversation with the man she loved. "I need to go back by myself. That's the only way I can find the person I was when I was with Moriah. You weren't there then, so you can't be there now. This is a journey I must take on my own."

"Damn it, Joyce, I know what you want me to say. But you want honesty too, right?"

"Of course." At least she thought she did.

"You want to go off on your own on a dangerous expedition in the forest. To you, this is logical. No, you don't have to correct me—to you it's *necessary*. But, honey, to me this is unthinkable. The wrong solution. The wrong answer to the problem."

"I need to do this, Will," she repeated. "I won't be able to go on like I have been if I don't!"

He shook his head. "I'm trying to understand. Trying to understand why you'd want to leave now."

Understanding pushed through the heat of their argument and punched her in the chest.

"Leave you, you mean? Is that what you think?" She waited until he nodded, then said, "Honey, I love you very much. But this is not about us. It has to do with me alone. I need to find my way back to myself, to who I'd become when I was there. I don't know how to do it from here. I've tried." She took a deep breath, wondering if she should push harder, and then she did it. Hit where it would hurt him hard. "You know about the nightmares. Every night, Will. I have them every night. I don't want that anymore." She steeled herself to hold his eyes. "And I know you don't want that for me."

When he blinked, she said, "I promise I'll come back no matter what I find. I swear to you I will come back." The more she talked, the stronger her resolve for the journey, but she understood how difficult her decision would be for Will. "Please, Will. Please try to understand."

He sighed. "Would you at least take Beau with you?"

Joyce smiled, knowing that she'd reached him.

"Darling, I would love more than anything to take Beau with me, but

I'm afraid that the trip would be too difficult for him. I don't want to have to worry about him. I'll be fine, I know the forest well; I made my way through it many times. After all, that's how I got back to Jenner, remember?"

"So . . . why don't we sleep on it?" Will said.

So maybe she hadn't completely convinced him. But she would.

~

As soon as Joyce was out on her morning run, Will phoned Dr. Gladwell. She'd requested that they contact her if anything was wrong, and Joyce's plan was certainly cause for alarm.

"She wants to go back to the forest by herself," he exclaimed, skipping the usual greetings. "She says she needs to find herself again and that going is the only way she knows how to do it. What can I do? How can I stop her?"

"I understand your concern, Will, but I don't see how we can stop her. We can't declare her incapacitated, because she has proven that she can function quite well since she's been back. The only thing you can do is give her every possibility to be safe while she's on her journey. I understand that to you it doesn't make sense, that it might feel like she's escaping, but it does make sense to return to the place of trauma and re-experience it in the imagination to overcome that trauma. Returning with strength allows the person to exert control where they didn't have it before. At least this way she can finally put her doubts about what happened to her to rest."

Will was terrified. He knew he had no choice but to let Joyce go. His only condition was that she enable the location tracer on her iPhone.

He helped her prepare for the trip so she would be as comfortable and as safe as possible.

He got her extra batteries for her phone and a solar charger in case the batteries ran out. He bought a walkie-talkie in case she was in an area with no reception and needed help. He got her compasses, both manual and electronic, and showed her how to use them. He ordered a subzero sleeping bag and paid extra to have it shipped overnight. He got the best hiking shoes that helped against slipping, a Swiss Army knife, condensed milk and powdered food in case she ran out, several lightweight water jugs, antibiotic ointments and pills, bandages and Band-Aids, eye drops, Vaseline and even a foldable toothbrush.

Rechargeable flashlights . . . His list of supplies kept growing, and over the next few days packages arrived at their front door one after the other.

Eventually, however, she packed her backpack, tried on her fleece jacket and hiking boots one final time and was ready to go.

Will concluded that no matter how detailed the prep, he'd never be ready to watch her leave.

But he did it anyway, feeling noble because he didn't beg her to stay and foolish for not following her.

CHAPTER THIRTY-SEVEN

The Abyss

THE THRILL OF the adventure filled Joyce. She felt no fear, only excited anticipation as the road spiraled along the meandering coast. It was a bright and crisp February morning. Almost a year had passed since that pivotal day when their lives had been changed forever.

Today she felt as strong and as healthy as she ever had. She'd mastered ways to overcome the lapse of memory she still experienced, and in the place of those memories was the enjoyment of new discoveries. She hoped to make many new discoveries on the trip.

The Tesla practically drove itself along the winding curves. She'd identified exactly where she wanted to go and put the info into the car's GPS, intending to stop at the exact spot where she had parked the car a year ago and figure out her way into the forest from there. Knowing that her destination could be anywhere north of the vista point from which she had started her run on the day of her disappearance, this made sense.

The GPS indicated the approach of her destination. Another turn and there it was, a small parking area that opened up to a huge panorama of cliffs, ocean and sky. She parked the car, got out and put on her backpack—already regretting promising Will that she wouldn't take out any of the zillion necessities that he'd so lovingly bought and packed—and started walking north along a narrow path by the road.

She controlled her steps, feeling a bit of vertigo from the expansive abyss on her left. About half a mile up the road she noticed a small beach that could only be reached by climbing down the hillside. She decided to explore it, as it might have been the beach where Moriah found her. She carefully and slowly negotiated the sharp descent. Her heart pounded loudly as rocks and pebbles rolled under her feet, causing her to slide, but she caught her balance quickly by grabbing onto a bush. From then on, she scooted rather than walked, keeping herself closer to the ground.

When she reached large boulders that seemed to protrude directly from the ocean, she began climbing down the steep side of the uneven rocks and toward the tiny gray sand beach below. Waves exploded thunderously against the rocks, spraying her with mist that dissipated in the air. When she got closer to the bottom, she noticed seals dotting the shore. A few lifted their heads and twisted their bodies awkwardly to follow her descent. She sent them a kiss of gratitude as she walked by them, remembering Moriah's tale of how they saved her from drowning. Only when she finally reached the beach could she see on the far side a narrow sandy path that led beyond the beach and to the forest. A scent of seaweed and kelp reached her nostrils, reminding her again of Moriah and their cabin. Her heart skipped a beat when she sensed she was getting closer to it. And then a gust of wind whisked the scent away.

Tired from the treacherous descent while carrying the heavy load, she wanted to sit down on the sand and take in the beauty of ocean, the gentle breeze and the waves' roaring. Yet as soon as the idea crossed her mind, she decided to push forward. She was on a mission and didn't want to get distracted from it on her first day.

She marched to the path and then into the forest, imagining what it would have been like to be pulled—by four huge dogs—down the narrow space inside a wooden boat. The feat would have been difficult but not impossible, if one were to believe it, she mused.

The forest seemed to swell around her the deeper she stepped, until it became thick in oak and pine trees, bushes and ferns. Sounds and smells engulfed her. The whispering of leaves in the wind, the crackling of twigs underfoot, the moisture of both earth and air, the fragrances of moss and pine awakened her previous experiences among them.

Joyce was immersed in the moment.

According to the light that drifted westward, casting longer shadows on her path, evening was nearing. She was prepared to camp for the night and for many nights if necessary, but she hoped she wouldn't have to, as she knew that Moriah's cabin couldn't be too far off. Maybe a few miles into the forest from the beach, at most.

She kept up her pace as well as she could while negotiating the increasingly complex terrain until she reached an area so thick with large trees that she could no longer see her way forward. In the depth of the forest, she felt lost, not having any idea which direction to go. Automatically she touched the tiny pinecone that hung from the red yarn on her neck and asked to be shown the way. She felt nothing. She asked again, this time calling for Moriah's help. A gust of wind lifted her hair, and a branch fell from a tree not three feet in front of her. A sign? She decided to go in the direction it was pointing. The idea of a sign gave her confidence and lightened her steps.

Yet when hours passed and there was no sign of the cabin or the meadow in front of it, she resigned herself to set up camp for the night. In the thickening darkness, it was becoming more and more difficult to see the path among the trees, so she started looking for a decent site. Far above, she saw the first stars glittering between the foliage, and then she blinked, clearing her eyes, when a glimmer of hazy light flickered in the distance. The night was unusually clear for the season, and that light seemed out of place. Instead of stopping, Joyce continued pushing through the thick trees, their bulging roots and the high bushes. The light stayed stationary, giving her a target, and a few minutes later the forest abruptly opened to a large field illuminated by an almost full moon. She raised her head in thanks.

The cabin must be close, because it was on the boundary between forest and meadow; she could spend the night there. "Thank you, thank you, thank you," she said aloud, dropping her pack. She stretched her arms over her head and rolled her shoulders. Her back was locked in pain. Why did she allow Will to convince her to carry all that gear?

She looked around, turning in a slow circle, yet didn't see the cabin. Was it hiding in the shadow of the forest? She walked along its edge. Nothing. She repeated her search—still nothing.

Her enthusiastic exploration was turning to despair the longer she searched.

She'd been thinking that she must be in the wrong place, but had it been merely a dream after all? Had she gone on this monumental journey in the hope of reclaiming her peace and joy and convinced Will to let her go, just to receive confirmation that the cabin and Moriah had never been there?

Disillusioned and disappointed, she sank to her knees.

"Ow!"

Her right knee banged against something hard, sending a jolt of pain through her. That was the last thing she needed. Anger rising on the back of frustration, she peered down at the ground. A mound of rocks. The moonlight revealed something soft covering them, probably moss. She pushed herself to her feet, limped to her backpack, pulled her flashlight out and walked back, directing the beam toward the rocks while dragging her pack on the ground. Nearing the mound, she nearly fell to her knees again from surprise at what she saw. The rocks that were neatly assembled on top of each other were encircled by yarn. What looked like red yarn. Next to them grew a young oak tree. And not a little seedling, but a thick and sturdy sapling.

"Is this real?" Her voice was her own, steady and clear, so surely she wasn't dreaming.

She looked around in amazement, picturing how it had been. Where the cabin had stood there was now an open field. Everything was gone—the cabin, the gardens. But the rock monument wrapped in red yarn that she'd erected at Moriah's grave was still there, and the acorn that she'd planted was now a tree.

Overcome, she fell to the ground over the spot where Moriah's body would lie underneath and began sobbing. Fat tears rolled down her face and were absorbed by the earth below her. She wept with remorse for doubting Moriah's memory. She wept with shame for abandoning Moriah and herself, the love they'd shared. She wept over the abandonment of her own mother. She wept for the confusion, fears and doubts that had plagued her since she returned to the city.

She wept until there were no more tears to give, until she collapsed from exhaustion into deep slumber.

The cold woke her, or maybe was it the gushing streams of wind sweeping by and whispering *Tikvah*. Surely she had dreamed that. But she was awake. She *felt* the dampness of the earth beneath her. She felt cool mist on her face.

She slowly opened her eyes to discover pale moonlight filtering through the heavy fog that hung low to the ground. She sat up shivering and reached for her warm sleeping bag. Before she got into it, she gathered a few branches and surrounded them with small rocks and lit a fire. Its glow spread through the air, illuminating the low mist. She closed her eyes and listened to the night. An owl called at a distance, the trees circling the meadow rustled their canopies, and what was that? *Tikvah* again traveled on the wind's whispers. She saw Moriah's eyes glimmering, soft, deep wells reflecting her own eyes back to her. Perhaps it was then that she fell asleep again.

The chatter of birds filled the air before the appearance of first light, waking her from dreamless sleep. She lay watching the light change softly. She felt cleansed. As though something heavy that had been lodged deep inside her had been released. She found a new depth of feeling she hadn't known before, not in this way. She felt completely loved, even with no one present to give that love to her. As though that place, with all that was in it—the animals, the trees, the plants and forest, even the light—encompassed her in endless love. She lay held by the love for a long time, reluctant to move. When sunlight hovered above her, she finally pushed out of her sleeping bag. Her thermos containing sweet tea was still a bit warm, and she drank thirstily while taking in her surroundings.

The ground wore its winter coat. The withering green grass was covered by a layer of tiny droplets of morning fog which hung heavily in the air. She remembered her first sight of the meadow, how foreign it seemed then. Unlike today, since now she knew its many facets through the seasons. Beyond the meadow, the forest stood in majestic darkness. How she used to fear it until it became her friend! It had taught her so much of what she now knew about herself. She gazed at the bold pines that surrounded her at a distance and marveled at their solid beauty. For a moment she thought she saw Gabi's gray mane appear between the distant trees, but then it disappeared, a fleeting shadow. She wasn't sure if he had been there, yet she could feel his presence.

Then she sensed Moriah. She lifted her head. At first the feeling was ever so subtle, like a gentle caress within her, but then it increased until it filled her. She sensed Moriah's strength and beauty just like she felt the strength of the trees. She sensed her protectiveness, just as she'd felt it in the passing glimpse of Gabi. She sensed Moriah knowing her like no one had before, and mostly she sensed her love, so powerful and so complete. That love echoed in all that surrounded her, in all that she felt and saw. It filled her senses, and it filled her soul.

She realized then that Moriah's spirit didn't exist only in this place; it existed within her, and she could carry her everywhere she went. She finally found a home, a home in herself. A home she could take anywhere.

At the thought of home, Joyce realized that she needed to assure Will that she was all right. She sent a text, not wanting to break the magic of the moment with conversation.

I'm fine. I'm safe. I've reached my destination, and I'm ready to come home.

Will's response was immediate. *I'm so happy, my love. Safe journey home.*

The road back to him awaited her, and she was eager to return. She packed up her gear while munching on a protein bar. She thanked the meadow, thanked Moriah and Gabi, thanked the sun and the wind and the moon. She cut a piece of the red yarn that was sticking out from underneath a rock and rolled it into her left chest pocket. Then she picked a tiny acorn from the young oak and buried it in a pants pocket. "I love you, Moriah!" she said. "And I firmly believe in you. You are always with me." Then she headed into the forest.

The way back through the woods was easy. She knew intuitively where to go to reach the road she once took to Jenner. There were no mushrooms or berries to nourish her, and although she had a backpack full of goodies, she didn't stop to eat. She felt filled, satiated by the certainty of Moriah's unconditional love, a certainty that she had forgotten for a moment but never lost.

Moriah's lessons paraded through her mind, a waterfall of wisdom and goodness filling her heart, expanding it. The expansion brought new awareness. She understood that part of her had needed to die in that fall in order to be reborn. Realized that her memory loss allowed her to open up to new senses beyond the cognitive ones that had previously consumed her existence. With Moriah's guidance, she learned to recognize the more subtle senses that connected her to her soul. In feeling that Moriah was always with her and within her, she recognized that the realm of the spirit contains no boundaries and can't be defined by a place.

She *knew* that she was shaped by what she allowed to matter and the meaning she gave those things. The meanings resided in her memories and in her imagination and were held in her consciousness by love and hope.

Deep in thought, she hadn't noticed the time go by, and she was surprised when she reached the road leading downhill to her car. The car unlocked itself as she stood next to it. Even the car remembered her, she mused, laughing to herself.

She was back on the road to the city, but it now seemed an entirely different road than the one she had taken to get there.

Memories of Moriah flooded her mind. She saw her at her loom, eternally weaving her love and joy into the world. Moriah's sparkle was fueled by her mission to help humanity—Joyce understood the truth of that now. *Her mission . . . mission . . .* repeated in her mind as she contemplated the word. The story Moriah told her about the girl who lost her mother and then lost herself to her mission came to mind. What was the lesson there?

What was wrong with her mission to overcome the pain of the mother's illness and death by saving others from a similar fate? Wasn't that a worthy way to spend her life? Her gaze drifted to the flight of birds circling the ocean, so graceful, so free. *Mission . . .*

Remembering that Moriah's intentions sprang from joy and love, Joyce suddenly understood what she'd wanted to communicate through the story about the young girl. And in a flash of realization, she understood that her own mission had been founded on grief and therefore could only attract and create more pain. She saw for the first time that her loss had shaded everything she had done from that point on, all her life choices and actions emerging from the loss and from her need to overcome it. Finally, she understood that she had sacrificed her happiness while trying to overcome her pain.

Once Moriah had told her that her loss of memories was a gift. Losing her past had never seemed anything gift-like until that moment, when she realized the deeper meaning of the story.

She had ingrained her self-image in the traumatic event of losing her mother in her twenties, which had guided her choices and memories from that point on. Creating her life from that dire perspective, she could never become her true joyous self, could not find her way to love herself and others and her world completely, as Moriah had.

That was a heavy sacrifice indeed, one that she'd been freed from when those memories were erased. But now she could make the choice to create her life based on love and joy; there was nothing in her to confuse or hinder her choice. Liberated from her past traumas, she was free to make choices from her true nature, which sought joy, love and peace above all else.

A hawk flew across the road in front of her car. She followed it with her gaze, feeling herself soar. She was as free as the hawk, able to rise without needing to fight a force intent on pulling her back or holding her down.

She was free.

She turned on the stereo and bounced in the seat, celebrating not only her new understanding, but her freedom.

Passing the gentle rolling hills that led away from the coast, with the farmlands she so loved, she knew instantly what she wanted to do.

She stopped at the gate to a ranch and climbed over it into an empty field that sprawled uphill away from the ocean. Several horses lifted their heads from their grazing and stared at her in surprise. So did the curious llamas that gathered along the fence in the adjacent enclosed yard. She spread her arms wide, hugging the vast space around her, loving it. From her pocket she pulled the piece of the red yarn she had cut from Moriah's tombstones and tied it to the gate. As she drove away, she watched the crimson cord flap in the gentle breeze, tying her hopes to this place.

CHAPTER THIRTY-EIGHT

New Vision

T HE MOMENT SHE opened the door, he was there. He swept her into his embrace and held her tightly, their anxiety unwinding as they remained locked together in their doorway. She let his love pour into her as she opened her heart to him. Then they kissed passionately for an eternal moment. She melted into his arms. She had herself again, yet she was his and he was hers.

Beau jumped around them joyously, wagging his tail, wanting a piece of their love. She kneeled down and patted his head, and he returned her affection with a big lick on her cheek.

They entered the living room that was filled, as usual, with her favorite flowers, lilies and roses mixing their fragrances with the aroma of boeuf bourguignon, which had become his signature welcome-home dish for her.

Yet there was something different. It was intangible yet palpable. She was fundamentally changed from the last time she was there, and everything changed along with her. She felt grounded in the fresh ability to receive love, knowing that she was loved unconditionally without effort or merit, gaining security in the knowledge that true love was never lost. She looked at Will, lovingly aware that he now trusted that she could take care of herself. The change was subtle, yet monumental, as it seeped into their glances, silently and gently casting roots into her heart.

When she came out of the shower, feeling radiant in her off-white winter dress, the table was already set, candles flickering. A glass carafe half filled with red wine, left to breathe and enrich its flavors, stood on the white tablecloth. They sat next to each other at the round dinner table, needing to feel close.

"You found what you were looking for?"

"It was miraculous. I don't know how to describe what happened." She began searching for the words and discovered that there were none grand enough to recount her experience.

Instead, she told him about her adventure, how she found Moriah's grave by stumbling on the stone marker she'd built for her and then discovered the oak tree that grew next to it. She showed him the photos of the tree and the stones wrapped in red yarn. She'd marked the coordinates on her cell phone so they could visit it someday.

"Darling, *I* never needed proof," he said, giving her phone a quick glance. "It was wonderful to receive your text and know that you were safe, and on your way back. All I care about is you being healthy and happy."

"I know, but there's so much I want to share with you about what happened to me while I was away before. I want you to know what I experienced. I just wasn't sure anymore if it was real, so I held back. I now know that I don't need to be sure; all that matters is what I believe to be true for me. I want you to know those things."

He listened attentively as she shared her experiences with Moriah and their four magnificent dogs, who might have been wolves, her gentle and protective playmates.

"Maybe you could write a book about your fantastic adventure someday. Honey, you'd inspire so many people." But she had other ideas in mind.

As the hours wore on, she eventually told him about the farm that she saw on her way back and how on the rest of the drive home, she had begun to plan it all out, how a cascade of new ideas could fulfill her mission, and she was on fire telling him about it. To her relief, Will immediately caught her enthusiasm smiling and nodding, his eyes alight. They talked deep into the night, moving from kitchen to living room to bedroom, and Will added suggestions, exactly what she'd hoped he'd do. It was exciting and satisfying to envision a whole new future together, one unlike anything they'd ever expected.

They made love like never before, moved in waves of passion ignited by newfound intimacy and hopes. Their naked bodies wrapped around each other as though they were one, entwined like the roots of an ancient oak tree. They were souls woven together by memory and destiny and a future they were creating together. He was in her, and she was in him, the two bound by trust and mutual love. Afterward they drifted into abandoned sleep.

In the morning Will suggested that they go to the farm she discovered. "I need to see this place that captured your heart."

"Honey, you captured my heart."

In a flying leap, he took them back to the unmade bed, with Joyce unable to stop laughing. She felt free and uninhibited. Capable of anything. *Happy*.

~

Will was driving—the top down, the heater and stereo blasting, and Beau sitting in the back—when she saw the red yarn she'd tied to the fence.

"This is it."

They left Beau in the car and walked up the driveway, stopping more than once to take in the ocean views, following the paved path surrounded by mature trees until they arrived at a large oak door of a two-story Victorian farmhouse. Joyce rang the bell. Minutes passed without response, and just as they were about to turn back to the car the heavy door opened. Behind it stood a diminutive elderly woman wiping her hands on her apron.

"Can I help you?" She asked with a broad generous smile.

Joyce introduced herself and Will and explained that she had been admiring this farm and asked if they could be shown around.

"Yes of course, You're not the first curios people who've knocked on our door lately. Are you visiting the area?"

Joyce swallowed. Were there other perspective buyers who'd scouted the area. Is she too late?

"Please come in." The woman widened the door opening and stepped aside to allow them to walk into a dark wood paneled foyer.

"I'm Wilma Linhart. Please forgive my appearance." She said brushing her hands again on her wide apron. "I just took out the cookies from the oven. My husband John is out feeding the cattle, but he should be back shortly. He probably saw your car pull up and won't be long. Would you like some fresh baked oatmeal cookies and tea while you wait?" Joyce nostrils picked up the sweet aroma of homemade baked goods and cinnamon and her mouth watered.

"A hard proposition to resist." She gave Will a wink, and he nodded his agreement with a large grin.

"Please come in, I'll just be a minute." They walked into a small sitting room at the front of the house across from a wooden staircase that led to the upper floor, while Wilma disappeared into the kitchen at the back of the narrow corridor. The room was simply furnished with heavy wood furniture polished by years and generations of use. Joyce glanced at Will to see, if like her, he registered the coincidence of the farmer and his wife's first names as being the same first letters as theirs, only with their gender reversed. The woman's name started with W-I-L, while her husband, John, began with J-O, clearly a good omen. But Will didn't return her glance as he was absorbed at studying the family photos covering the mantle of the stone fireplace, which dominated the room. They sat on the small faded floral sofa while they waited for Wilma.

The scent of fresh baked cookies and strong tea filled the room with Wilma's return as did her cheerful and warm energy.

They chatted pleasantly about the area, when Joyce told Wilma about the house that they used to own on the coast close by. Wilma disclosed to them that the cattle farm had belonged to her husband's family for generations. Each generation kept increasing its size, acquiring more land and cattle, which is how it ended up encompassing the entire hillside all the way to the road in front of the ocean.

"But the buck stops here." she added with a sigh. "There is no more money in cattle farming as it used to be, and the government subsidies are drying up for small farms such as ours. So, we had to let go of most of our workers and give up most of our herd since it's just John and a couple more hands now to do the job, and he's not getting any younger. Plus, times have changed. Our kids aren't interested in farm life. They like it enough to come visit every so often, but they don't want the work. I don't blame them. It's not an easy living. I was a city girl from Chicago when John and I met, I was working for the Chicago Tribune and writing an article about how the changes in farming policy were affecting small farms all over the country. Well, I interviewed John for it and that was it. Never did complete the article, but I sure know a lot about small farms now after fifty plus years!" She winked at Joyce who smiled back at her imagining the young bright and, unusually for her time, career woman, a big city journalist, who had given up her job to live this difficult yet undoubtably rewarding life.

"I never regretted my decision! Not for a single moment." She added as if guessing Joyce's thought. "This land, this place has given me so much, and of course John and our four kids... hard to believe it's been more than fifty years since I've left the city, tough."

At that moment John walked in, dressed in heavy jean overalls and a wide-rimmed straw hat. He beamed a smile at Wilma and then to the unexpected guests in his sitting room.

"Well, we got company again!" He greeted them as if wasn't surprised to see them.

"I'm John!" He said extending a wide and course hand to Joyce, who felt John's strength in his solid handshake.

"These are Joyce and Will. They would like to tour the farm, if that's ok with you, dear." Wilma's face radiated love, and Joyce wandered if she would be still looking at Will that way when he came into the house in thirty years.

"Of course, and what brings you to these parts?" John lowered himself into a worn leather armchair after removing his hat and boots by the front door. Joyce cleared her throat. A lot was riding on this conversation and she knew that what she was about to propose to Wilma and John might come as a surprise.

She told them how much she loved the region and the land. Loved farming and hoped to expand the sustainable practices she had learned. When her hosts continue listening and watching her attentively with nods and smiles, she took the leap of faith and told them about her vision for creating a place where scientific and spiritual practices will inform each other to help people heal, and that she hoped she and Will could acquire a farm like theirs and set up an operation like she'd described in a place as magnificent as the land outside the farmhouse door.

"I like your vision." John beamed at her and looked at Wilma who nodded back with a knowing smile.

"I'll be honest with you, things have not been easy here at the farm for the past few years as I've had to let go of most of my field workers, and I'm getting on in years myself, so I don't know how much longer we can sustain the little farming we still do here to maintain our needs." He was echoing much of what his wife had told them earlier.

"Word gets around, you know, when times are tough. You're not the first to come knocking on our door with lofty propositions. Although, I must tell you of all the proposals we've heard so far, yours in the only one that I could stand for."

The couple obviously had been thinking their circumstances might push them towards selling up, Joyce thought, her heart in her throat.

"The thing is," John pauses looking intently at both her and Will as though reflecting on what he was going to say next. "I can't leave this land where I've lived my whole life, and where eight generations of Linharts have raised cattle and children." He wasn't looking at Joyce anymore. His eyes were fixed on his wife, who sighed in resignation.

"I'm sorry you two came all this way, for nothing. But at least you got to taste Wilma's famous oatmeal cookies." Joyce stared at the half-eaten cookie on her plate. She forgot all about the cookies. It was Will who interrupted the loaded silence.

"What if we only acquired part of the land, and you were able to stay at your home for as long as you like." He interjected vehemently. But John was already getting up to leave.

"Just wait a minute, hear us out." Will voice rose to try another suggestion. Joyce knew where he was going with it. Sensed that he was going to try to coax them to change their minds with a financial offer "they couldn't refuse." She also knew that it wouldn't work, not with people like John and Wilma, who've already sacrificed so much to keep the integrity of their land in-tact. She put a hand of Will's thigh, who understood the gesture implicitly and stopped midsentence.

"What my husband it trying to say." Joyce spoke slowly, weighing her words. "Is that we understand and respect your choice to stay here. We would probably have done the same." John nodded his appreciation at her expression of understanding, and before he could say anything else, Will quickly interjected.

"Here's my card and I wrote down Joyce's cell phone on it as well in case you want to reach us." He handed his business card to John. "Or invite us back for oatmeal cookies." He added with a smile. The Linharts both smiled back at the mention of the cookies and the strained atmosphere in the room relaxed. Will sure knew how to work his charm and was always prepared, Joyce thought, her heart swelling with appreciation for him.

They returned to the car and despite Beau's exuberant greeting remained silent. Will started the motor and gave Joyce a sympathetic glance, waiting to hear her thoughts, before putting the car in motion. Still, she didn't say anything. She needed time to reflect and absorb what had just happened. Joyce didn't like to be told "no" especially when it came to something as important and existential as her and Will's entire life plan and mission, but after reconnecting and integrating Moriah's spirit and unconditional love she noticed a shift in her reaction to this rejection. She knew deep in her core that her path forward will be determined by her highest love for herself. Her trusted adage "the universe conspires for my highest good" had never felt to her as true as at this moment. She was only able to acknowledge this conviction and change in her because of John's adamant refusal to grant her wish, even though she was convinced that it was the best path forward for everyone.

"It'll all work out, Will!" The words flowed from her as she found herself once again consoling Will for what had been her disappointment. It was her mission and her vision, and Will took it on whole heartedly, knowing it was the path to her, and to their ultimate happiness. In the dimming daylight the landscape lit in a golden glow. As the car sped forward, she glanced back on her hopes reflected back to her from the side-view mirror and caught a glimpse of the red yarn still tied to the fence blowing a gentle goodbye in the soft evening breeze.

~

Undeterred by the disappointment, during the next few days Joyce feverishly wrote out her vision and plans in her diary. Will told her that he was overjoyed to see her so intent on her mission but worried that the hinderances along the way might set her back emotionally as when Stewart rejected her research plan.

"This is different, Will." She reassured him. "And I'm different. I have nothing that I need to prove to myself in order to feel ok." She meant it! Her reinvented mission was giving her wings to surge and none of the usual fears that habitually lurked under the surface, those self-doubting voices that she had learned to ignore her whole life, pestered her anymore. Instead, she felt equanimity in the assurance that everything will work out for the best and all will be revealed in time.

After three days of incessant writing, of laying her notebook down, only to return to it a few minutes later with another idea, she finally stopped. Her over-active mind needed a rest and so she headed to Chrissy Fields with Beau in the evening. The sky's pinks and orange hues reflecting in the serene water of the bay washed into her heart as she pondered what she hoped to create without having any idea how and where to go about it. Yet again, the uncertainty did not deter her peaceful conviction that as the creator of her reality, she will find a way. She remembered Moriah telling her that her mission was a life choice leading her to her greatest joy and not a condition she needed to achieve in order to prove her worth, her reason for living. This recollection of Moriah's teaching strengthened her resolve that nothing in the pursuit of her mission could take away her joy, not even setbacks and momentary disappointments. She smiled to herself, to the sky, to the ocean, as she patted Beau's head and lingered just a moment longer to savor this realization. Her jogging pants' pocket buzzed startling her to the realization that she forgot to leave a note for Will that she was going for a walk. He was probably looking for her and Beau when he got back from the gym. But when she glanced at her phone's screen, she was surprised to see an unknown number, as few people were calling her cell phone these days.

She hesitated for a moment before pressing the green button.

"Hello?"

"Joyce?"

"Yes...?"

"This is John, from the ranch. You came by with your husband a few days ago."

"Yes, of course, hi John." She said trying to sound as nonchalant as possible. But who was she kidding, her heart was racing!

"Wilma and I have been discussing your proposal; To be honest it was she who convinced me to think it over. I can be a stubborn goat, as she says. Then we talked it over with our kids. And..."

There was a long pause, so charged with tension that Joyce could hear John's difficulty in coming up with the next words."

"Well, Joyce." His voice was horse but determined. "I'm happy to tell you that we've decide to let you have the ranch!"

Her breath caught.

"Thank you!" She mumbled.

"You still want it?"

"Yes of course! She raised her voice realizing that in her astonishment she might have sounded hesitant. "And everything we promised you, still stands."

"Well, we'd like to stay at the house, but the rest of the property is yours... We'll have to approve of all your plans though, but from what you told us we're all aligned with what you're wanting to accomplish here and would love to contribute to the creation of it. Believe it or not, it was the kids who convinced us to accept your generous offer and invest the money, so we can live comfortably and not have to struggle anymore to maintain the farm.

"That's wonderful, John..."

"There's one condition we haven't discussed that will have to be added to the agreement."

"What is it?" Joyce couldn't imagine what the Linharts could want more than what was already promise to them.

"There has to be a stipulation that the land will remain farmland for perpetuity and can never be sold to a real estate developer or hospitality group. Would that be acceptable to you?" His voice regained the firmness she recognized from their previous discussion.

"John, this is absolutely in line with my mission! And I'm happy to put it in writing."

"Then we have a deal!"

"Thank you John, and please thank Wilma and your children."

She hung up and jumped from the bench lightening her steps to rush home. "Com'on good boy!" she said to Beau while fastening his leash. "We've gotta' hurry back to tell your daddy the good news! Our lives are about to change again!"

CHAPTER THIRTY-NINE

Hope

OVER THE NEXT few months, they put together their plans. The Linharts were consulted on each step along the way, and Joyce and Will made sure that they were on board with everything they wanted built on the property. Most projects were met by the Linharts' enthusiastic approval, and John even helped with some of the planning such as extending the well and agricultural plots, and the new breeds of cattle they added. Joyce and Will even got to meet their children and grandchildren as they came by to pick up old belongings they stashed in the sheds. They too were thrilled by the plans for the land and that their parents could remain there and take part in the exciting cutting-edge developments.

When the property was theirs, Joyce and Will built a contemporary house up the hill, with a large glass facade overlooking the ocean, for their own home. Everything was built to sustainable standards and the entire property was made to be self-sufficient.

Solar panels on all the roofs assured an ample supply of electricity. The well was deep enough to accommodate their watering needs for showering and feeding the animals and watering the garden. Additionally, they built a water purification system that cleaned rainwater that was gathered in large containers around the property and they were looking into designing a desalinization plant that used solar power.

In April of the following year, Joyce and Will walked hand in hand, with Beau leaping by their side, surveying all that they'd created in the year since they'd purchased the farmland, and its horse stables. They passed the vegetable garden, overflowing with greenery in neatly lined plots. Suzanne and Joshua were weeding, but they stopped when Joyce and Will approached. Both couples smiled broadly.

"Hi, Suze, hi, Josh," Will and Joyce said. "How are the squashes coming along?" Joyce asked.

"Everyone is doing fine, including Suzy!" Josh said, laughing.

Suzy, who'd been diagnosed with early dementia, had been showing positive signs of improvement since coming to Woodland Ranch three months earlier. The work in the gardens, along with a vegan diet designed especially for her and the spiritual learning she enjoyed at the ranch, seemed to have contributed to enhancing her memory.

"Make sure you join us for music and dancing tonight at the cabin!" Joyce called out as they continued their stroll toward the lower pastures, where the horses and sheep grazed.

They watched Tom being led on a horse by Mark, one of their instructors. Tom had come to the ranch with a diagnosis of Parkinson's, yet he was showing no signs of motor degeneration in the past month. He held the reins of the horse and looked frustrated at being led and not allowed to gallop on his own.

"Hang in there!" Joyce said as she held the horse by the muzzle and patted his head. "And you," she said to the horse. "Tom is ready to ride you but go gentle on him the first time."

Beau dashed towards the meadow unable to restrain himself from herding a few sheep that strayed from the flock. Seeing how the sheep had multiplied since the beginning of spring, there would be a generous shearing this coming season, she thought as they passed the hilly meadow. Will suddenly started running, and he pulled her down the hill with him, whooping and hollering. She was grateful that he hadn't tackled her to the ground to roll down the hill, a trick he tried to pull every other day. She enjoyed the fun, but her white jeans wouldn't have liked tumbling through damp clover.

Their jog stopped as quickly as it had begun, and Will pointed at one of the sheep.

"Beautiful head of hair on that one. Think I should let my hair grow long and curly?"

"Funny." She punched his arm. "You're vain enough now." He shot her a wide-eyed look. "Me vain?"

"No. Not really."

He smiled and began humming.

No, he didn't have a vain bone in his body. He was generous and loving and willing to try anything she suggested for the ranch.

She was so glad that they'd kept the animals and added more, even though they hadn't planned on using them for meat. All the animals had proven useful for grazing and for enhancing agricultural practices, and they were actively looking for additional animals. Maybe geese. She wouldn't mind getting used to something new and unusual, although they had cows, horses and dogs and llamas and sheep. Plus they *had* recently acquired a kitten, much to Beau's delight.

The biodynamically diverse farm, where plants and animals sustained and fostered each other, had proven wildly successful so far. The rich variety of produce from the vegetable gardens and fruit trees provided all that was needed for them and their guests. Will had suggested maybe prepping for sales to the public the following year.

A wave of satisfaction washed over Joyce. The gardens buzzed with butterflies, insects, worms, bugs and growing plants. Loyal to the practices she learned from Moriah, Joyce kept separate plots for rodents and insects, creatures that somehow knew to keep themselves separate from the rest of the crops. The meals prepared primarily from the farm's fruits, vegetables, dairy and eggs were cooked by a trained chef and his team to be delicious, healing and nourishing. Meals at the dining hall were festive experiences which often ended with guitar and drum music, singing and dancing.

The same simple wooden fence separated the ranch from the road and the neighboring farms as when Joyce had found it. The red yarn, she'd tied there, withered and sun bleached, still marked the gate. A small oak tree protruded from the ground by the entrance. It could have easily been missed if it hadn't been encircled by stones when Joyce planted it with the acorn she had picked from the oak that grew from Moriah's grave. Now a young oak was budding its head through the earth. Joyce and Will stopped there in reverence and gazed at the ocean as they often did. It was surprising to see the acorn sprout so soon after it was planted the year prior. Yet they accepted this miracle along the myriad of others that they had experienced recently. They had come to expect miracles as the way of life.

Will felt proud and humbled and loved. Joyce, he knew, felt that and even more. He'd had his own experiences with becoming the man he'd been meant to be, but he never tired of hearing her talk of Moriah, the cabin, the wolfdogs and all that she'd learned. Their shared hope was to make all of that possible for the ranch's visitors too.

"We've come a long way," Joyce said, her voice sounding as though it was spoken from a distance, although she was standing close to him, her gaze fixed on the horizon. Knowing that she was in deep reflection, Will didn't interrupt her.

"My mission had always been to help other people. I've come to realize that I can only do that if I really love myself and my life. Now I can truly say that I do! And I love you so much, Will! Thank you for sticking it out with me."

She turned to meet his eyes. A lump lodged in Will's throat and his eyes teared. He wanted to respond, but the words remained stuck. He hugged her tightly. He had loved her from the time they were young adults through all the dramatic changes they had gone through. That love coursed through him now from the depth of his being, and yet still the words wouldn't come. Instead, they kissed, and everything around them melted away. Only the sensations of their mouths exploring each other and the feelings of bliss, love, joy, ecstasy, remained, until even those dissolved. They let go of each other in a spontaneous rapture of rolling laughter echoed by the hills, the ocean, the bright blue sky with seagulls flying overhead and the rustle of the leaves of the young oak.

"Look what I found this morning when I unpacked our last boxes from storage."

Joyce pulled out a leather-bound notebook and opened it to a page marked by a dry leaf before handing it to him. Will took it from her and immediately realized what it was, recognizing her meticulous handwriting. He knew she had taken up keeping a diary since her days at the clinic, but she had never offered to share it with him before, so his curiosity was piqued, and he wondered why she would do it now.

Feb 9, 2021

My hope in creating Woodland Ranch is for it to become not only a biodynamic farm, but also a healing center and a campus for transcendental learning . . .

He gave her a knowing smile, recognizing the vision for their creation which they'd often discussed, particularly in the early planning stages. Then he continued reading. His breath caught when he read the last paragraph. He pulled it to his chest.

"Will, what is it?" she asked, her voice tight with suspense.

The insight was a lot to take in, and he wanted to assimilate the meaning of each word, so he read out loud.

"It feels like the ushering in of a new world, where data guided by intuition allows the creation of possibilities never before imaginable. Where experiences rather than results are the core focus. Where people come to heal rather than to be cured. Where nature determines the human experience rather than the other way around.

It's a place where nature loves itself and knows that there is no life without love!

It is an homage to Moriah!"

His voice choked when he read the last sentence.

"What's the matter?" she asked, clearly baffled by his reaction.

"Joyce, this is beautiful." His eyes held hers. "I never saw this part of your vision, but now I understand."

"I wrote it right after I got back from my trip to the forest, when I found Moriah again. Well, at least her grave and her spirit. Remember?" She paused, struck by a thought. "My ideas about all this were already forming, even before I saw the Linhart's ranch on the way home."

Of course, he remembered. They had spoken of nothing more for days afterwards, but now it seemed so far away, another lifetime.

"That's amazing, honey. You had it all laid it out just over a year ago, and it all came true, and now we're living it!" He hugged her shoulders, elated, yet still astounded by what they were able to accomplish through their inspiration and hard work in such a short time.

"Maybe we could add some of this description to our website," she suggested. "Let people know what the vision is, so those who need us can understand what this place is about and be able to find us."

"I think that's a great idea!" He beamed extending her notebook back to her.

He had taken on her vision wholeheartedly from the moment she got back from her trip to the forest. She'd been transformed by her experience of reconnecting with Moriah's spirit; he'd felt the change instantly. And her transformation changed him. She had come back to *him*, to love him, just the way he was, with all his fears and shortcomings. She didn't need him to take care of her anymore, probably never had, as he'd wanted to believe all those years, so he could feel secure in her love. It had taken over twenty years and tremendous trials to get there, but he finally felt that they were truly together in a way he never dreamed possible. He was full of gratitude for Moriah, whoever she was. She must have been a miracle worker indeed!

They returned to Moriah's grave together once afterwards, since Joyce wanted to show it to him. But after that visit Joyce had concluded that Moriah's spirit could be found anywhere, so there was no impetus to go back to the site of her burial.

"Let's go say hi to Ravi at the lab." Joyce's chipper voice interrupted his musing. "I'd like to show this to him as well." She pushed the diary back into her bag. She took his hand and they climbed up the hill to where Ravi and his team of researchers had been setting up the lab in a new state-of-the-art facility they'd just completed building.

They walked in a sweet silence enhanced by the sounds of nature. After the brief visit with Ravi, who was still unpacking, they headed to the large wooden cabin that had been inspired by the cabin where Joyce had gone through her life-changing experience. It was a large structure of seven sides. They used the space that could accommodate up to two hundred people for seminars and conferences by luminary philosophers, spiritual teachers, scientist and artists. It was also used as a party and dance space on special occasions. It was named Moriah's Cabin.

"Come on, JoyTi. Some important and impatient people are waiting for us."

Will loved to tease her, since everyone at the ranch had taken to calling her JoyTi when she added Tikvah as her official middle name.

"I'm coming."

Their daily stroll ended at the wide entrance of the cabin. Will escorted Joyce to her place at the side of the auditorium, making sure she had all that she needed as she listened to the talk on empathy and healing. She settled into the rocking chair that she'd installed inside Moriah's

Cabin. Beau slumped down beside her, resting his head on her foot. The murmur of the participants and presenters filled the space as the audience took their seats. After sharing a few greetings around the room, Will blew a goodbye kiss in Joyce's direction. But before leaving for his office, he lingered by the door, leaning on the wall to glance one more time at his love.

Joyce picked up her weaving and began humming and rocking gently. In a pouch on her lap, she cradled their baby girl.

Their precious Hope.

EPILOGUE

J oyce jolted awake, her senses prickling as if someone had softly called out to her. But it wasn't a voice that had stirred her, more a whisper caught in the night breeze. And that whisper hadn't called her by the name she lived by now, but the one Moriah had given her—Tikvah. Fully awake, she turned her head to the crib where Hope lay, her little chest rising and falling in peaceful slumber. Will, too, was beside her, deeply asleep. The thin beam of moonlight filtered through the slightly open window, casting a gentle glow on the leather-bound diary on the night table—an artifact from a time she had nearly forgotten, recently rediscovered amidst the routine of unpacking.

The diary beckoned her now, whispering its own silent call. That evening had been unusually warm, prompting her to leave the window ajar for the ocean breeze. Moving with the careful grace of a cat, Joyce slipped into her robe, picked up her flashlight and notebook, and tiptoed to the door, making barely a sound.

Outside, the stars hung low, as if leaning in to listen. She settled herself into the old rocking chair on the deck, a faint hint of jasmine teasing her senses. It was their first bloom, she realized with a small smile. The deep silence was punctuated by the distant, rhythmic lullaby of the waves and the occasional whisper of wind through the foliage.

She began to rock gently, her mind slipping into the past, to nights where Moriah would sit in her own rocking chair, sharing stories and wisdom under a similar canopy of stars. A deep peace enveloped her, a familiar embrace. Eager to delve back into those cherished memories, she opened the diary and illuminated its pages with her flashlight. The words she had written so long ago now danced before her eyes, evoking reflections on Moriah's teachings, her own growth, and sometimes, a laugh at her youthful naiveté.

The night sky drew her gaze again. The memories flowed—of belonging, of the deep connection Moriah had instilled in her. Now, she carried that feeling, weaving it into the life she shared with Will, their daughter, the farm, their colleagues, friends and guests. Her eyes traced the familiar constellations, landing on Sirius, twinkling like a sentinel of old lessons. Suddenly, it all crystallized in her mind—the pattern, the order to Moriah's lessons, like a carefully woven tapestry.

Each lesson was a step, a building block:

~ Finding the acorn had connected her to her hope, the bedrock of her life.

~ The search for the smallest pinecone had granted her intuition, guiding her hope towards her truest self.

~ The night under the stars with Moriah had revealed her sense of belonging, to the world, to her time and space, and most importantly, to herself.

~ From her sense of self, the mushrooms had shown her the interconnectedness to everything in her universe.

~ Saving the crop from the geese had taught her that with hope and intuition, she could create a reality of her highest good.

~ Learning the meaning of Moriah's weaving had made her aware of her impact on her world and others through her intentions.

~ Devotion to their garden had fostered the understanding that all she did flowed from love.

Joyce felt awe wash over her. The old pen from the clinic, still wedged in the diary, called to her. She had to record this epiphany, to share it with Will in the morning, and perhaps others. It had always been there, waiting for her to see it with the clarity that only time could bring.

The lessons laid out before her, a path to her own joy, intricate and beautiful, created by the weaver's hand.

ACKNOWLEDGEMENTS

The inspiration for this book has been a tremendous gift to me. I have grown and learned so much in the process of creating the story and writing it. Shawn Randall's and Tora's teaching of connecting to spirit and higher realms of consciousness, fostered this inspiration, and for this I am forever grateful.

My deep gratitude to my fellow spiritual travelers, Rainya Dann, Robert Klein, George Fermin, Marcy Haines and Ed Hunt, who share the multidimensional journey with me, empathetically listening, and supporting me through the process of creating this book, particularly Ed Hunt, who sparked the inspiration to write this novel by revealing my own aspiration and motivating me to get going with it.

A huge thanks to my considerate early readers, Tori Arthernack, Patricia Blanc, Kimberly Heart, and my mom and dad. Their enthusiasm let me know that this is a story worth sharing. Patricia and my mom even read different reiterations of the manuscript, each one longer than the previous version.

Beth Hill, my dedicated editor, who patiently guided me in the craft of constructing a novel and helped enhance and mold it without suppressing any of the magic. Alaina Bixon, who put the final editing touches in place with her sharp-eyed proofreading. I am honored that Jeff Lyons, an accomplished writer and Stanford writing professor, shared his resources, and knowledge about publishing.

My gratitude to Elvin Durant, wherever he may be in this grand universe, for translating my ideas for the cover design and website into digital form, and to the guys on his team, Carlos and Brian who completed the designs.

Heart-felt thanks to my close friends (they know who they are) who listened to me talk endlessly about the book during the past year, encouraging, and celebrating milestones with me. Writing can seem like a lonely journey, but thanks to my dear friends, it hadn't been.

My loved ones inspired this story, particularly my loving and supporting parents. Jeff, my life partner, always believes in me, even at moments when I doubt myself. Not to be forgotten, a joyful thanks my doggie Max, who has a way of tugging on my heart strings like no one else.

And I am so ever grateful to you, dear reader, for reading this book all the way through, even to the acknowledgments, and sharing it with your friends and loved ones, for we are all creating it together.

For more from The Weaver, please visit the website:
www.theweaverbook.com
and subscribe to our email list.

Further reading about some of the subjects in this book:

~

Beresford-Kroeger, Diana, To Speak for The Trees: My Life's Journey from Ancient Celtic Wisdom to a Healing Vision of the Forest, Random House Canada, Sept 24, 2019

Dr. Alexander, Eben, Proof of Heaven: A neurosurgeon's Journey Into the Aferlife, Simon & Schuster, Oct. 23, 2012

Moorjavi, Anita, Dying to Be Me: My Journey from Cancer, to Near Death, to True Healing, Penguin Random House, Sept 1, 2014

Moorjavi, Anita, Dying to Be Me!, TEDx Bay Area, Nov. 30, 2013

Stamets, Paul, Mycelium Running, How Mushrooms can Help Save the World, Ten Speed Press, Oct.1, 2005

Stamets, Paul, Fantastic Fungi, Film by Lyn Davis, and Lourie Schwartzberg, Moving Arts, 2019, Netfix 2021

Ramachandran, Vilayanur, The Neurons that Shaped Civilization, TED, March 4, 2014

Hegarty, S. Dec. 5, 2011, "What Phantom Limbs and Mirrors Teach Us About The Brain", *BBC News*.